The Ghostly Diva

by

Sandra L. Young

The Ghostly Diva

Cover Art by *Diana Carlile*

The Wild Rose Press, Inc.
PO Box 708
Adams Basin, NY 14410-0708
Visit us at www.thewildrosepress.com

Publishing History
First Edition, 2024
Trade Paperback ISBN 978-1-5092-5522-1
Digital ISBN 978-1-5092-5523-8

Published in the United States of America

Dedication

With this final novel in the Divine Vintage trilogy, I send a huge shout-out to my local community. The reception for the books, set in our Northwest Indiana county, has been utterly fantastic. I'm so grateful for all the happy readers - plus presentation, media, and book club opportunities. Another big kiss to my fave super fans: Rick and our Corgi pup, Sopa. Thanks for indulging my demanding schedule and huge vintage collection!

Chapter One

January 2010

When the mannequin's hand clattered to the floor for the third time, Justine Saunders reached her limit for patience. She muttered an expletive as it bounced under a hoop skirt large enough to hide three kids and a dog.

She glanced around the cavernous lower level of the LaPorte County Museum, past a mastodon jawbone and the salmon-hued fins of an Edsel. Luckily, no one lurked nearby. Her boss would shrug off a complaint of his assistant curator cursing, but their government overseers would not. With LaPorte County's current financial distress, she shouldn't place herself in the cost-cutting crosshairs.

Justine stifled a sigh and returned to changing out the clothing. The best part of her job was curating their vintage clothing collection, ranging from pioneer calicos to 1960s chic. Having passed the New Year's mark, she now switched from 1930s holiday frocks to Civil War-era winter garb. She lifted the metal hoop, releasing a rustle of pine-green taffeta, and stretched low into the darkness for the bothersome hand. Beyond the ruffled bloomers, she latched onto the digits, disturbing the dust beneath. Her sneeze jabbed pain into her lower back, in an unsubtle reminder of avoiding yoga class for weeks. She clutched her back, staggered upright, and glared at the mannequin. "Are you playing with me?"

Across the room, the dozen lightbulbs that framed an antique hotel sign blinked. A charming effect...except she knew the sign wasn't plugged in.

Her lips pursed. "Cut it out. I'm busy."

Physical manifestations weren't new here. On Halloween, when she'd heard notes tinkling from the Victorian parlor's upright piano, she bobbed her head in rhythm and continued on her way. The week after Thanksgiving, Justine had watched a transparent figure glide across the Edwardian library. When she asked, "What's your name?", the thready voice sent shivers down her body. "Hazel" walked through a table and disappeared.

Her boss, Carl Olsen, expressed a hint of jealousy after she relayed the incidents to him. The director himself had never experienced spooky encounters, though volunteers through the years swore to similar happenings. Justine reasoned some artifacts—and ghosts—exerted bursts of psychic energy, waiting for the right person to intercept them.

The mannequin, however, was just a modern pain in the butt. A fur muff could disguise the problem—handily. On a mission to find one, she snickered at the pun and ran up the concrete staircase to the main floor, where rows of cases resembled parallel train tracks.

Carl sat in their shared, glass-enclosed office and turned at her approach. She waggled the mannequin hand in a friendly wave. His laugh sputtered out with a spray of coffee, and he pointed an accusing finger before composing himself to answer the ringing landline.

Entering the back doorway into the storage area, she jolted when the intercom buzzed. Carl's muffled voice floated into the room. "Justine, pick up line two. Some impatient dude wants to donate clothing." Cold symptoms transformed his usual mellow tone to gravel. "Drumroll...his mom was Liza Maddox. The actress. What if he wants to give us some costumes?" Excitement also colored his words; her boss was a star-struck movie fan.

Justine wrinkled her nose. Before returning to their shared hometown of LaPorte a year prior, Liza Maddox only performed small roles in a couple dozen movies and television shows. But at least the woman had been *in* the movies, instead of spending Saturday nights at home watching them, alone.

"I'm on it." She pushed the blinking button and adopted a cheery tone. "Good morning. This is Assistant Director Justine Saunders. How may I help you?"

"I'm supposed to talk to you about donating these old clothes?"

He did sound gruff and harried. She imagined a frowning, older man, irritated at being kept on-hold.

"Yes, I can help you, sir." She ramped up the polite factor to calm him. "Could you tell me more about the items you've got?"

"What I've got?" He exhaled with force, annoyance cutting over the line. "I hoped *you* could tell me what I have. Look, I'm no expert here, but my mother and grandmother left reams of old stuff I thought might have historical interest. If not, I'll call the local thrift shop."

"No." Taken aback by his curtness, she jumped in. "We definitely prefer to see your items. We can set up an appointment for you to bring them to the museum."

"You can come here. I don't have the time or the inclination to schlep it out to you."

Part of her wanted to tell him to haul it to Goodwill, and don't let the door hit him in the… Yet the temptation to delve through a treasure hoard of vintage clothing was too enticing to ignore. She'd go in the daytime. If the vibe felt off, she'd leave. "All right. Were you thinking of a timeframe?"

"Tomorrow afternoon. I need to unload the stuff as soon as possible, before heading out of this slow-motion town."

Where did this rude, impatient person live that ranked so superior to her beloved hometown? She bit the inside of her lip to avoid slapping him back with a defensive zinger. LaPorte, Indiana, showed progress in the downtown revitalization. The latest efforts provided fun activities in a new plaza and supported entrepreneurs to open businesses, including a coffee shop and an artists' gallery.

She countered the caller's attitude with a civil tone, glad he couldn't see the snarky expression on her face. "How about three o'clock?"

"Fine. 2506 Michigan Avenue." He clicked off.

She glared at the intercom. "Goodbye to you, too. Jerk."

As she ran the address over in her mind, she scanned the metal shelving units in the cavernous storage room. The staff hung sturdier vintage garments on racks, but other items were stashed in labeled plastic containers. She found the small fur pieces and mused about the call. Michigan Avenue. The grand old street boasted maple trees and lawns edged with tended bushes and flower gardens. Despite the nasty conversation, she wanted to see the place and sort through the clothing. If they couldn't use the offerings at the museum, some could be donated to Little Theatre, where she enjoyed costuming plays and musicals.

Her own phone buzzed in her pocket. For a moment she froze, thinking the nasty caller caught the sign-off comment and called back to berate her. Foolish. His call came in on the museum line, not her personal cell. She dug the vibrating phone out of her tan slacks and took a peek.

Drysdale Museum flashed on the screen. After the county's financial predicament worsened over the past months, she applied for positions on a job-match link. Her pulse thumped in her throat. Despite the effort, she really hadn't anticipated receiving any responses. She swallowed hard and answered with a pleasant tone, ignoring the quiver of tension skimming through her body. "Hello. This is Justine Saunders."

"Ms. Saunders, my name is Lynn Redmon, from Human Resources at the Drysdale Museum in Chicago. I'm calling to set up a skype interview for the curator position."

"Thank you. That's wonderful news." She fanned her suddenly warm face with her free hand.

"We're scheduling for Monday with Executive Director Samantha Chan. Are you available at eleven o'clock?"

"Absolutely. I'm honored to have the opportunity." Her mind whirled to recall her upcoming calendar. Wait. She worked on Saturday. Monday would be a day off. She wouldn't have to concoct a reason to be gone for the morning.

"Good." The woman continued with brusque efficiency. "I'll forward you the Skype information via email."

"The Drysdale is a lovely museum. I look forward to meeting her. Thank you again."

They exchanged goodbyes and clicked off. Justine blew out a shaky breath and stuffed the phone in her pocket. Carl's assessment of the most recent county budget meeting sounded dismal. Through no fault, tax collections were snagged, creating a drastic need for reductions in expenses across all departments. He reasoned the museum was certain to take a hit because local artifacts didn't draw enough attention. People exited the town of twenty-two thousand residents and accelerated, zooming past their sprawling, red brick building surrounded by cornfields.

The next day she launched a discreet job hunt.

Despite the unstable situation here, she had to force herself to apply for the position. Yet she couldn't deny a thrill of exhilaration. The Drysdale, a mid-sized Chicago museum, was interested in her. Granted, not at the same administrative level, but a post in the city could be a stepping-stone to greater things.

With a fist pump in the air, she returned to the storage box to pluck out an oversized mink muff. She halted, fingers sunk in silky fur. Her life would come off super boring in an interview. For three decades she'd lived in this smallish town, leaving only to achieve her history degree at a downstate college. Eight years prior, she accepted the assistant position straight out of school. Yes, she stayed on because she loved it. But also, partly, out of inertia.

She closed the box and headed toward the door, reminding herself of the basic, underlying reason for the job search: better to resign on her own terms rather than face the axe. If she left, that might even protect other positions and programs.

Nerves churned her stomach. Moving to Chicago definitely would shake up her dull lifestyle. In LaPorte, family, friends, and work dominated her world. Would she fit into the big-city hustle of traffic and humanity? What would be worse? Remaining here unemployed, or failing to meet the standards of a demanding new workplace?

The implications of a move seared her brain as she clutched the muff and the mannequin hand and left the room. Outside the storage area, a shadowed figure stood waiting at the end of the hallway. Justine stopped and stared. The woman, garbed in a sweeping cloak and a plumed hat, appeared more solid than the ghosts she usually saw.

When the arms stretched toward her, Justine backed against the door and heard one word whisper in the air. "*Mine.*" Gloved fingers beckoned to her.

The insinuation clicked. "This is your muff." Tempted to roll it along the floor, she held the black fur aloft to discourage an approach. The spirit nodded once and dissolved.

She sucked in a breath. These darn manifestations were growing bolder. They didn't scare her, exactly, but she preferred they leave her alone. After taking a few moments to regain composure, she attempted to tiptoe around their office to avoid Carl. Not because of the ghost. Her face might give away her deep secret. She wasn't ready to share about the job search, or interview, at an early stage.

Carl's boss radar pinged. He motioned her forward.

So much for stealth. Justine rolled her eyes and joined him in the cluttered lair. A pencil remained clenched between his teeth, a signal of writing the weekly newspaper column to share events, updates, and donation lists. Not that he used the pencil to write. Carl was computer-literate. He believed chewing on a pencil like an old-time newsman bumped his journalistic juices. She always winced when she grabbed one of his bite-marked writing implements by mistake.

He pushed back from the desk and gazed at her over the top of his wire-rim glasses. "Ow'd da call go?" His voice was a muffled growl around the clenched pencil, his thick lenses reflecting the fluorescent light. After working in the shared space for years, she could interpret the garble.

"Peachy. What a dick." She plopped into her desk chair and rolled beside him, avoiding the tower of papers tilting near his keyboard. "I mean, the guy's downright rude. He insisted I go to his location to check out the clothes, rather than bringing them here. I almost refused, but I couldn't resist the chance to unearth something fabulous. Of course, I caved."

"En're ya goin'?"

"I thought I'd go tomorrow and end the day there. Does that work for your schedule?"

He spat out the pencil to croak, "Hey, July. Come in here a sec."

Their lead volunteer wandered out from behind the entrance counter. July—as in "born on the Fourth of"—was a retired teacher who volunteered a few times a week to greet and direct visitors and collect the entry fee.

If they'd been in the south, Justine would have termed the woman's walk a "sashay," with plump hips swishing a pleated skirt around her knees. She wore another of the fanciful winter / holiday sweaters that kept her warm in the frigid northern Indiana air. This oriole blue favorite sparkled with snowflakes, rhinestones, and a scatter of silver sequins. "What do you need, honey?" The low voice dripped sugar.

Carl cleared his throat. "Nice sweater." He made the running-joke almost every day and usually kept a straight face. Even when her patterns veered to the extreme, such as the chorus line of high-hoofing reindeer. "Will you be able to stay tomorrow through five? I've got a horrendous budget meeting with the county finance committee. They've been busting all the department heads with this tax fiasco hanging over us." The chair squeaked as he slumped against the cushion. "I won't be able to escape before we close up here. Justine will be out, connecting with Liza Maddox's son to go through her clothing for a possible donation."

July's heavy-lashed brown eyes widened. "Oh, my goodness. I read she was in a couple of those beach movies. You know, with Frankie and the crew." Her lips lifted in a dreamy smile. "I just loved those films. So much fun in the sun."

His round face puckered, akin to a jolly elf. "Yeah, you really liked watching the buff guys. Sorry—no sexual harassment intended. I think Liza made at least one movie with our favorite Mouseketeer, and also did TV cameos. I'll have to Google her." He reached across the desk to grab a tissue and blew his nose with a resounding honk.

Justine rolled back in her chair to avoid a spray of germs and stood, recognizing the conversation could wind into a movie gab fest. "Great. Sounds like a go for tomorrow. Maybe the son's got some '60s-era bathing suits. I'll ask him to donate a photo or let me borrow one to copy."

July clasped her hands over her sweater-clad bosom. "Such a striking lady with that black hair set off by smoky gray eyes. Remember the gorgeous photo they ran in the paper when she passed? Now Liza's son, I imagine he could be a looker, too. D'you think he's single?" Having been happily married for decades, she'd determined to help Justine find "a good, honest man."

"Sorry to burst your bubble, but the man's pushy, impatient, and gruff." Justine shifted the muff and the mannequin hand in her arms and inched toward the door. "I wouldn't be interested in him even if he were young and single. I am only going over there to check out the clothing. Hopefully, the trip'll be worthwhile."

The older woman grimaced. "We all know your first love is musty old clothing. I just wish someday you'd find a nice gentleman."

Half expecting violin music to waft through the room, Justine brushed past another inference that her life was incomplete without mating with the right man. She did get lonely, but wasn't that normal? Not that she wouldn't like to have someone special to kiss first thing in the morning, without even caring about morning breath. But since that someone hadn't materialized, she got on with the mundane "everyday" of her life.

She edged out into the hallway. "I'm happy. Really," she affirmed to herself as much as her listeners. "I've got a great job, wonderful co-workers, and good friends. My mom and dad are active and healthy. I love spending time with my sister and her sweet babies. When, or if, the time is right, I'm sure I'll meet someone worthy of me," she assured, tongue firmly in-cheek.

Maybe in Chicago. A new start. Her traitorous mind

swung to the interview request. Her grip loosened. The mannequin hand escaped once more and rolled under Carl's desk. He thrust out a loafer-clad foot and bent low to pull it closer. She gulped as he held it out to her, trying to maintain a poker face.

July continued, undeterred. "Anyway, hon, what's the boy's name?"

The boy? Oh, she meant the old crab. "I don't know. He didn't bother to tell me, and I didn't care to ask."

Carl swiveled his chair between them. "He introduced himself as Jackson Maddox." His pale brows drew together. "Interesting that he has her last name. I don't recall seeing anything about his father. I'll have to Google it."

Chapter Two

The next afternoon at the Michigan Avenue address, Justine stepped out of her car smack into a calf-deep snowdrift. Frigid cold sliced through her wool slacks while clumps of snow invaded her ankle boots. She leaped out of the drift like an ungainly doe and shook the snow off her pants before plowing up the sidewalk toward the dark-brick house. The two-story was a generic square design with tan shutters framing mullioned windows. A red door provided a pop of color.

The three steps leading up to the door weren't shoveled, either. The old curmudgeon could at least have cleared the walk and the stairs. On the thought he might suffer a heart condition, like her father, she excused the oversight and placed her boot onto the bottom step. Her own heart cartwheeled as the heel slipped. With a shriek, she flung her arms out, trying to grab the wrought iron railing. Her hands shoved through inches of snow to clutch the rail. Miraculously, she remained upright. Winded and panting, she hoped none of the neighbors were watching out their windows.

A wet drop splatted her nose. She shivered and peered up. Snowflakes swirled around her hat and upturned collar. She knocked and waited. And waited.

Maybe he was hard of hearing, too. Just as she raised her mittened hand to pound harder, the door flew open. Startled, she dropped it to her side, trying to see into the dim hallway.

"Ms. Saunders?"

"Yes." She recognized the curt tone of voice. The door opened wider to sweep her in, along with more snow flurries. Disoriented, she stood in the foyer and stamped her feet on the entry mat, trying to hide her shock.

Jackson Maddox was not old. Or decrepit.

He stretched beyond six feet with a body type she'd call lanky, toned rather than skinny. His straight, brownish hair was streaked with blond. Tanned skin also spoke of recent hours in the sun. Trendy, dark-rimmed glasses perched above high cheekbones. A hip goatee graced his chin.

An attractive guy, except for the disdain curling his lip. Probably in his mid-thirties. She couldn't quite superimpose the image over her previous mental picture, but definitely recognized the grouchy attitude. He didn't speak further, just crossed his arms over his ski sweater and stared.

She stuttered to fill the conversational void. "The snow's starting to come down out there again. We sure don't need another foot."

His dark brows arched.

What an ass. Well, the sooner she finished, the less she'd have to endure his company. She broke eye contact and stretched to pull off the red wool hat, knitted by July. Her fingertips tingled with electricity as she freed the halo of hair, which sprang around her head like an erupting science experiment. She reached up in a futile attempt to tame the mass.

Jackson Maddox shifted to a full-fledged frown. "I can't wait to get out of this frozen tundra. No wonder my mom moved to California." He leaned against the wall, arms still crossed, not offering to help as she shrugged out of the knee-length down coat.

He still stared, taking her full measure, and apparently finding her lacking in the khaki-colored slacks and navy sweater. Justine fumed, aware her cheeks must be flaming as she tried to balance holding her bulky outerwear while pulling off the boots. She ducked her head, glad she didn't make any special effort with her appearance. A ballgown wouldn't impress this jerk. He hadn't even bothered to thank her for traveling to the house in nasty weather.

When she straightened, he finally extended a hand for her damp items and lumped them on a rack by the door. Her mouth fell open as he tromped away down the paneled hallway, tossing back over his shoulder, "We'll start with my mother's room."

Didn't they believe in manners in California? Nasty digs simmered in her head as she trailed behind him, her wet socks leaving splotches on the dark wood floor. But bare feet would be even more unprofessional.

The irritation and concerns derailed as her eyes began to roam. To her left, a multitude of antiques graced the cozy parlor. Her feet slowed as she passed a stained-glass lamp, the light enhancing muted aqua and green florals. She wanted to dart in to seek a manufacturer's mark but didn't dare lose sight of him. He'd already continued past the next doorway, which revealed a rectangular dining room with a crystal-drop chandelier. Her lips parted in pleasure as she halted in the arched entrance. A carved Victorian sideboard across the room displayed figurines, vases, and glassware.

A kinder, gentler host would indulge the time to

appreciate the items, and even be pleased about her admiration. J. Maddox was all business. He'd already disappeared from view. She quickened her steps down the hallway and turned left into another connecting hall.

Empty. Where did he go? She peeked into the first doorway. The high-ceilinged room flaunted dramatic rose paint. A magenta and sage green floral spread covered the bed, with matching throw pillows. The coordinating drapes were drawn tight. Her host, standing next to the shuttered window, gave a brief, emotionless nod.

She interpreted it as permission to enter. Her gaze wandered further to take in a massive white makeup table. A jumble of cosmetics, creams, and other toiletries littered the surface, as if Liza just used them then flitted out of the room. In the attached mirror, three vintage, gold-framed movie posters reflected from the opposite wall. Ignoring his silence, Justine stepped closer and gasped. "Oh my gosh. Did he really sign this?" Her finger quivered when she pointed at a well-known actor's scrawl over a blazing action scene.

"Looks like he did." From across the room, he offered a negligent shrug. "My mother ran with a lot of those folks from the late sixties through the nineties."

He must've grown up in a Hollywood lifestyle, yet how could he be blasé about such famous connections? She burned to ask whether he knew any big stars but didn't bother. He'd peg her as even more of a hick. Then she'd be mighty tempted to slap the smug, judgmental sneer off his face… She turned away from the enticing posters. "Was your father in show business, too?"

If he heard her, he ignored the question and moved toward the closet. "Should we pull the stuff out so you can see it better?"

Was he being a deliberate creep? *Keep your cool, stay professional, and wrap this up as quickly as possible.* She paused for several weighted seconds before adding a hint of frost to her tone. "We need to handle the garments carefully. Vintage clothing can be fragile."

Swallowing her irritation, she joined him in the walk-in closet where a bare bulb provided illumination. Annoyance dissolved into anticipation while scanning the neat contents. Now she'd take charge. "Let's separate the items in piles, with the modern clothes on the throw rug. We can lay vintage pieces on the bed. If you need help telling the difference, just ask."

He winced. "I'll leave the decisions totally to you. Obviously, that's why I called."

"Fine." *Just trying to be polite. A foreign concept in your world.*

She ignored his presence and started at the end of a hanging row. Soon her mood lightened, finding couture items scattered among the modern silky blouses, tailored slacks, skirts, and dresses. Liza Maddox's clothes exhibited great taste. Justine could imagine herself in the clothing, making herself over in a new job, a new life, a new town. Leaving behind her current beloved workplace, family, and friends.

Her fingers clenched around a wrap dress at that sad aspect, including hiding the Drysdale interview from Carl. They truly were good friends as well as co-workers. She wasn't afraid to tell him about the opportunity, but why stir him up if nothing came of it?

Besides, the choice might well be made for her. At this moment, her boss was mired in the county meeting where they could vote to axe their entire budget, or at the least, slash it deeply. Her hands shook at the serious musings. Nothing she could do about that here, and she had a task to complete. Liza's moody son paced past the closet door, checking his phone, face mirroring impatience. He'd probably set the stopwatch function to time her. Well, too f'ing bad. She wouldn't let him rush her.

The silent dig returned a grin to her face. She refocused to comb through both sides of the closet and decided to pull several couture garments. He hadn't stomped by for a few minutes; she raised her voice to address him. "I don't see anything truly vintage in here, but these classic designer pieces are nearing the twenty-year mark and they're worth holding onto."

No response. She draped them over her arm. "You could sell these outright or consign to a specialty secondhand shop."

His head poked around the doorway. He held up both hands. "I definitely don't want to mess with that process. They go with you or to Goodwill."

"We'll be happy to curate them." She hid her triumphant expression at introducing Prada, Chanel, and Dior labels in their museum. Special treasures to educate and entice future generations.

To her surprise, he stepped into the closet. "I'll carry these out."

To keep his precious, efficient timeline, she imagined. "Put these pieces on the bed. Carefully, please."

He smirked, standing close enough she could see the dark growth where he hadn't bothered to shave. His arms opened, as if welcoming an embrace. She clutched the clothing to her chest and tamped down a rush of embarrassment at the silly thought.

The load was heavy and slippery. Her toes in the damp wool socks bumped against his athletic shoes as she attempted to arch her arms to propel the mass toward him. His arms encased hers as the garments slithered between them. Within seconds, the clothing shifted, but they remained hooked together. Maintaining the precarious balance, their eyes locked.

Thick-lashed, sky-blue eyes hovered inches above hers. "Pull out," he instructed. She could feel his warm breath on her cheek. In a rom-com they'd warm up and their lips would quiver and lower…

Justine hiccupped out a nervous laugh, released her grip, and edged back to allow the fabrics to settle in his grasp. Yet he didn't leave. Those startling blue eyes probed behind the hipster glasses. "Just how did you get so knowledgeable about this stuff?"

The question jolted her. She'd grown used to his avoidance. "I've always liked history. I majored in it. Vintage clothing is an important element in the big picture." She skimmed a hand over the nearest garments. "The clothing people wore helps to identify their personal status and the eras they lived in."

He tilted his head. Was he interested?

Okay, she'd continue. "I got the job at the LaPorte County Museum right after graduation. For accuracy, I researched. You don't want someone complaining the mannequins are wearing Civil War clothing in the Edwardian parlor." The subject relaxed and warmed her. "Eventually, a friend asked me to help with costumes at LaPorte Little Theatre and my interest kept growing. I've even collected a few pieces myself."

He shifted his armload higher but didn't leave.

"Authenticity's critical. Don't drag people out of the story."

"Exactly." She mulled the insightful comment. "We do what we can here on the local level, but we can't match Hollywood budgets in providing magical illusions. We settle for portraying accuracy."

Budgets. She flashed again on the unhappy thought of Carl defending their work with the county committee. She drew a deep breath and distracted herself with a question. "What made you call us? Not to be crass, but you don't seem impressed by all this."

He arched his brows over the dark frames. "Let me dump this load first."

Justine imagined his confusion. The country mouse had a backbone. When she glowered at the term "dump," he snickered and backed out of the confines. She didn't expect him to return and snuck a glance to see him release the clothing—gently—onto the bed and smooth it. Her pulse kicked when he sauntered back to join her.

He stood framed in the doorway. "As if you couldn't guess, my mother was all about appearance. Clothing, makeup, hair. She'd get a kick out of being immortalized at the museum." He looked beyond her, his expression mellowing. "Local girl makes good. She didn't hit the big-time in Hollywood, but she acted in recognized movies and shows. And she loved living the lifestyle."

"Who wouldn't?" Justine kept pulling out additional garments, grudgingly impressed he contacted them to honor his mother. Even the biggest narcissist could have a soft spot for his mommy. But what about his father? The earlier brush-off about whether the man had been in show business stung.

He placed a tanned hand on the rack in front of her.

"Let me guess, you're the veritable hometown girl who stays put. Goes to college—maybe even commuted from home—and afterwards lands a sweet little job to fill the days before marriage and kids."

The smug comment pierced. She swung toward him. His lip lifted, but she didn't appreciate the attempt at humor. A slow burn coiled up from her chest and into her throat, lacing her words with heat. "I don't know if you're trying to be funny, or snide. Since I'm here in a professional capacity, I'll be the bigger person and give you the benefit of the doubt." She didn't dare say more, or risk losing her dignity and the vintage haul.

His mouth flattened. "Sorry," he muttered. "I've been told my dry humor sometimes misses the mark."

She broke eye contact while he backed out of the space. Darn her quick tongue. Quick to justify. Quick to defend. A behavior honed through the years to slap off judgmental slights from catty high school girls. On the other hand, he deserved the sharp comeback. How nasty to poke fun when he'd barely met her. She could describe her life as mundane. He hadn't earned the privilege.

They lapsed back into prickly silence as she evaluated the closet's contents. Somehow, J. Maddox's presence loomed just as large out of sight. Prepared to carry the next load of fashionable clothing herself, she pulled back when he stepped inside the closet again.

His features remained passive. "Load me up."

She half expected him to kick her out. But they could pretend their way past the tension. The intense gaze still rattled her as she concentrated on draping a load of clothing over his arms, keeping distance this time. Her tone veered toward clinical. "Unfortunately, all of this is modern. Lovely, but not for the museum. Are there older pieces in another closet or an attic?"

"Maybe." He moved out, balancing the pile. "There's more in the guest bedroom."

The possibility of acquiring one of his mother's actual costumes was too enticing to ignore. Much as she'd prefer to escape their growing tension, she wouldn't miss the opportunity. Justine followed him out of the closet and gaped when he opened his arms to drop the tangle of garments to the floor. She pressed her lips together hard enough to melt the lip gloss. Touché. No words needed. He'd hit her with a most effective silent comeback.

A slow grin rolled over his face, probably recognizing how she itched to smooth everything into a tidy pile. "I'll stuff this into bags later," he said, with emphasis on the word *stuff*. "Maybe I'll find time to run it to Goodwill. Or leave it at the curb." He nudged a silk scarf with his foot before heading out of the room.

Leaving her standing like an idiot. Justine gritted her teeth. He wouldn't dare dump these items. Would he? She closed her eyes, counting to ten and attempting to re-center herself. A scent of floral perfume wafted past her nose. Her lids fluttered open.

A fleeting movement at the edge of her vision led her to swing around. Her mouth opened in shock as she took in the semi-familiar person slouching on the bed. She squeezed her eyes shut, slapped her hands over them, and shook her head. Surely, when she opened them, the impossible image would have disappeared.

She peeped through her fingers and gasped. Liza Maddox lay propped on the bed in a royal blue miniskirt. Raven-dark, chin-length hair waved back from her stunning face in the ultimate Charlie's Angels style.

Nose straight and petite, lips full and pouty as a collagen injection. Dark brows winged over silver-gray eyes. Except for the hairdo and late '70s dress, she appeared natural and...human.

Justine shivered, with her gaze riveted on the apparition. In disbelief, she pinched the tender flesh of her own forearm and winced at the stab of pain.

Liza threw back her head and chuckled, baring her long throat. "Yes, dear. You're very much awake. I hope you're not too startled, but I thought maybe you could use some pointers in dealing with my obtuse son."

"Oh-my-Lord." Justine's breath panted out as she stood frozen. This. Could not. Be. Real. Yet a few hesitant words slid out of her mouth. "Has Jackson seen you here?"

"Of course not. You think he'd believe in ghosts, my gruff, no-nonsense progeny?" She paused and looked away. The smug expression sobered. "He did believe in magic when he was little. Until he figured out I couldn't give him the one thing he really, truly wished for."

"I, uh, I'm sure you meant well." Justine stuttered. She actually was having a conversation with a ghost. Or she was majorly delusional. She squeezed her eyes shut again and counted to ten. When she opened them, the apparition remained, though the edges grew hazy.

Liza's arresting face remained downcast. The voice grew faint as she faded. "Unfortunately, my priorities were skewed."

Justine scrubbed her hands over her cheeks and stared at the now-empty bed. She didn't dream the encounter. Liza Maddox was haunting this house. No way she could she tell her cynical son. She ran out of the room, heart pumping double-time, to catch up with him.

Chapter Three

Liza, June 1963

With her mother's voice droning outside the closet door, Liza ignored the familiar nagging tone and dropped to her knees to find her special-occasion black heels. The patent stilettos were unearthed in the far corner beneath a quilted robe. She pushed the robe aside as another item destined to stay in LaPorte. The pink pattern was much-too-demure for her pending California lifestyle. Rising with a dancer's grace, she extracted the heels and tossed the cardboard box aside.

Outside the closet, she caught her mother's stern expression and tight-crossed arms, a further contrast against the sunshine-yellow walls of the bedroom. Liza swallowed her annoyance. For once, she wasn't braced for a fight. She just wanted to leave with quiet courage, like an adult. She slid the shoes into a suitcase splayed open atop the eyelet comforter on her bed. The new white furniture and the overstuffed armchair seemed chic when she entered high school. Now the decor grated as babyish and unsophisticated.

Her mother moved, towering over the side of the bed. "Couldn't you at least give college a try? You could take a couple of classes while you figure out what you'd like to do."

Ignoring the strain in Mama's voice, Liza focused

on the mounds of clothing, folding and shoving pieces into her case. "I know what I want to do," she repeated, with as much patience as she could muster. "I'm taking the bus to California to work in the movies. You were proud when I won the best actress award for both the junior and senior plays."

Margaret Maddox's deep maternal sigh seemed to echo in the over-quiet room. For once the boxy record player sat silent. "You really think that's all you need to get cast in the movies? You're not the only perky young ingénue fleeing small-town roots in the hope to capture fame. There are hundreds of pretty girls who haven't had a drop of luck in landing a movie or even a commercial. Thousands probably. What makes you think you're so special?"

The jab hit home, as intended. Liza dropped the folded red cardigan and straightened. She expected to meet the hard glint of battle. Instead, tears shimmered in the luminous eyes that mirrored her own. Her irritation floated away, akin to a released balloon. Her stoic Midwestern mother never cried. She hadn't seen her eyes well up since daddy's—her husband's—funeral. They'd both cried buckets then.

"Mama." She reverted to her childhood term of endearment. "I know there's no guarantee I'll have any more success than those other girls who want to make it big. I'm realistic about both my assets and my chances out there. But I'm committed, persistent, and can work the charm." She flashed a smile, trying to coax one from her mother, who uncrossed her arms to swipe a finger under each eye.

Liza grasped the damp hand in her own. "Aren't you relieved I'm staying with Linda Townsend? She's from a good family and has lived out there for five years. I'll learn from her how to negotiate the town and the business."

Thankfully, she'd met this cousin of one of her local friends during summer visits. Linda invited her to stay in her small apartment. While trying to break into modeling, she could use the extra cash. "I know I can find waitressing or a secretarial job. I have skills from summer work and my school classes." The cajoling tone often disarmed disappointed teachers and demanding boyfriends.

Her mother sniffed loudly before pulling her into her arms. Liza registered the scent of lavender soap and felt silky, dark hair against her face, passed to them from Irish ancestors. The Celtic bloodline also embraced dogged determination—or downright stubbornness.

Margaret's voice murmured next to her ear. "Sweetheart, I know you think you have it all worked out, but I can't help but worry. Two thousand miles is such a long way. Los Angeles is a very big city. Not everything out there is shiny. People will try to take advantage. You'll have to be on your guard." She pulled back to capture her daughter's eyes.

Liza met the stare, willing herself to come off as completely confident. She couldn't let her see the underlying uncertainty beneath the bravado. Though she was committed to this course, the move was huge. Especially for a sheltered girl from Indiana.

Her mother's hands still encased her arms. "I know you think the little trust your father set up will go a long way, but everything's much more expensive out there. Be frugal and be careful." Worry lines, on the face devoid of makeup, had aged her beyond forty years.

Vanity had never been one of her mother's vices.

Yet it topped her own list of personality flaws. Liza lifted her chin to project strength and resolve. Traits she'd have to rely on, along with her looks. They'd be her main lucre in this adventure. Milky skin, full lips, and dark-lashed eyes an admirer compared to shifting fog over a lake. She'd make the most of her appearance while she could, because didn't she know better than most girls that life could change in an instant?

The image of her beloved father floated into her mind. Dear daddy maintained a smile for her, even when he couldn't lift his head from the pillow. *"My little sunbeam. You should be an entertainer when you grow up."* Sadly, he knew he wouldn't be there to witness it. A decade had trudged by since they'd diagnosed the cancer in his blood. Despite weeks of harsh treatments, the disease clung, refusing to be beaten.

Afraid she'd turn to quivering jelly at leaving her mother alone, in the big old house, she shoved the thoughts from her mind. Her shoulders squared. Margaret O'Connell Maddox was a strong, capable woman, who now could get on with her own life. Maybe even open herself to find a new man to love.

Her chest burned at the thought. She leaned in to tighten her arms around her mother again, registering the strong muscles. Before today, she couldn't remember when they last embraced. After slamming into her teen years, Liza rebelled against any closeness, concern, or boundaries.

She dropped her arms and reestablished a cool distance. If she didn't leave immediately, she'd get caught in the web of a pleasant, boring life. Ending up here for the rest of her years, married to a fine but simple man and raising two to three precocious kids.

Both of them could pursue new dreams, she told herself. Even as she watched the mist of tears cloud her own eyes in the dresser mirror.

Chapter Four

Jackson stood in the doorway of the second upstairs bedroom and glanced at his watch. He'd figured thirty minutes, max, to help the woman from the museum jam clothes into garbage bags and haul them to her car. Instead, more than an hour had frittered away. Somehow, he'd gotten sidetracked in observing her immersion in the clothes. As a screenwriter, he observed human emotions and interactions, yet rarely indulged in them himself.

Multiple expressions flitted across her face: brows knit in concentration, wide eyes at a recognizable label, exasperation at his careless handling of the "treasures." He stared down the empty hallway, recalling their strained introduction. He didn't ask her there for polite entertainment. His goal—and he was known for being single-minded and a stickler for detail—was to finish as soon as possible to focus on the rest of the house. And return to his life in Los Angeles.

Impatient to begin, he couldn't help but size her up as she shuffled out of the lumpy coat, revealing a shapeless long sweater. About five-foot-seven in stocking feet. The top of her head would graze his nose. When she'd pulled off the knitted hat his lips twitched as wavy blonde hair with a tinge of red sprang to attention. While her hands shot up in a futile effort to tame it, a blush colored her cheeks. To his puzzlement, he found that a tiny bit endearing. He couldn't remember the last time he'd seen a woman, of any age or social status, blush. Unless the script called for it.

After leaving his mother's bedroom minutes ago, he expected the woman to follow. She probably couldn't help herself and stayed to straighten the mess he intentionally left. He started to holler down to hurry her along and heard the soft pad of footsteps.

He waited, scratching his head that the out-of-character, sentimental attachment to his mother and grandmother propelled him to call the museum. He definitely was out of sync here, in the house where they both passed. Why else would he get a weird kick out of someone's enjoyment in sifting through outdated outfits?

Her joy hadn't dimmed, even after his not-so-witty observation about her life. The poor girl had been an easy target, a channel for his ire at handling these final tasks. Alone. Liza gave birth to only one child. A bastard.

The visitor popped into view at the top of the stairs. Her eyes strayed to the right, lingered, and snapped straight ahead. He imagined her disapproval at the crumpled towel lying on the bathroom floor. Perhaps another blush would stain those cheeks if she glimpsed the tangled sheets on the bed in his grandmother's room.

In actuality, as she neared, she looked a little paler than before. He stepped inside the guestroom with the twin bed, dark wood dresser, and a lumpy padded armchair under the window. The blinds were shut. He switched on the floor lamp before moving straight into the closet, to avoid chitchat.

Seconds later she joined him. Color returned to her features as she literally bounced, as if her feet longed to dance. "Oh, yes. Yes. Gorgeous." She touched a springy net formal the color of fresh creamed butter.

"Must have been Liza's," he guessed. The dress was sexy, draped over one shoulder to leave the other bare. Down-to-earth Gran wouldn't spare any time for seduction and pretense. His mother had mastered that art. After all, she captured three men in marriage. Excluding his nameless, faceless "father."

"Have you ever seen a photo of her in this?"

The question drew him back. He shook his head while she gathered the voluminous gown in her arms. He flattened himself against the wall to give her space to whoosh it out into the bedroom. A whiff of scent floated as she brushed by. Warm and sweet, with a hint of vanilla. He didn't think before asking, "What are you wearing?"

The eyes rounded in alarm. "Wha-at do you mean?"

"You smell like something familiar. I was trying to place it."

She seemed to inhale a calming breath. "Warm Sugar Cookie" from The Body Shop. My friend, July, bought it for me for Christmas."

"That explains it." His grin turned wicked. "You're supposed to smell good enough to eat."

A full-out flush traveled from her face and down her neck. "Not my intention," she shot back. "Though July probably thought that very thing."

"What kind of name is July?" he parried, wondering why he cared enough to ask. Maybe he was trying to rattle the hometown girl. He had to give her points for showing unexpected backbone.

"My friend was born on the Fourth of July during war-era patriotism. Several times a week, she joins us to volunteer." She chuckled, clutching the dress against her chest. "And no, before you ask, she doesn't look like a 'July'."

She spread the dress on the quilt, sewed in a log-cabin design by his Gran. Her face brightened. "What a wonderful prom dress from the early '60s. Do you know if your mom was in the court?"

"Court? Um, no. I mean, I don't have a clue." He didn't know anything about proms. Except for watching horror movies. He'd gone to an all-boys prep school.

"I'll check the yearbooks at the museum. Do you know when she graduated?"

He searched his memory. "LaPorte class of 1963 sounds right. Within a week, she jumped a bus toward a glittery future in Hollywood. Where she dabbled in acting, made the rounds of the best parties, and whirled her way through a revolving door of male companions." He clamped his lips shut. Yeah, being in this house messed with his head. Years ago, he finally accepted their living situation and moved on to make his own way in the world. His own success. He didn't need to ride anyone's parental coattails.

The woman seemed to sense a reluctance to continue and fluffed the gown again. "Such a striking look. I imagine all the girls were pretty itchy, encased in stiff netting." The skirt expanded to cover the spread, rising up like a sail catching the wind.

He tapped it with a finger. "Their boyfriends were probably happy to relieve them of the misery at the end of the night."

She frowned, straightened, and made an effort to smooth her face. He hadn't intended to shock, just to distract his dark thoughts. He ignored the tinge of regret and swung back into the closet. "What else do you want out of here?"

"Hopefully, most of it." Her voice regained an edge of reserve. She stood in the doorway. "Do you have any photos of your mother I could scan? If there are any of her in this dress, or other pieces, we can pair them together. If we're lucky enough to find an actual costume, we could match it to photos from that time, or movie stills."

Jackson shook his head. "No way would she have been allowed to take costumes, unless a show was low-budget, and she had to wear her own clothes."

She dropped her eyes to the carpet. "Right. I'm an idiot. Sorry."

"No, you're not. I grew up around movie sets, so I have inside info." Man, he was a yo-yo here. Wanting to hurry this woman out of the house, sniping at her with uncouth comments, then showing concern about hurting her feelings. "I don't remember what's in them, but there are photo albums downstairs. You're welcome to copy things."

"Thanks." She stepped past, evidently more intrigued by the clothing than further conversation. He couldn't blame her. After handling more items, she ventured, "Did your mother grow up here? I wondered how long the house has been in your family."

Jackson pondered to recall the stories from his youth. Nobody in California was interested in where his family came from. If you didn't boast a recognizable last name, they assumed you were a nobody until proven otherwise. He worked doubly hard to convince people in the business to give him a chance. "The place came down through my great-grandmother's family. I think Liza was a baby when they moved in. After eight years, her father died of leukemia. His passing left my grandmother a young widow, but she never remarried."

Nostalgia gripped him at the thought. Having a grandfather might've helped smooth his own edges. "I guess he was her first love, and this old house was the second. We came back a few times when I was growing up—extreme culture shock from swinging California."

Her lips curved. "I bet your grandma loved having you visit."

He thought back to the summer when his mother and dismissive second stepfather dropped him off before their European honeymoon. "When I was ten, I spent two months here with her and we bonded. She was old enough to retire from her work as an elementary school secretary, yet she enjoyed the kids too much to give it up. That left her free in the summer to take me on day trips to Chicago and Michigan, and to visit the shores of Lake Michigan."

With her deep Midwestern roots, she provided a strong grounding influence for him that continued through occasional visits, long distance calls, and lots of letters. Mainly from her side of the mailbox.

Justine tilted her head. "See. We're not all cornfields and cows in the Midwest. Our history is important to us." Her face softened. "I imagine you miss both of them a lot."

He ducked a direct answer. "They were two strong, impressive ladies." With his mother, the feelings were too mixed to unravel, her unexpected passing too new to process. Yes, he missed his grandmother, especially in this house, which embodied her homage to the family ancestry. Jackson brushed away a tinge of guilt at his intent to dismantle that heritage. "As for this place, the house is also impressive. Not my style, though."

"Really? What is your style?"

He peered out into the bedroom, comparing the ambience. "My condo's in a converted warehouse, second floor. Lots of glass. Not many walls. A few minutes' walk to the beach. Great restaurants and shops." He lifted his brows in a mocking expression. "Urban chic."

She stared him down. "Personally, I would love to live in a place like this, surrounded by beautiful antiques. But I work in a museum. And I better get back to the job at-hand." She broke off to resume the closet search.

Despite the congenial tone, the memories left him a little unmoored again. He retreated to sit in the armchair to check his phone for texts and emails. He flew out here in a break between film projects but couldn't afford to linger because he might miss a fleeting opportunity.

His head flew up as she whooped an enthusiastic, "Yes!" Intrigued, he spotted her kneeling at the back of the closet. He joined to peer over her shoulder. The letters "CA" were written on a large cardboard box. The tight confines didn't allow them to open it inside. "Here, let me." He edged past her to carry the box into the bedroom.

She dropped to her knees and together they yanked back the flaps. Justine's eyes shone as she pulled out flirty mini-dresses, a silver formal, and a couple of '60s-era beach bunny bathing suits. Notecards also were tucked inside. "She jotted down when she wore these. We love that kind of provenance." She held up her arm, inviting a high five.

He snickered at her enthusiasm, extended his hand,

and slapped it against hers. She wagged her head. "You must think I'm crazy."

"I respect people's passions. I'm glad you've found one. That's how I feel about my writing."

"You're a writer?" Her lips pursed. She sat back on her heels. "I'd have guessed a more detached, physical job. Architect, or engineering."

The pointed jab amused him. "Screenwriter, to be precise."

"Not to be gauche, but would I recognize any of your work?"

"You might. One of my projects was *Winter Frost*."

Her features reflected an amazement she clearly struggled to tamp down. "I loved that movie."

"I'm blown away you even saw it here. The critics were fairly kind, though the general public didn't flock to the big screen." The words slipped out before he could stop them. "I wrote it for myself. Catharsis, I suppose. Pulled a lot from my mother and grandmother's relationship."

He stared above her head, recalling Liza's pleasure at the veiled immortality he bestowed. Of course, she also pointed out areas he could have improved. Gran had already passed by then, or he could have counted on her to crack a clever quip and pull him close for a teary-eyed hug. Damn. While the emotions toward his mother definitely were complicated, he did miss both those feisty women.

He looked up to find Justine watching him through soft eyes, as if trying to peel away the protective layers he'd spent years building around himself. He scrambled to his feet to divert any further probing conversation. His fragile, young-boy core shriveled and died long ago.

Chapter Five

Liza, April 1979

"Miss Maddox, you are definitely pregnant."

From the doctor's stern expression and knitted bushy brows, Liza gathered the man didn't approve of mingling "Miss" and "pregnant" in the same sentence. If she'd been rational, instead of rattled and jumpy, she would have given a fake name to set up the appointment with this new gynecologist an hour from her Los Angeles apartment. Or she could've prefaced her name with the social acceptability of a "Mrs." But since missing her second period, she hardly slept. Coherent thought was a stretch. She even turned down an audition to grab this first open appointment at the small clinic.

His confirmation exaggerated her fears. Liza couldn't control the panic that gripped her mind and body. Her limbs trembled hard enough to rustle the paper-covered exam table where she perched. She wrapped her arms around her mid-section, wishing the words inspired joy, rather than dread. The joy they'd found in the act of creation.

The man's weathered face seemed to mellow. "You're about two months along."

There were no words big enough to address the monumental situation. She envisioned a script assistant standing in the corner with a cue card bearing the correct, happy expression: *"Oh, how wonderful!"*

Despite the spectral prompting, she couldn't say the line. While she was a good-enough actress, it would take the dramatic chops of Katherine Hepburn to pull off even a hint of pleasure at the news. She drew in a deep breath and pushed it out slowly.

The doctor glanced down at the chart, then at her ring finger, before meeting her eyes. "I take it you're not married. Or engaged. Is the father in the picture?"

She stared at her lap, where her manicured nails dug into the cotton gown. "Not really."

"Well," he tapped his fingers on the clipboard. "I'll prescribe pre-natal vitamins and the nurse will give you some helpful brochures. You can set up another appointment with the receptionist."

"What if I'm considering other…options?" Her voice came out low and strained.

"That, young lady, is not something I can help you with." His tone cooled. He walked to the door, snapping it shut behind him.

Slumping in defeat, she knew she had tough calls to make. First, she'd find a more sympathetic doctor. One more open to supporting a woman's choice. Eventually, she'd decide whether to call her mother back in LaPorte.

Imagining the maternal disappointment that would wrap around her own heart, she closed her eyes. A tear slid down her cheek. The first she allowed herself since the suspicions arose. Despite their differences, she found herself longing for homey comfort and support. Her move here had only widened the chasm between them. She truly didn't know if they could reach across it, burdened by this crushing issue. Especially with Margaret's Catholic faith driving her opinions.

Landing small parts in movies and TV shows didn't impress her. Nor had her daughter's early marriage and quickie divorce. The revelation of dear hubby's drinking and cheating might've swayed her opinion, but Liza was too proud to admit she fell for a smarmy cad. Especially when she ignored her mother's concerns after dragging the bum to Indiana to meet her.

She bowed her head. Not praying but straining for every ounce of mettle she could muster to decide how—or whether—to approach her mother and the father of the child. An unwanted pregnancy might sever both relationships forever, depending on how she chose to proceed.

Chapter Six

Justine couldn't believe this aloof, sarcastic guy wrote the incredible script for *Winter Frost*. When she talked her friends into seeing it at the local theater, they all teared up over the tale of a dying older mother reconciling with her wayward daughter. If he could write such a touching story, perhaps there were hidden sensibilities behind his cynical façade. Not that she had any interest in probing them.

He closed down any hint of vulnerability, jumping to his feet and tossing a dismissive, "time's wasting" comment.

Right. He'd asked her here. To help him. She ground her teeth and stood to return to the closet. Better to take stuff and sort through it at the museum than spend more time in his company. Or the ghost's. She shuddered at the reminder of the earlier encounter. What would he do if she informed him about the conversation with his mother? Probably dial 911 and restrain her until the police arrived. Better to let sleeping ghosts lie.

If they were willing to. She stiffened, sniffed the air for floral perfume, but didn't detect the scent. Yep, she should finish quickly and run. Yet back in the closet, her resolution dissolved. An emerald-bright dressing gown beckoned from the rack. Her fingers tingled as she smoothed them down the slinky brocade satin. She held it against her torso—so entranced she forgot he was watching beyond the doorway. Looking up, she caught his gaze. Self-consciousness overrode the enchantment. She rehung the garment. "1940s. Gorgeous, but not your mother's generation."

He eyed her lazily from behind the hip glasses. "Then why don't you keep it."

A smile teased her lips before propriety reared. "I couldn't. These gowns fetch a good price."

His blue eyes sharpened. "I don't care. You've done me a favor coming over here. The green color's killer with your eyes."

She hesitated, surprised he even noticed. And he finally recognized her extra effort in coming to the house. A second refusal hovered, but the offer was impossible to resist. She'd report the gift to Carl, who also wouldn't care. Releasing a hint of buried rebel, she accepted. "Thank you. Dressing gowns are among my favorite vintage items. I've collected a few really fine ones."

The corner of his mouth lifted, bewildering her anew with the unexpected behavior shift. Just when she thought she had him pegged, the guy turned her assumptions on end. Realizing she was standing like a dolt, she gave herself a mental kick and returned to the remaining garments. The dull glow of the closet bulb created a cozy cocoon while she separated out vintage treasures. They didn't speak as she finished with the hanging rack and passed him items to move into the bedroom. Finally, she could focus on shoe and hat boxes on a narrow shelf above. She climbed onto a two-step ladder and stretching on her toes to grasp one.

"Hey, I can reach those…"

His offer faded as the ladder wobbled. The box

slipped toward the floor while her body angled back. She shrieked and flung out her hands to grasp the rack—but missed. Expecting the impact, her back thudded into a hard surface that wasn't a wall. She heard him grunt and felt the exhalation of air by her ear as his arm slung around her. Under her breasts. His other arm grabbed her waist, sliding under the bulky sweater as they crashed backwards.

Justine's feet dangled several inches off the floor. Stunned by the impact, it took her a moment to tune in to the hard body cradling hers. Next, she recognized the oh-so-intimate placement of his hands. One was splayed against her bare skin; smooth, cool fingers spanned her stomach, from the waistband of her slacks to the bottom of her bra. A flood of heat spread through her body, part embarrassment, part heightened awareness. Squirming free would only magnify the super-awkward situation.

Even more torturous, to let her down gently he had to ease his grasp. His right arm brushed over her breasts as she slid along his body, her nerve endings registering every sharp plane. For a lanky guy, he was taut and toned. She knew her face was flaming, and her female parts were a tad heated, too. Her socks hit the carpet and she scooted away, trying to compose her face. To calm her body's reaction.

She sucked in a deep breath and turned slowly to face him. "I'm s-so sorry." Her voice betrayed her. "Thank you for catching me. Are you okay?"

"I should be asking you that." He sounded hoarse, as if the wind had been punched out of him. Yet his eyes were intent on her, behind glasses that had been knocked off-center.

Without thinking, she straightened them, and her

fingers brushed the skin at his temples. His eyes drilled into hers, mere inches away. Blue. Vivid. Calling up the sky on a lovely, cloudless day. She snatched her hands back and stepped away, ignoring the renewed flutter in her body.

Something crackled beneath her feet. Thankful to break the mounting tension, she looked down to see a scatter of white envelopes. "The box is full of letters." She stooped to gather the pile and held them out, waiting for him to acknowledge the find. He glared back at her, his jaw working, but didn't move or speak.

Exasperated, she stuffed the envelopes back inside the shoebox and skirted around him to settle the contents on the bed. Moments later he joined her, gaze trained on the find. The silence expanded between them. She wondered what held him back. With such a cool discovery, she'd longed to drop right down on the closet floor to read them. Out of historical curiosity.

Jackson waited several more beats before plucking up an envelope. He regarded it with such intensity she pondered snapping her fingers to remind him of her presence. Yet she stayed silent as he rifled further into the box, seeming to examine the postmarks. Something mysterious was going on, but it wasn't her business to ask. She'd finish the vintage mission and head on her way.

She cleared her throat to voice that intention as he pushed a hand through his hair, knocking his glasses askew again. He didn't seem to notice. She wasn't about to repeat the intimate gesture. Seconds ticked by before he seemed to register her presence.

"They're from my mother." His voice was low and somehow tentative. "The date stamps are during the time when she was pregnant with me."

Chapter Seven

Liza, June 1979

Liza rolled from her stomach to her back in the poolside lounge chair and glanced at her watch. "Could you hand me the lotion?" she asked her friend, Jewel. "I'm starting to sizzle."

Palm trees waved above them, stirring a slight breeze. She lifted her face to it, appreciating the opportunity to spend the day at the private pool. At four months her mid-section formed a marshmallow-y mound under the blazing orange one-piece suit. A week ago, she shoved her bikinis to the back of the drawer and purchased a more conservative number with a hidden maternity panel.

Her figure and looks represented a defining asset to her career success. Which was on indefinite hold as the stretchy panel would expand soon to cover a basketball-sized bump. At this point, someone meeting her for the first time would believe she was a little out of shape. Or at least, that's what Liza told herself.

Her companion, a dyed-blonde starlet from the beach movie circuit days, had become a close friend and confidante. The woman passed a bottle of sunscreen and looked over the tops of her rhinestone-encrusted shades. "You told me you wanted to talk today. So dish."

Liza took her time squirting lines of lotion onto her

tanned arms and legs. She added another dollop in her palms and sat the container between them on the patio fronting an oval pool. "I talked to my mama this week." She smoothed the protection over her legs and affected her former Midwest drawl. "What a surprise, she's not thrilled with my news. While she didn't say those words, I could read between the lines. She's so glad my father isn't living to witness my shame."

Jewel frowned and reached for her margarita, the red matching her bikini. "Was she really that awful?"

Liza considered the question. Even without drinking, her head felt sluggish as her body in the LA heat. "No. That's not fair of me. She tried to act cool about the baby. But I know it crushed her. Especially when I stated there's no chance of marrying the father. With the added kicker that I wasn't sure how to proceed with the pregnancy."

"Wow." Her friend drained the glass and rolled toward her. "Did she think you were talking about an abortion?"

The word stung. "I was. Or adoption." She paused to rub lotion onto her face, sadness tugging at her. "To be honest, I still didn't know at that point if I wanted to keep the baby. Motherhood is a damn big deal, you know." Jewel was the proud mother of two little girls who were napping inside the Spanish-style bungalow.

"I do. I love my babies so much, but it's hard raising them, even with two parents. I admire that you've decided to go it alone."

"I wrestled the decision over many sleepless nights. I hope I look less haggard than I feel."

"You are always beautiful. I hope the bastard— whoever he is—kicks himself every day for letting you get away."

The blunt words drew a tiny smile. "He probably will. I didn't tell him till last week either. His face lit for a second, before the implications set in."

"Such difficult conversations." Jewel reached to take her hand. "I'm so sorry, hon."

She returned her friend's squeeze. "He argued the options. I need to let my mother know I've made up my mind to keep the baby. Maybe I'll take the easy road and write this time to avoid the Catholic guilt. I just hope I'm making the right decision." She smoothed her free hand over her stomach. "Last week, after I talked to both of them, I started to feel these little flutters of…life. I realized I couldn't get rid of him or her. Or give the child up to someone else to raise. This baby was conceived in love, even though we'll never be able to marry."

"You never know if—"

Liza held up a hand to cut her off. False hope would only drag out the misery. "Yes, I do know that he and I aren't meant to be. His father-in-law would destroy him. And me." Her lips curved softly. "But this baby, I have the strongest notion he's going to make a difference. He's not a mistake."

Chapter Eight

The letters were from a pregnant Liza Maddox. That would be a good thing—right? A joyful time. Yet her host's actions indicated otherwise. He seemed to be warring with himself. Justine watched him flick open an envelope with the tip of a finger. He pulled out the letter and pushed the box aside to sit on the end of the bed, below the net formal.

She stayed standing, unsure whether to slip back into the closet to give him time alone. He'd apparently tuned her out again. After several moments of reading, he looked up. His face mirrored a naked vulnerability that wrenched her. "I never knew my father." His voice roughened with emotion. "Don't even know who he was. Liza only told me he was famous. When I pestered her about it—when I still cared—she said she couldn't tell me more until he passed away. I suppose he may still be living." His eyes lowered to the letter where his fingers clutched the pink notepaper.

Justine experienced a wave of compassion for the small boy hoping to connect with a father. And for the man who pretended he no longer cared. "Do you have any idea who it might be?" she whispered, not wanting to shatter his confessional mood.

He shook his head, which resettled the glasses on his nose. "No. I doubt the answer's in this box. Gran swore she didn't know. She could be pretty damn blunt, and when I was in my early twenties, she told me she only knew he was married at the time of my conception. Plus, she muttered a few choice comments about that 'self-indulgent era.' She was old-school conservative. Didn't approve of the wild life her daughter lived in California."

"That had to be difficult for you." She couldn't imagine growing up without her own loving father. Or mother. There'd have been a huge hole in her childhood without their constant care and guidance. No wonder Jackson seemed cynical. From the sound of it, he'd practically raised himself. She watched the cool, detached façade slide back onto his face.

He released the letter into the box. "I did get a taste of having fathers. Stepdads." He held up two fingers. "Liza also got married way before I came along, for a year in her mid-twenties. I never met the guy." He smiled wryly. "There were always boyfriends before, after, and in-between. She liked men and she was a babe for her time."

Yeah, she'd seen that for herself—in the semi-flesh. Justine shook away the disturbing thought and noted he referred to his mother by her first name. As if trying to override his somber memories, he rose and headed to the door. "Sorry to get heavy. Let's wrap up and send you on your way. I'll grab some garbage bags."

So he could brood alone? Her eyes riveted to the letters. Evidently, Jackson had great willpower and would wait until he was alone to probe into the painful past. Or he'd hide the box in the dark recesses of the closet and forget he'd ever seen them.

She shoved down her own curiosity to peek inside the envelopes. She had no right to intrude on this history uninvited. He returned with a roll of bags, and they transferred the sorted materials into them. The box marked CA and the dressing gown he gifted would go with her. They'd also have to collect the couture items from Liza's bedroom. *No—he could do that.* She wouldn't risk encountering the spirit again.

Jackson gathered bags in his arms. "Make sure you take what you want. The rest will go to Goodwill. If the theater will use them, they're welcome to the clothes." He stepped past her. "If there's anything else you want personally, take it."

"Don't tempt me." She'd love to help herself and might have to war with her conscience later. One last look in the closet assured her no treasures remained. He had left just one bag for her to carry. She hefted it, reminding herself to check out the framed photos on the hallway walls and any albums before leaving. But as she started down the stairs, he met her halfway, his brows furrowed.

"We've got a problem. The lake effect snow machine dumped a load while we were buried in the closet. Buried being the operative word."

****

Jackson turned on his heel and headed back down the stairs, irritation twisting inside him. He trudged into the parlor and halted in front of the picture window. Though darkness had fallen, the streetlight illuminated the outline of her car, invisible under a snowy mound. Heavy flakes continued to drift, adding to the multiple inches on the ground. At her approach, he kept his eyes trained forward. "With the drapes pulled in the bedrooms, we didn't see the snow coming down like this for the past," he glanced at his watch, "two-plus hours."

"Umm, do you want me to come back another day

to look at the photo albums?" Her voice registered a hint of alarm.

"Ms. Saunders. You aren't going anywhere." He didn't remember her first name, as she hadn't repeated it earlier. He flung a hand toward the frosted window. "Not only is your car covered, apparently a snowplow shoved several more feet across the driveway. I couldn't even find a shovel here to clean the walk. My mother must've paid someone or cajoled a neighbor to plow her out."

"B-but, I can't stay here."

He shot her an annoyed look. Was he that repulsive—or fearsome? "You don't have a choice unless you want to wade through several feet of snow to trudge home. Don't worry, I promise I'm not going to attack you."

Her posture stiffened as she shot him a defiant glare. "No, I'm sure I'm not your type. Believe me, that's the least of my worries."

Though he definitely was annoyed by the situation, he couldn't help snickering. "I'm not sure I have a 'type' anymore. And no, I won't be a good host. There's hardly any food around here. I've been eating out and carrying in. Which reminds me, I haven't eaten since breakfast at good ole' Round the Clock."

She crossed her arms over the front of the baggy sweater.

His lips tightened. He wasn't thrilled, either, but he wasn't going to burrow through the drifts with his bare hands. "Look, I agree this is far from ideal, but unless you can call someone to plow or blow out the drive, we're probably not going to get it opened up tonight. Is there anyone you can call who'll brave this mess?"

The fluff of hair bounced with her head shake. "No.

My dad had a stent put in last week. My sister's husband is on a business trip. Carl will be at his mom's already celebrating her birthday." She stopped. "Sorry, too much information. Nope, no one I can call."

He stifled the growl that threatened to climb up his throat. "My grandma would kick my tail for being inhospitable in her house. I suggest we accept the situation and go forage in the kitchen."

****

Beside him, Justine watched the flurry of white through the window, mirroring a shaken snow globe. Her mind searched for another solution. One unsavory option was to walk more than a mile home. In below-zero weather in a swirling snowstorm. On uncleared sidewalks.

She thrust out a discouraged breath. "Since Mr. Pussufus died last summer, there's no one expecting me home." She tried not to wince at how pathetic that must sound. Really, why had she confided to him about the passing of her beloved fourteen-year-old furball.

"Mr. Pussufus?" Jackson snorted with laughter. He stopped to catch his breath then resumed, guffaws echoing as he wheeled to head out of the room. He offered a lazy, backhand wave. She accepted it as an invitation to follow.

"Just what would you name a cat?" she challenged his retreating back.

At the kitchen doorway, he turned to face her with a devilish grin. The expression made her want to smack him upside the head, hard enough to muss his sun-kissed hair. She crossed her arms over her chest again and glared.

"Well, I've never had a pet," he drawled, oblivious.

"But I'm sure I'd name it something manly, like Diesel, or Max. I hope your cat was spayed, 'cuz otherwise you de-balled him with that wuss name!"

She opened her mouth to defend the choice, but crap, he was right. "Yeah, but the wussy name suited such a huge, furry guy. Like something from the musical *Cats*."

"Don't even go there. Never seen it and never plan to." He stroked the trimmed goatee on his chin. "Speaking of names, I don't remember yours. Seems a little formal to call you Ms. Saunders all night."

She thought about making one up—Esmerelda or Guinevere—just to see how he'd react. "Justine," she muttered.

His brows furrowed, but at least he didn't laugh. "The perfect, swooning Regency heroine." Evidently, he was finished with the conversation as he turned and entered the kitchen.

Really, were polite segues that difficult? Though how would she have responded? Her mother had, indeed, been inspired by a romance heroine during her first pregnancy. She apparently felt less enchantment during her second, naming her sister a basic Kelly.

She followed him into the mid-sized kitchen, painted a soothing powder blue. The central counter balanced appliances and cabinets on both sides. The counters were topped with an adorable white starburst pattern. A granny's 1960's kitchen. She traced her finger over the kitschy Formica as he opened cabinet doors.

Next to the dated stove, he finally grasped a couple of cans and waved them toward her. "We have a choice of soup, soup, or more soup."

"Good thing I'm in a soupy kind of mood." She

hesitated to rummage through a stranger's kitchen. But what the heck, he didn't live here either. She opened the cabinets nearest her. In the third she found a bounty. "How about a side of peanut butter and crackers. And microwave popcorn. This is getting good." She turned and caught her breath.

His lean torso stretched, reaching toward a high cabinet above the refrigerator. The sweater inched up to reveal a band of firm, tanned skin. Hmm, he must work out. The memory of clinging to his taut body in the closet drifted heat through her system again.

She darted her eyes away as he swung toward her with two bottles of wine. "Even better. We might survive the night after all."

The comment reinforced the reality of the situation. She couldn't leave if she wanted to. Even if things got weird in some way. She gulped and tried for a nonchalant grin. "Excellent." Fighting a jitter of nervousness, Justine broke eye contact and bent to search through the lower cabinets for a pan to heat the soup. Sharing food should be a calming way to pass time and get to know each other, in a friendly, surface kind of way.

Chapter Nine

Jackson grasped the wine bottles, hard, as the visitor leaned to look into the cabinet beside the stove, giving him an eyeful of tight butt. He pushed aside the tinge of interest.

A one-night stand with this small-town girl could only end uncomfortably. The sex wasn't worth the drama. He spun away, clacked the bottles onto the counter, and found openers for the cans and the wine. The safest bet would be to eat then separate to spend the evening apart. But for some reason—maybe the nostalgic dive into his mother and grandmother's closets—he welcomed a distraction from his dreary thoughts and solitude. Before the call to the museum, he hadn't spoken to anyone here except waitstaff and delivery people. At first, he relished the downtime. Now the quiet haven just seemed lonely. And a little pathetic.

He turned with the openers and jerked to find Justine standing behind him with a saucepan. She flourished it toward the stove. "Let the feasting begin."

Fifteen minutes later, they sat at the old, carved dining room table eating vegetable soup and peanut butter crackers and drinking a passable white wine. He sipped and lifted his glass. "Leave it to Liza to stock the bare necessities in groceries, but to stash away a few bottles of decent wine."

He hadn't meant it as a toast, but she clinked her

glass to his. "Alcohol definitely improves the ambience of the meal. Here's to your mom and grandmother for keeping their lovely clothing, and so many other treasures." She gestured toward the glass-paned sideboard full of vases and figurines and her gaze lingered.

He had to dispose of all this stuff, too. Maybe hire a company to do an estate sale. None of it would suit the décor of his sleek, modern loft. But the contemplation of his grandmother watching all her favorite things go to the highest bidder saddened him. He swigged more wine. "Did you grow up in this town, in an old, antique-filled house?"

"Is it so obvious?" Eyebrows raised, she pushed away her empty bowl. "Yes, and my parents still live there. My sister Kelly lives a couple blocks from them, married to a great guy; they have a four-year-old daughter and a two-year-old son. Adorable, but a handful. Luckily, auntie gets to go home after a couple hours of playing with toys that make ear-splitting noises. Not to mention Bruno the Chihuahua leaping a perpetual Mexican hat dance around my knees." She snickered. "Sounds awful for me to admit, doesn't it?"

"Sounds like reality." He grabbed two saltines and crunched them in the remainder of his soup. "You've never been married?"

Her expression grew guarded. "No. Not been engaged. Never lived with anyone. Had a semi-serious relationship that just...fizzled. LaPorte isn't exactly a dating mecca." She looked down, her eyes trailing to his bare ring finger. "How about you?"

Damn. He didn't want to talk about himself or his failures. But he stupidly opened the subject. He could ignore the question but didn't want to be the total ass who pried into her life and clammed up in return. "I was married for a year. The story ended badly. 'Nuf said." He grabbed the wine bottle and poured the last of it into their glasses. "It's pretty easy to meet women in California, if you're looking." Feeling overexposed, he pushed back his chair and stood. "I'll handle clean up."

****

For several flustered moments, Justine sat, wondering how they were going to make it through the long evening. She didn't want to overanalyze his actions, but questions bubbled in her mind. The marriage had been bad enough to leave him scarred and negative? Never having known his father, that rejection might've pierced him even harder. Without having been in a deep relationship herself, she couldn't fully empathize. Yet she grew up a shy kid who endured being left out of a lot of activities. Such rejections had helped shape her—into a person who came off as if she didn't mind being kicked a bit or ignored.

Apparently, J. Maddox had built a solid wall of gruffness around himself to avoid any lengthy interactions, positive or negative.

Leave the sleeping bear alone. She wadded her paper napkin into a ball and leaped up to avoid being discovered loitering at the table. Her feet carried her to the living room / parlor. Maybe she could find a distraction there. Through the drapes, she could see the still-blocked driveway. The escape route hadn't opened.

How strange. Tonight, she wasn't a guest, but rather an unwanted interloper. Actually, her host had adjusted pretty quickly to the forced intrusion. Resigned to the situation, she scuffed back to the floral couch and sat to check her phone for messages. She had one text, from Carl.

—Budget meeting was a free-for-all. Fill you in tomorrow. Weather's getting worse. Stay home and safe tonight. Hope I don't get snowed in at mom's.

She gripped the phone. Had the council narrowed toward a decision? She didn't dare ask. No need to pile on more bad news. At least Carl would be comfortable tonight with his family, and not cooped up with a mercurial stranger. She imagined he'd be concerned to know her circumstances, but she didn't feel unsafe, thank goodness. Despite the mood swings, Jackson didn't toss off any threatening vibes. Still, she should alert someone to her whereabouts. Someone who wouldn't freak out.

Her good friend, Marcy, might've also gotten stuck in Chicago, where she commuted from LaPorte to earn a fine arts degree. Her pal's Zen nature positioned her as the person most likely to take the news in stride. Justine dashed off a quick text.

—RU in Chicago?

—Yeah. Brrr. Didn't want to chance the roads. Bunking at a friend's dorm.

—Stay safe. I'm snowed in at 2506 Michigan Ave. Went to investigate a vintage haul. Big time snow dump buried my car. Guy's harmless, thank goodness.

—Guy? How old?

—mid-30s

—OMG! RU sure? Lock your door and call 911 if anything feels wonky.

—Really, he's okay. Just wanted to let someone know. I knew you wouldn't panic. RIGHT?

—No panic. I'll trust your gut. Long as he didn't lure you there.

—NO. The clothes lured me. Gotta go.

She shoved the phone into her pocket as footsteps sounded in the hallway. The buttery smell of popcorn floated into the room. A peace offering?

Jackson entered with a red ceramic bowl, their wineglasses, and the second bottle. He settled the snack between them on the couch as he lowered himself onto the cushions. "Want to see if there're any movies on TV?" He now acted as if this was any mundane evening between friends, reaching to fill her empty glass and topping his.

She stared straight ahead and didn't bother to infuse enthusiasm into her answer. "I suppose."

He clicked the remote and the flatscreen above the fireplace reflected a snowy white image similar to the one swirling outside. On every channel. He tossed it on the table with a clatter. "That's a bust. No cable."

"We could read, maybe?" She stood to wander the spacious room, admiring porcelain and glass knickknacks arranged on every surface, covered with dust. Maybe she could find a cloth and clean them. No. Way too quirky, even for her neatness compulsion. She stepped past paintings adorning the pale-yellow walls and stopped in front of the jammed bookcase. Classics mingled with magazines, cheesy romances, and games. "How about we play trivia?"

He crunched a bite of popcorn and grimaced. "Is that the only choice?"

"Oh, come on," she cajoled. "You have the advantage of growing up with ties to the movie and TV industry. You should be able to nail those questions." At least it would kill time until she could say a polite good night and head... To which bedroom? Her nerves zinged.

She would *not* sleep in Liza's bed, after what she'd seen. Glimpsing the tangled sheets in the first room upstairs indicated he slept there.

Another type of woman might evaluate the situation as the perfect hook-up. A good-looking guy with no strings, why not indulge? No one would know.

Justine would take the guest room. And lock the door. If she had to, she'd leap through the snowdrifts and flag down a passing car. In LaPorte, she'd either know the driver or share a six-degrees connection. She drew a deep breath to calm her thoughts, carried the game to the coffee table, and concentrated her attention on the set-up.

Her companion whooshed out an exaggerated sigh and stood to tune a radio on the nearby desk. He found a local light rock station and headed to the white brick fireplace as she arranged the pie wedges. Gas flames leaped in tendrils of orange and gold. He warmed his hands before returning to sit on the floor across from her.

****

His guest crossed one slim ankle over the other as she leaned against the couch. Her socks exactly matched the drab-colored slacks. He watched her wriggle for a moment, trying to get comfortable as a pop ballad on the radio thumped the sultry beat of an '80s make-out tune. Awkward.

Suddenly she shifted toward him, right hand outstretched. His body zinged interest in sniffing that tasty sugar cookie scent he'd noticed in the closet. Was the girl going to make a move on him? Talk about still waters. Off-guard, but preparing for her touch, he exhaled as she reached up toward his face. Her hand angled up behind him to grab...a throw pillow.

Could he really be disappointed? Or was the letdown feeling just a product of his hyper-active imagination? As a screenwriter, he sometimes caught himself dramatizing everyday encounters. Now, he realized if he adjusted slightly left, his mouth would land on her sweater-covered—

His hands curled into fists. He inched back.

Justine settled the pillow behind her, apparently unaware of the havoc she'd wreaked on his system. "What color pie do you want?"

Pie? The reference to the game piece took a moment to sink in. Pissed off for mistaking her intentions, he skidded the blue plastic circle across the board and took another long drink of wine. They were in for a tedious night. Though his body might be saying otherwise, he wouldn't take advantage of the situation, even if she was willing. Which was beyond doubtful.

Her lips curved as she set up the hot pink pie for herself. "Don't sulk. You can roll first."

"Gee thanks." He didn't modulate the sarcasm and shook the dice. "I'm not sulking. Games aren't my forte. I haven't played anything in years. Being here is like stepping into a time warp." He released the dice. They flew across the board to land on his least favorite topic: sports. He couldn't contain the groan. "I almost expect my mom and grandma to come in and join us."

She fell back at the words, eyes widening. "Are you saying there are ghosts here?"

Even with his own vivid imagination, he never strayed that far. "No, of course not. Don't tell me you believe in that stuff."

She ducked her head. "Our museum volunteers share some interesting stories."

"I bet they do. You'd have to spice up the tales in a one-horse town or go slowly insane."

The trivia card trembled in her hand. "Thanks for reminding me that living here is a path to insanity. Here's your frickin' question." She rattled the information off in a terse voice.

The comment had been a joke. Another poor attempt. Were his social skills really so rusty? Again, he'd touched a nerve, but his own unease in the town and the house didn't allow him to apologize. Another glug of wine fortified him to attempt the sports answer. Sure enough, he whiffed it. When she rolled and landed on the history category, the correct answer tumbled out immediately.

On his second try, he hit sports again. "The game's rigged."

A mischievous glint lit her eye. "I'm sure you're used to winning but buck up."

She seemed to be mellowing with the wine. He kind of liked this bolder persona. Their interplay had begun to reveal the intelligence and humor behind the rather drab façade. Drab because of her clothing choice, he mused. The pale green eyes were striking against the mane of hair. But again, he reminded himself he was here to score against her, not with her. His competitive nature was the driving force to earn at least a couple of wedges. Her total had mounted to four.

His luck improved as they continued to maneuver around the board, nailing some questions, slapping their foreheads over others. Science and nature proved his best category, while ironically, she excelled in the entertainment category. "You didn't tell me you were an entertainment savant." He grabbed another handful of popcorn and crunched into it.

Justine rolled her eyes. "My boss, Carl, and my friend, July, are huge movie buffs. They discuss this fluff all the time." She stretched to round up the remaining kernels in the bowl. "I boned up over the past eight years to hold my own in the conversations."

"Eight years? Seriously, do you plan to make a career there?" Too late, he realized his voice held a touch of incredulity. He was his own boss as a freelance screenwriter. Partnerships worked fine, but he would chafe under a micro-managing employer.

Her lips twisted. "I might've stayed that long. But the county is in budget-slash mode. My job could be gone overnight." She concentrated on wiping her hands with a napkin, cleaning each finger individually. "Not something I can impact, so I'd rather not talk about it."

A touchy subject, he got that. He hadn't meant to mock her—that time. She could guide the conversation from here on. Though another compulsion had continued to nag him through the afternoon and evening, tightening his chest. Finally, he'd had enough wine to blur his inhibitions. "Do you care if we ditch the game? I concede to your supremacy."

Her expression became a bit wary. "Fine by me. People go to bed early in one-horse towns." Without hesitation, she swept the game pieces, dice, and cards into a pile in the center of the board.

Fortified by wine and false bravado, he stood. "You can go to bed if you want, but I'm going to look at those letters."

Chapter Ten

Justine clasped her hands in her lap, unsure if he meant for her to help, or leave him alone. "I don't mean to intrude. If you're not comfortable—"

"I've spent way too many years pissed off. Telling myself it didn't matter. That his actions didn't affect or define me." Jackson shoved his free hand through his hair, spiking it in the front. Not seeming to care. "They didn't define me. But yeah, they've haunted me. And my mom. She's gone now, and maybe I should buck it up, search for the truth, and let them both rest."

The words rocked her. Floral perfume suddenly filled her nose. She yanked her head up and glanced around the room. No Liza, thank goodness. "Moving on could be...healthy," she ventured, watching him for a reaction to the scent. He didn't seem to notice, and the fragrance receded.

"Maybe it will be easier with a neutral bystander. Hold on. I'll go get the box." He bounded out of the room.

She put away the game and waited, hoping she wouldn't be treated to another ghostly visit. Could she be considered neutral about the letters and his situation? Good Lord, she'd seen and spoken to his mother. That conversation had hinted at years of longing and regret. Justine's curiosity was piqued, yet she also worried how reading the letters might affect him. Maybe they'd be everyday ramblings. But in her line of work, people held onto items with a level of meaning to them.

For comfort, she stretched her legs and moved from the floor to the couch as his footsteps echoed in the hallway. A flush reddened his cheeks. He situated the shoebox beside her and plopped down next to it. Seconds ticked until he pulled out a fistful of letters and handed some to her. "I grabbed this notepad upstairs. How about we jot down anything important. With the wine I've drunk, I might not remember any of this tomorrow."

"Good idea." She clasped her hands together and waited for him to open the first letter. When he didn't, she immersed herself in hers, reading silently from the pale pink paper.

"June 23, 1979. Dear Maman. I apologize for not writing or calling sooner, but I can't unhear the disappointment in your voice when you learned I was pregnant. And still unmarried. I know you live by firm beliefs, but mine are more...flexible. Truly, I've hashed out the options day and night. My decision isn't rash.

I hope you'll be pleased to hear I've decided to keep the baby. Such action would ignite considerable gossip in LaPorte. Attitudes are more open here.

I've told the father, but the situation won't change. Not that I expected it to. I know you were shocked when I told you he is married and not going to divorce his wife. He has a big movie coming out at the end of the year. The bad publicity could derail his career. His wife's connections could kill it, as well, and I just can't do that to him. He has such potential to present brilliant productions. I will not be the one to rip away his future, or his family, as there are other children involved.

I told you this wasn't a casual fling. I went into it

knowing the score. If I hadn't gotten pregnant, we'd probably still be seeing each other. Yes, I love him. He feels the same.

I'm sorry if this all sounds tawdry. You'll probably never meet him, or even know his identity, but he is a good man. He hasn't just disappeared from my life—which he easily could have done. To help, he's quietly giving me money, because I can't get hired for movies or TV with a bun in the oven. Ha ha. She had scratched through those last two words.

Mama, I'm not trying to make light of the situation. But I am being realistic. I can almost hear you snorting 'it's about time.' Yes, I guess it is time I started acting like a grown up. I'm trying to pull my act together before the baby comes in November.

Do you think, maybe, you could come out to stay with me for a while? Please say you'll think about it and let me know. I really do want to be a good mother to this child."

She'd signed it "with love." Justine clutched the letter, saddened at the private family issues she had no right to see. Liza's appearance complicated the issue for her, infusing the letter with a distinctive voice—which had flipped from teasing to regretful during their brief encounter.

To keep from feeling like a voyeur, she'd try to regard the information as a historical record. "You'll definitely want to read this one." She thrust the paper toward him.

He hadn't opened his own but took her letter. His jaw worked as he stared down at it. "This is harder than I thought it would be. I'm kind of surprised grandma kept them."

"They represent a huge milestone in all three of your lives. People are often compelled to hold onto such mementos." Her voice gentled, empathizing with his indecision. "We don't have to continue."

"I need more wine." He poured the rest into their glasses, drank deep, and took his time resettling the glass. Finally, he opened the note. "Maman," he muttered. "Always the flair for the dramatic." His lips tightened. He slumped against the couch and read on.

She hesitated to dive into another letter, wanting to gauge his reaction to the revelations. To be a sounding board if he needed one.

His focus remained on the words, and after a few moments, he tossed the letter on the coffee table. "Wow. I'm not shocked, considering the circumstances, but to see in print that she might've considered adoption…or other alternatives…is challenging." The tense demeanor hung on in his expression and twitchy movements. "This is going to take time to process. One takeaway I hadn't considered is that raising me was a brave decision. Even in laidback California."

She fingered the edge of the shoebox, moved by his realization. By the emotion flitting across his face. "Her actions were brave. Both to have you and to protect him."

He rubbed a hand across his neck muscles. "To get through these, I have to dwell on the purely research aspect. The guy had a big film coming out in the last quarter of 1979. That knowledge narrows the scope." He scribbled notes on the pad. His head lifted but he stared beyond her. "Though he could've been an actor, director, or producer. Wouldn't take much to search the internet to determine the main men linked to these late-year productions. One could check out if they were married.

Maybe even who the wives were connected to." The pen tapped the paper, leaving a scatter of ink dots. "We could cross-reference to see if any of them link to mom's acting gigs."

We. An invitation to help him probe further? "The internet's a wondrous tool." She kept the comment generic, not wanting to sway him either way. The decision had to be pursued on his terms.

He gulped another mouthful of the wine. "I'm not ready for such a huge step, but I think I could handle a few more letters."

They both opened envelopes and grew silent to examine the fine lines of cursive handwriting. Justine spoke first to paraphrase her note. "In late September, Liza talks about how big she's getting and asks your grandmother again if she can come out and help her when the baby is born."

"Gran really must've taken this hard. Their relationship probably already was stressed, but eventually she came around." He waved his letter. "This one is dated November 1, a week before my birth."

"Dear Mama. I'm looking forward to seeing you next week. Hopefully, the baby will wait till you get here! I'm absolutely huge now but couldn't resist attending a Halloween costume party this weekend. Dressed as a pumpkin. Apropos, eh? I just needed to get out and remind myself I have friends and can move on, before my time becomes wrapped around the baby.

Then he and his wife walked in. We were both staggered but hid it well and didn't talk to each other beyond a false, cheery 'hello.' The blonde bitch of course had to insert herself, patting my tummy with condescension and saying, "Your patch is especially fertile this year."

Get it, pumpkin patch? Everybody laughed, and I gritted my teeth. But no, she doesn't stop there. "And where's Peter Peter the Pumpkin Eater?"

Can you imagine her face if I'd pointed to her saintly spouse? But I didn't—for his sake, certainly not hers. You see how vicious she is? If she found out, she'd take him down and smear him, so he'd never work in this town again. Neither would I. I have to think about the baby and make a living for us.

I shouldn't even tell you this, because I know you won't approve. But since I decided to have the baby despite his efforts to convince me otherwise, we've struck a pact. I'll stay mum on his fatherhood, and he'll continue to help us out along the way.

"Son of a ..." Scowling, Jackson bit off the oath. "Nice to know they could strike a cold, civil business transaction." After a few contemplative moments, his jaw relaxed. "Maybe that was the only way she could afford to raise me. At least the lowlife did help out financially."

He gripped the letter tight. "I'm glad my grandmother decided to go out there. Despite their personality clashes, she loved my mother very much and doted on her. I imagine she was heartbroken about the whole situation and trying to influence her to move back here. As you might guess, a strong streak of stubbornness runs in our family." Jackson paused and checked the clock on the mantel. "It's almost ten. If you're tired, we can make up a room for you."

"Totally your call. The letters provide fascinating insights. Mine refers to his mansion in Beverly Hills and wonders if the baby will have blue eyes like his father."

Justine tilted her head to search his face. "I guess you do."

"Not sure I needed to know that tonight." He plucked off the glasses and scrubbed his palms over his eyes before grabbing the notepad. "Before we stop, here're the highlights of what we've read. He was 'famous,' in the actual words of my mother, and connected to a movie opening toward the end of '79. They had friends in common, indicating they all may have been involved in some earlier film or TV projects. His eyes were blue. Also, he slipped her money on the side. Probably cash, so his wife couldn't track it." He slipped the note into the envelope and returned it to the box.

Justine did the same. When he didn't move to grab another, she gathered he was indeed done. "That's a load of valuable information. The wife was blonde, bitchy, and had strong connections. Perhaps money, or the mob. That would entice anyone to stay in her good graces."

Chapter Eleven

Liza, November 8, 1979

Giving up all pretense of bravery, Liza opened her mouth wide and screamed. The sound echoed through the room as she gripped the hand holding hers, grinding the knobby bones. The pain ravaged through her body with searing intensity.

Although the death grip must be hurting her, too, her mother didn't let go. "You're almost there, sweetheart." She offered words of encouragement and lifted her other hand to stroke the hank of damp hair off her daughter's sweaty forehead.

Liza closed her eyes against the sharp overhead light and panted as the contraction eased. Over the past hour, the pain increased to blinding waves, swamping her. Pushing her to the edge of endurance. The epidural barely dimmed their power.

The young obstetrician stood at the foot of the bed, with a clear view under the sheet. His voice sliced through her haze. "Gather your strength for one more big push. We're almost there."

We. She considered kicking him in the groin, to truly share the pain, but didn't want to deplete her dwindling strength.

Oblivious, he knelt to position himself between her lifted knees. He apparently hadn't taken time to shave after the pre-dawn summons, and pale reddish fuzz bloomed on his full cheeks.

After twelve hours of labor, Liza no longer cared that her most private parts were exposed, and her face must be swollen and mottled from the straining effort. Her entire being focused on expelling the source of the agony wrenching her body. She gritted her teeth and bore down with a moaning grunt.

"There's the head. Push now, Liza. Give it everything you've got."

She did, her voice rising to a shriek as she forced her exhausted muscles to the limit. The doctor knelt so low she could only see his ginger-haired scalp. She registered a tinny cry, surprising her with the volume.

"Hey, we've got a boy!" Dr. Callahan lifted a squirming, slimy bundle above the sheet.

Her lips trembled into a smile. She caught the matching, radiant beams of her mother's and Jewel's flashing teeth, and beyond them, the bouquet of two dozen red roses without an identifying card. She knew who they were from, as her friend delivered the pre-arranged, vague-coded message when her labor started.

The baby was placed in her arms, a warm, squirming weight. Blue eyes cracked open. His father's eyes. "Welcome to the world, Jackson Maddox," Liza whispered. A burst of maternal love flooded her tired body. She carried no regrets.

Jewel rubbed a finger over his downy, dark head. "Such a cutie. Don't worry, your mama will forgive you the pain of that eight-hour delivery."

Her own mother hadn't spoken. Liza craned her head up to see tears rolling down the usually stoic face. Holding her gaze, Margaret Maddox sniffled and swiped a handkerchief across her cheeks. "He's a strong boy. Let's hope he hasn't inherited our stubborn streak." She reached out to cover a tiny hand. The fingers curled beneath hers as the baby emitted a snuffling sound. "I imagine he'll be hungry soon."

Liza's heart expanded at her mother's support. "They'll clean him up and feed him and then we can visit again. Won't we, little man?"

To Mama's chagrin, she'd decided not to breastfeed. Returning to work to support them meant regaining her figure. The thought brought an unexpected pang at missing out on a very special connection. She'd have to make it up to him in other ways. As both mother and father. She dropped a tender kiss on his forehead, noting the tiny, drooping eyelids.

The nurse who assisted in the delivery bustled back into the room. "Congratulations on a lovely baby boy. How about I make him more presentable for his big day." She stretched out her arms.

Reluctant to let him go so soon, Liza acknowledged he'd be more comfortable cleaned, dressed, and fed. She lifted Jackson, supporting his head. "Can we go down and watch?"

"Most certainly." The nurse bundled him into her arms. "Roll down to the viewing area whenever you're ready."

Liza's eyes traveled to follow them into the hallway, and her pulse leaped. A tall man in a suit stood near their doorway. His eyes trailed the nurse as she carried his son away. They returned to meet hers. The full lips lifted, and he raised his fingertips to blow her a kiss.

Her mother and Jewel were conversing near the window and didn't notice. She lifted her hand to return the gesture as an orderly pushed a woman past in a wheelchair. When they cleared the spot, he was gone. Leaving her alone with her support system. And their child.

Chapter Twelve

Suddenly, Jackson preferred to be alone. The implications of the letters nagged at him, even while he attempted to drown his bitter thoughts in wine. "I'm wiped out. Which room do you want?"

Justine's expression flattened. "The small one upstairs will be fine."

"Understandable. Liza's room carries an air of a shrine, underscored by that dressing table littered with her cosmetics and jewelry. I can't bring myself to clear it off." His chest tightened. He ran a finger around the rim of the popcorn bowl. "She died of an aneurysm here on the living room floor and wasn't discovered till two days later, by a friend who lives nearby. When she couldn't reach Liza, she stopped by. A truly sad and tragic ending."

He stood to join her, picking up the bowl, leaving the box and the memories behind. "Believe me, I'm not trying to make light of it. Just relating the facts in case you didn't know. The woman found my contact in my mother's phone." The admission still stung. He hadn't called his mom often enough and sometimes waited a couple of days to respond to her messages.

His guest looked stricken. "I'm so sorry."

"She was only sixty-five. The call was a massive shock." Surprised at his candor, he turned to stalk out of the room. "I'll help you make up the bed."

"Don't worry about it." Her voice followed him. "You seem to need some alone time."

He swiveled toward her. "Sorry if I'm coming off rough. The letters and stuff have put me on edge."

She didn't answer, probably afraid he'd lash out. Though truly, that wasn't his usual style. He just wasn't handling the trying circumstances well. He let her walk ahead through the dim hallway, recalling how in childhood, he badgered his mother for details. Especially on his birthday and at Christmas. She never budged, even when he cried and pleaded. As a teen he heard her sobbing in her room after one of his inquisitions. He swore never to ask again. Now Liza was gone and the direct opportunity to learn about his paternity was lost.

And what would he say or do if he found the man anyway? Confront him? Punch him? Ask how the hell he'd been able to abandon him and his mom so easily?

After dumping the bowl in the kitchen, he jogged up the staircase. Justine waited outside the bedroom door, face passive. A hint of nervousness expressed in the fingers jittering against her legs. At the hall closet he stopped to dig for sheets, finding a flannel set to cover the bed. Soft footsteps padded up. He closed the door with his hip and thrust the load into her arms. "I'm a lousy host, but I saw an extra toothbrush in the bathroom, and towels. Help yourself to anything you need."

Her brows furrowed. "Thank you. I'm sorry to impose."

"You're not. Really. Sleep well."

Ashamed of his inhospitable behavior, he strode away toward his grandmother's room.

****

Justine bit the inside of her cheek as Jackson

disappeared through another doorway, the one with the tangled bed sheets. Should she follow him to offer comfort and apologize? But for what? Deep down, she knew he wasn't upset with her. Apparently, the man hadn't learned to deal with his feelings. He probably squashed them because he'd never been given the opportunity to meet his father, or even talk about him. She was super lucky to have loving, attentive parents who supported her at every turn.

Carrying the armload, she entered the guest bedroom, thinking Liza may have had good intentions. Yet she made a mess of the relationship with her son. Too bad Justine was the one dealing with that fallout tonight.

Her fingers fumbled on the bedroom wall to find a switch. Light spilled from the overhead fixture, illuminating a shadowy presence in the armchair. She swallowed her startled yelp and the flannel tumbled to the floor. "I really, really hoped I'd imagined you."

The image brightened in color and intensity, highlighting Liza's natural beauty. "Oh, no. You are one hundred percent awake and alert." The notes of her perfume swirled around the room. "I'm enthralled that you can see and hear me. Though I have no idea about the logistics. How long I can connect, and so on."

"Or why you're here?"

"Unfinished business, as they say. Rather fascinating to speculate, isn't it? Would you concur I haven't fully 'crossed over'?" She made quote marks in the air.

"No clue. I'm Methodist, not a psychic." Keeping her eyes on the figure, Justine gritted her teeth, regathered her composure, and bent to collect the scattered sheets. She bundled them in her arms, welcoming the solid bulk against her body.

A smile curved Liza's pouty, red-glossed lips. "He'd never admit it, but Jackson must need me, too."

Justine couldn't help snorting. "I can't see that man admitting he needs anyone or anything."

"He rather seems to like you, which is unusual." Liza crossed her bare, tanned legs. The stack of clothing they placed on the chair earlier lay pooled near her feet. "I also have a good feeling about you. Which is partly why I exercised the prerogative for another little girl talk."

A little girl talk—with a ghost. Though she did believe her eyes, she couldn't quite convince her head. "Better exercised than *exorcized*, in your case. Wait, why do you look so young? No offense."

"None taken. How could it be Heaven if you weren't able to live as your ultimate self?" Liza stroked her waving hair. "I happened to be at my best in my early thirties before Jackson was born, so you and I are practically contemporaries age-wise. As for coming here…well, I was blessed with a very strong will and personality. I suppose I'm exerting it extra-specially for the time being." She leaned forward. "Tell me what you think about my son. Isn't he handsome?"

Off guard at the swift topic change, Justine answered truthfully. "Yes, he is good looking. And annoying."

"Much as I love him, he can be a real ass."

She pressed a palm over her mouth to squelch the chuckle of agreement. If Jackson heard her, he'd definitely think she was insane. And maybe she was. May as well indulge the madness. "Still, the more I get to know him, the more the gruff exterior cracks to allow a glimpse of a nicer guy. I think his snark is a defense mechanism after all those years of tumbling around fatherless in California." *Whoa, talk about snark.*

Her companion's dark brows rose. "Please, don't hold back your opinions to spare my feelings." She waved a slim hand. "Actually, I admire spunk as much as Jackson. You are perceptive and correct. The circumstances I thrust upon him were not ideal."

"No. They definitely weren't. But if you've been watching, I think finding those letters shifted his balance." The idea of the ghost monitoring their conversations was a little creepy. Yet her distaste changed to empathy as tears began to glisten in the smoky eyes. She drew a little closer to place the pile of sheets on the bedspread, keeping her eyes trained on the chair.

Liza's fingers clenched in her lap. "The letters don't name his father. He'll have to search for the answer."

"Or you could tell me." Though how in heck would she convince Jackson Maddox she suddenly knew the name of his father?

A lone tear rolled down the pale cheek. "I promised years ago not to disclose his name while he was living. Jackson must adjust his thinking and want to find him." Her form began to fade. "I'm glad you're here, darling. He could use a supportive friend to help handle the process, and the revelation. The letters were a start."

"Hold on." Justine unlocked her stiff knees and approached the chair.

"Another time, dear."

The response was so faint she wondered if she imagined the words. The chair stood empty. Justine stared at the cushions and shivered. What had she unleashed with her presence here? In her keyed-up condition, she half expected to encounter an eerie coldness next. Or the smoothness of actual flesh.

Sleeping in here lost all appeal, too. She trembled and spun to check out the dark corners, to peek in the closet and under the bed. But even if she didn't see anything, Liza had proven a ghost could access all corners of the house.

She wrinkled her nose and gathered her courage. "Hold it together, girl." Her eyes roamed the room again. "And you, behave tonight." With new resolve, she stripped off the quilt and put on the flannel sheets. While tackling the final corner, she debated sleeping in her clothes versus her undies.

But first, she had to visit the bathroom. Liza was a ghost with a purpose, not a creeper. She wouldn't intrude there. The silence in the house was a little unnerving now. On tiptoes, she left the room and crept down the hall. Inside, she shut the door and searched for the extra toothbrush and towels. After using the toilet, she brushed her teeth and rinsed her face with water. On the stealthy retreat toward her room, a crash and a curse halted her in her tracks.

"Damn it!" The words bounced out of the office doorway she'd glimpsed just off the stairwell. Something—or someone—had toppled or crashed into something.

Already regretting the impulse, but unable to check her curiosity, she sprinted toward the commotion. An overturned desk chair blocked the entrance to the room. She grasped the doorframe with both hands and panted out, "Are you okay?"

Jackson stood, arms akimbo, frowning down at the chair. "Decided to do some web searching and I needed liquor fortification." His words slurred at the edges. "Must've pushed back too hard."

The shoebox lay on the old rolltop desk, contents strewn across the surface. She kept her voice calm and non-judgmental. "Any new clues from the letters?"

"Nothing new-new. But I got the stupid urge to search." He scratched his nose and squinted. "Meh, I'm over it."

Liza's words echoed in her brain. He had to want to find his father. "You have internet access here?" She stayed in the doorway to block any escape attempt.

"I do indeed." His expression didn't lighten.

"You decided to run a search for him?"

"Yes…No. Either way, I need booze. 'Scuze me." He righted the heavy chair and attempted to brush past her.

She didn't budge, only lifted an eyebrow and stared him down. He latched his hands onto her shoulders and scooted her aside. Not roughly, just a smooth little adjustment. "Hey—"

He left the room. She sagged against the wall. Should she stay and play the supportive friend like Liza suggested? Maybe then the ghost would leave her alone.

Although, with more liquor in his system, he'd possibly pass out with his head on the desk. Before she could decide, footsteps pounded again on the stairs. He entered the room with a grin, a half-full bottle of whiskey, and two glasses. Apparently, he expected her to stay. The bottle sloshed when he plunked it on the desk. "Pull up a seat."

Curiosity rooted her. She dragged a wooden chair

forward as he sat and began to pour. A squat crystal glass landed before her.

"*Slainte.*" He didn't wait to clink and glugged down the amber liquid.

She sipped, wincing as heat trickled down her throat.

"You've gotta chug." He held up his empty glass.

Twice today she conversed with a ghost. Whiskey might take the edge off to help her sleep. She tipped back her throat and emptied the contents. A fireball inflamed her tonsils and trailed down her esophagus. "Good Lord." She wheezed out the words, shoulders shaking.

He didn't hide his amusement.

Justine narrowed her eyes as the liquor settled in her stomach. When it came to drinking, she definitely considered herself a lightweight. With whiskey topping their earlier wine, a pleasant wooziness rolled over her. How sad—she couldn't remember the last time she'd been buzzed. Or sat this close to a man who wasn't her boss or a family member. Maybe she needed a new job to jolt her out of such a dull, complacent life.

Jackson booted up the laptop and tossed his glasses onto a sheaf of papers. Sneaking a glance, she recognized determination in the set of his jaw. He typed and muttered, "Top movies 1979."

Before she could read the loading entries, he clicked on one. Ten movies were listed, with six she recognized. The others reflected sci-fi and horror with violent undertones. Not her preferred genres.

His movements stalled. He stared hard at the screen.

"Now we need to look at release dates," she prompted.

He avoided her eyes and grasped the bottle. This

time he swigged directly. When he leaned it toward her, she did the same. The burn lessened, but the buzz intensified.

With the bottle resettled between them, his shoulders stiffened. Seconds ticked away, until she nearly leaped up and grabbed the mouse herself. Finally, he poked out a finger to rap the touch screen. A film poster emerged, with two men poised in a tense shoot-out stance. Below, they read that the gritty western had opened very early in the year. Not a fit for the timeframe in the letters.

They scrolled on. The second film, an outlaw buddy pic, landed in September.

The blockbuster sci-fi hit in June.

But the coming-of-age drama landed onscreen in mid-December 1979.

Neither of them spoke. She barely dared to move or breathe in fear his resolve would crumble. He lifted the bottle to his mouth for another slug and passed it to her. Anticipating the burn, she tried to contain her reaction as the heat reignited.

Their eyes locked as hers watered. His solemn expression cracked as he snickered. "We're missing the dramatic mood music. If this was my script, the tension would be unbearable."

"I'm about to faint with the anticipation already." She gripped the desk with both hands. The words felt sluggish rolling off her tongue.

Face sober again, he shoved back from the desk. "Me, too. I don't know if I'm ready for this."

Of course, this was his decision to make. She bit down the disappointment and knew she'd check out the film on her phone when she returned to the bedroom. If they didn't follow the truth together, she could make an educated guess. Gathering herself to stand and leave, her head spun. She hoped she wouldn't wobble down the hallway. Or fall down and pass out.

She jumped when he leaned forward, lightning fast, to click away on the keyboard. A cast and production list popped up on the screen. Squinting to read the small type, Justine drooped against his shoulder. Four males had shared the lead and supporting actor roles.

Jackson's eyes trained ahead. "Now we follow a process of elimination." He highlighted the first name, and new search results popped. They scanned the bio information and photos.

To her disappointment, the man didn't meet the scant criteria from the letters. "He was married to a brunette who wasn't in show business, which should rule him out."

The second came out as gay in the '80s. He grimaced. "While an affair could've been possible, it's less likely. Looking at the others, that guy"—he pointed a wavering finger—"is a huge stretch age-wise to be with her. Leaving…British-born actor Peter Nevins." He grasped the bottle again. "A toast to the joys of cyber-stalking."

After his drink, the whiskey level dropped noticeably. He motioned in her direction with the bottle.

"No, thanks." Settled into the buzz, she preferred not to push toward hangover territory. If she could make it into work tomorrow, she'd need a clear head to digest Carl's insights about the county budget meeting. She winced at the nasty thought as Jackson cracked his knuckles and resumed typing. Nevins' info popped onscreen. Age thirty-two. Handsome. Dark-haired. Blue eyes. A prolific list of television and screen appearances. Justine blinked to clear her vision. Yes, the woman identified as his wife in one photo sported light, streaked hair.

He caught the detail and pulled up her bio. "Ah, daughter of a Vegas casino magnate. Didn't you mention mob ties?"

"Sure did. A cliché, but possible. They stayed together a long time before divorcing, with two children." The revelations made her feel smart and sassy. Kind of like the sparring detective couples in the popular 90's series that she watched as a child. "How about the director?"

He scrolled to the top. "Lawrence Reynolds. Yeah, I know his work." Another click revealed more factoids. "At thirty-nine, the age could fit. Besides movies, he also directed television shows." Jackson rubbed a hand through his hair. "Some of these sound familiar. Both of the guys were involved with several shows during their career peaks. I'll have to check 'em against Liza's resume." His words slurred more noticeably. "Can't forget about wifey, either." At his tap, a picture of the blonde spouse filled the screen.

"Run a search on her." Justine's fingers tightened on his arm. "She had a prominent studio mogul father. One with the power to crush a promising director. And look, she starred in a couple of her husband's movies in the '70s and did guest spots on some of his television gigs." She bounced in the chair.

"Hot stuff. They stayed married until her death a year ago, with three children together."

"My gosh. These two are likely candidates." Her eyes darted around the room, half expecting Liza to shoot a thumbs up or point to one of them.

No such luck. Jackson's shoulders slumped, as if the search drained him of energy. He drew a deep, halting breath. "I never thought much about him having kids until tonight. They'd be my half-siblings." She cringed when he leaped to his feet, rolling the chair into the wall with a loud crack. "Why the hell did I think I wanted to get into this?" He lifted his chin toward the ceiling. "Why couldn't you have just told me?"

Chapter Thirteen

Justine's heart stuttered. Did he converse with his mother, too?

No, his question was rhetorical. Guilt snaked through her system. Her visit here had revealed the shoebox; she figuratively dumped the letters in his lap. She grasped his arm with a firm, calming hand. "What you'll do is take this information and sleep on it. You'll think about all the angles and decide what's right for you as a next step."

They both recognized the two paths that yawned ahead: either stop the search here and ignore the possibilities or follow it through to a potential father who denied his existence for three decades. To offer some small comfort, she slid her hand down to cover his where it braced on the desk.

****

Despite his bleared thoughts, Jackson realized all the whiskey in the bottle couldn't cushion the devastating consequences of this moment. He'd been irresponsible and crazy to pursue any level of information about the man who knocked up his mom. Being in the house, reading the letters, loosened his tight defenses. Along with the sympathetic woman sitting next to him.

Frustration simmered through him, overriding the liquor buzz. A gentle palm covered his hand. Sad eyes met his. Screw that, he needed more than a pat on the hand. He needed a distraction to strip the whirling innuendos from his mind. He leaned to close the inches between them, to place his lips on hers.

Soft, and oh-so-sweet. His mind blanked to ride the surge of sensation. Meeting zero resistance, he deepened the kiss, lips plundering as he cupped her cheeks with his hands. With a tiny moan, she opened to him. Desire surged as he glided in to taste the whiskey lingering on her tongue.

Mouths were not nearly enough. He tugged her up into his arms. Hers linked around his neck, melding their bodies together as lips and tongues offered and explored. His brain switched off. Every erotic shift and movement sent an electric charge through his body.

Her hands dropped to his shoulders. He felt a nudge of pressure there and loosened his hold, blinking heavy-lidded eyes.

She stepped back, separating their bodies. Her gaze didn't quite meet his. He read embarrassment in the flushed cheeks. Man, he'd crossed a line. For purely selfish reasons. No matter that they both seemed to respond equally. What an ass. "I'm really sorry. I got carried away."

She focused on rolling the desk chair back to its location, between them. "You were worked up. And drunk. I'm buzzed. No harm."

He took in the swollen lips and tousled hair and wondered why he'd ever regarded her as plain.

At least she didn't flinch away from him. His body protested, but with a willful effort he pulled back mentally and physically. "Do you need anything before you turn in?"

"No. I found the towels and toothbrush. So I'll be going. To bed." She glanced past him to the door.

He pressed himself against the desk to allow her plenty of room to skirt past. "G'night. We'll get you out of here in the morning."

Smart girl—she fled. He waited till he heard the bedroom door slam down the hall and collapsed into the chair. *He was frickin' falling apart.* Liquor always reduced his inhibitions. That catalyst had allowed him to slide back to a place he'd hoped never to return. A vulnerable boy hoping for any crumb of information about his paternity.

Chapter Fourteen

Justine dashed through the door of the bedroom, slammed it behind her, and didn't bother to look for a lock. Despite the confounding kiss, Jackson Maddox wouldn't try to force himself on her. She'd identified the lip lock realistically—a whiskey-sodden attempt to expel frustrated energy from the dad search.

She caught her reflection in the dresser mirror and groaned at the wild hairdo. At the time, she reveled in his hands sliding through the waves. But the sensual caresses left her with a lion's mane. Kind of apropos to her unexpected, uninhibited response. She smoothed down the curls with a flare of mortification, mingled with a tinge of curiosity. If she hadn't pulled back, would she have allowed him to maneuver her into his bed?

No. Even revved up, she wasn't tempted by casual intimacy. At least she held to some of her principles. She slumped on the edge of the bed and couldn't stop the bubbling laughter. If they'd made it to the bedroom, stripping her down to pink long underwear would've killed any hint of desire.

****

Down the hall, Jackson tossed in his grandmother's double bed, still regretting the impulsive actions. What kind of ass pushed himself on a woman trapped in a house overnight? No matter that she responded. He had no right to initiate the kiss. Yet his core temperature soared when their tongues entwined.

Dogged by guilt, the letters, and the internet revelations, he only dozed for a couple of hours during the night. He woke to the scent of brewing coffee. With a pounding headache, courtesy of the Irish alcohol. Pulling on last night's jeans and a sweatshirt, he swallowed two ibuprofens before wandering down to the kitchen.

Justine sat on a stool at the counter, sipping from a mug, wearing his grandmother's green dressing gown. Faint color under her eyes indicated she didn't sleep well, either. "I hope you don't mind that I wore this today. My wardrobe choices are limited." Without asking, she stood to pour him a mug featuring a smiling cartoon rabbit. She handed over the coffee.

He joined her to sit, impatient for the pills to kick in. "I told you to take it. Why not start now?" It didn't look wrinkled. He wondered what she'd slept in…

He diverted his horny mind with a gulp of the steaming brew. Dark and hot. Heaven. "Do you have any suggestions of how we can get you plowed out of here?"

"Usually, I could call my dad to bring over his snowblower. I'd rather not after the stent operation. Carl might have a shovel or two he could drop by. He should've been able to leave his folks' place because they have a tractor and a plow."

"Your boss?" Jackson asked, taken aback by the little tug of…jealousy?

"Yes. The one who initially took your call. He doesn't live too far from here. He could drop them by on his way to work." She ran a finger around the rim of her mug and her eyes dropped to his arms. "We have to physically shovel."

The caffeine slid through his sluggish system. "Don't worry, I can hoist a shovel. I think I'd rather dig out myself than face a questioning father at this time of the morning." Besides, the demanding exercise would be a welcome physical outlet.

Her cell lay on the table. She punched in a number and brought it to her ear. No speakerphone. After the space of a couple of rings, she muttered, "Hey, I'm glad I caught you. Do you have a shovel or two I can borrow?" She listened briefly. "No, I'm not at home or in a ditch. The lake effect buried my car at the Maddox' house, and the plow threw a huge pile into the driveway. I ended up snowed in here." She pulled the phone away from her ear with a pained expression and lowered her voice. "Don't even go there. Could you please just drop the shovels on your way to work? Great. Thanks. Oh, and I suppose I'll be late."

She tapped off and tucked the phone into the robe pocket. "He should be here within a half hour. He has to do his own drive first because he didn't try to come back from his parents' place last night."

Hmm, he'd get to lay eyes on the boss she enjoyed such an easy relationship with. The guy had a deep, throaty voice, he recalled. Her coworkers undoubtedly would pose curious questions about her overnight adventure. But somehow, he knew she'd maintain the confidence of their search for his paternity.

"Don't worry, I'm good at keeping secrets." Her words eerily confirmed his thoughts. "I won't tell anyone about the letters or the information we dug up."

"I appreciate that." But what about the sensual kisses? Maybe she wouldn't share them with the boss, but girlfriends often dished the dirt. Hopefully, she'd paint a sexy scene and not one where he'd pushed a drunken advantage. He massaged his temple, gulped the rest of the coffee, and stood to rinse the mug in the sink.

She did the same. "I'd better get dressed so we can tackle the shoveling right away. I've got a snowbrush in my car and can work on clearing it off."

Minutes later she returned and bundled into her coat and boots while Jackson donned his less-adequate leather jacket and cowboy boots. Hearing the blast of a car horn, he dragged on a knitted cap and mittens he found in the closet. They headed out the door, blinked into the sunshine, and slogged through inches of amassed snow on the sidewalk and drive. The frigid cold wrapped around him, trying to steal his breath. Trees and bushes hung heavy with glistening white loads, dropping powdery gusts when the wind whistled past.

Their feet and calves sunk into the drifts. He shivered as his face tingled and the cold inched up his legs. "How the heck do you live in this?"

She smirked. "You adjust. Our skin thickens in the winter." Her hand shot up to wave at a car idled on the road, separated from them by a three-foot mound of snow. Justine trotted over, but he didn't have the energy to hurry. When he reached the barrier, the man left the car, and she made quick introductions. He noted a round, pale face, trimmed brownish beard and mustache, and silver spectacles.

Her boss extended a gloved hand. "Thanks again for your generous donation. We love the opportunity to share your mother's Hollywood connections. I even watched one of her old movies the other night."

"Wow. That's great to hear." *Verging on extreme.* "Hope you enjoyed it."

"Definitely."

Justine interjected. "While I'm sure Jackson would love to talk to you about it, I know you've got to open up at the museum."

The man blinked. "Oh, right. Work. Yeah, I'll see you there." With a grunt, he heaved two metal shovels over to them. "You've got your work cut out for you here. I had less to do in my drive. I'm happy to head off to my cozy computer while you two labor away. Just drop those off inside my garage on the way home, if you want." He got back into his running car and drove away.

Jackson didn't detect any spark between the two. The cold wind whipped the thought away. He tucked his hands under his arms. "Go ahead and work on your car. I'll shovel a space for you to back out." *He was going to freeze to death out here.*

"No, let me help you first. Not to question your muscles, but you've probably not shoveled like this in a long time—if ever. The lifting is heavy, grueling work."

Together, they bent their backs to the task, scooping the clumped snow and tossing it further into the yard. After twenty minutes, they cleared a passable path behind her car and out to the street. She set to cleaning her car with the long-handled brush, letting it run to defrost the windows. "Please go inside and warm up," she urged.

He wondered if his nose and cheeks were as red as hers. "I'll grab the clothing bags and bring them out." Inside, he did take his time, savoring the warmth pumping out of the old radiator system. After making two trips to load her backseat, he stood, sweaty and winded, by the driver-side door.

"Well..." She stared past his shoulder and exhaled

forcefully. A puff of frosty steam floated between them.

"We-ell," he echoed. "Thanks for coming over to help me sort this stuff. I really am grateful. And my apologies for catching you up in my personal saga. The revelations have given me a lot to think about in the next few days, as I wrap things around here." The goodbye felt loaded. They'd known each other less than a day. Yet those hours were crammed with intimacy. Only his ex and Liam, his best friend and writing partner, knew the gist of his upbringing.

Her face fell. "Darn, I can't believe I forgot to look at the photos."

"We were a little preoccupied. I'll pick some out and bring them to the museum before I leave." He needed to be alone, to re-center himself. In a few days, their interaction—and the town—would be a vague memory. He lifted the shovels and stepped toward her trunk.

Getting the hint, she released the latch for him to stow the dripping implements. She slid behind the wheel, closed the door, and lowered the window. "We appreciate you donating the clothing to the museum. I'm already planning the tableau in my head. If you have any ideas, please feel free to share them."

"Not my forte. I'm sure you'll do fine." In fact, he might never see the display. Nothing remained to draw him back here, unless they needed him to settle the estate in some way. Most everything could be handled electronically these days.

"Okay then." She rolled her lips together and started the car. He watched as she reversed and maneuvered through the narrow slalom of snow, keeping her eyes on the rearview mirror. No goodbye wave.

He trudged back into the house. After a half hour of

shoveling, he did feel physically depleted, but his mind remained restless. Escapism, that's what he craved. First, a long, hot shower beckoned. Afterwards, he could head out for a hearty breakfast in his mom's car. Which he'd have to sell, too. Later, he'd work on the screenplay he'd been tweaking.

Keeping busy would help push the questions about his paternity to the back of his mind for a while, to let them simmer—the same way he attacked his writing: take an idea, mull it around, mentally work through scenarios. He would retreat and avoid working on a piece, sometimes for days at a time. Usually, he returned with new clarity and a heightened sense of nuance.

What did Justine say? "You'll think about it and make a decision that's right for you." He sure hoped she was right.

Chapter Fifteen

Justine stripped down at her house and stepped into the steamy shower, both to clean up and to warm up after the frigid shoveling. She lathered her hair, wondering if she'd ever see J. Maddox again. While first presenting as a nasty jerk, she also uncovered a somewhat softer side. He could be playful—when he wasn't caught up in an intense, conflicted situation.

And most definitely passionate. Her body tingled in recalling the startling kiss. Yet while she felt awkward this morning, he appeared to have forgotten it. Too much liquor loosening both their inhibitions, she supposed.

Did he really forget, though? Or did he prefer to avoid complications in trying to wrap his duties here and vamoose? She snickered, again imagining a possible reaction to her conversing with his mom. The dude might've barricaded her in the bedroom until he could boot her out into the cold. Locking the door behind her.

With distance from those spooky encounters, she now began to marvel at Liza's flawless appearance and form. Unlike other ghosts, she presented as solid and remarkably…human. Before dissolving into the ether. Justine rinsed the conditioner from her hair and a scary thought gripped her. Hopefully, Liza was tied to the house and wouldn't be able to pop up other places.

Unless she was tied to her clothing. *No, do not go there*. She shivered, wiped her eyes on the towel, and couldn't resist peeking around the shower curtain. Whew. Still alone. With no eerie message scrawled on the steamed mirror.

But while she got dressed, a new concern consumed her. Carl's budget meeting news couldn't be good, or he would've reassured her already by text or at the house. Darn it, she hated living in limbo and not being in control of her world. Today everything was tilted and off-center. Once she heard the news, she could pin down her plan of action.

Bundled back into her coat, she drove to the museum as quickly as the slushy roads would allow. They likely wouldn't see much traffic today, but she had plenty of projects to keep her busy. Including thinking through the Liza exhibit. The sun popped out as she neared the building, the rays glinting off snow piles lining the roadside. Thankfully, their parking lot was clear. Lugging the bags of clothing in the back entrance, she hurried toward the shared office.

No visitors lingered on the upper floor as she bumped through the aisles. Carl heard her noisy advance and swung around in his chair. "I didn't figure I'd see you for another hour."

"We made quick work of the shoveling together then I ran home to clean up. No frills or makeup today." After shedding her coat, she pulled items from the bags and arranged them on the center worktable to distract her growing anxiety. "I figured you'd be bursting with updates from last night's meeting." When he didn't answer, her hand stilled over the skirt of Liza's poufy formal where it spread across the table. "Do we still have jobs?"

His face crumpled. "For now. They—" He halted at

the sound of footsteps. July bustled toward them in a siren-red sweater, luminescent with white-frosted trees. A loopy, hand-knit scarf draped her neck.

She poked her head in the doorway. "Sorry I'm late. The snowplows are taking a while to make it through all the neighborhoods."

He waved away the apology. "I was just going to share about last night's meeting. Why don't you sit down, too, because the info will be in the newspapers soon."

Her lips thinned, and she unwrapped the scarf and joined them, sinking into an extra chair. Justine remained at taut attention, smoothing the clothing items. She wanted to cover her ears and run from the room, recognizing she might be forced to secure another job, ASAP.

"Relax, ladies." Carl attempted to reassure them. "We're not directly listed on the chopping block yet. But we are a non-essential service. For most of the evening, the council members shouted back and forth, suggesting possibilities to cut the budget with others shooting them down. Of course, we were mentioned."

Worry continued to nibble at her. "No one wants to raise taxes, I bet."

"No. They discussed applying for a loan or issuing bonds. Some cuts finally were agreed to." He rattled off a short list, including a couple of personnel positions in county departments.

July rubbed her hands together. "Those poor folks. I feel kind of bad to be happy they passed us by. I'm an unpaid volunteer, but you all are such a great staff. We couldn't handle everything without your leadership."

Their boss coughed into his elbow. His cold

wouldn't quite let go. "Having volunteers actually puts us at greater risk," he croaked. "We didn't get by unscathed. One member asked why our operation couldn't be handled by more volunteers. A couple of others stood up for us. Don't be surprised if a contingent of county council members visits to assess our operations. If they do, please be honest in your assessment."

Justine's adrenaline drove her back to sorting through the piles of clothing, seeking solace in her passion. "They'll be impressed by what they see. We're a skeleton crew out here."

"I agree. But let's stay on our A-game. Maybe come up with some special events to wow the public."

Inspiration sprung up from the groovy fashions. She lifted the formal gown, her mind spinning with possibilities. "The Liza display. We found some great pieces of era-appropriate clothing from her beach film days. What if we hold a grand unveiling on Valentine's Day and wrap it around a fundraiser? Maybe a dance and a silent auction?" She hugged the dress against her torso and twirled, wishing she could fit into it. The actress was a couple sizes smaller in those days.

The suggestion broke the gloomy mood. Carl's fingers tapped on his desk. "What an awesome idea. We have time to plan and get the promotion out if we hustle." A smile brightened his face. "All the attendees can be encouraged to wear vintage outfits."

July chimed in. "Liza Maddox, LaPorte's Sweetheart. What a wonderful, fun tribute. I can imagine her smiling down on such an event."

Hopefully, she wouldn't show up to join them. A chill darted down Justine's spine. She released the formal onto the table.

The volunteer stood to join her. "My, these are lovely. Can you use them all?" She stroked a beaded cashmere sweater.

"We don't have space to keep everything here. Jackson said I could take additional garments to Little Theatre. Or keep some myself." Oops, she shouldn't have opened that door.

The woman's eyes grew huge behind her glasses. "I almost forgot to ask about the son. Is he handsome? Debonair?"

"Try snarky and rude. Though to be fair, he did mellow as the evening wore on and he found himself forced to entertain me."

Carl rolled forward in his chair. "July doesn't know that you got snowed in with him last night. Do tell. We're all ears. By the way, he is a handsome fellow." He provided a pithy description as Justine tried to come up with an excuse to make a quick exit. He cleared his throat to draw her attention. "How did he entertain you?"

Visions of scattered letters, internet searches, and hot kisses flooded warmth to her cheeks. "We played a trivia game and went to bed early. Separately." She gathered an armload of garments, prepared to flee to the storage area.

Her audience chuckled. Carl picked up a bathing suit that slithered off the table in her haste. "How soon does he leave? Any chance of seeing the boy wonder again?"

She started toward the door. "Maybe. He said he'll bring out photos of his mom. But I wouldn't count on it."

Chapter Sixteen

The next morning, Justine loitered in her closet. Usually, she grabbed an outfit without thinking. Despite chiding herself not to care, today she wondered if Jackson might come in with the photos. Not to try to impress him, but she didn't always dress so basic. Or did she? Most of the items hanging before her ranged from dull to monotone. Easy to match, but boring.

She rifled a hand over the nondescript pieces, halting at the slippery-satin vintage dressing gown. The emerald hue did pop her eye color and complement her pale skin. Maybe she should go shopping with Marcy and add a few fun, colorful items. The girl had an artist's penchant for color and pulled off crazy pattern mixes that shouldn't have worked but did.

A deep-teal cable sweater beckoned from the back, a birthday gift from her sister. She plucked it off the hanger to wear with her gray pleated skirt and tall boots, accented with the coordinating scarf her sibling had tossed in. If nothing else, she'd feel good—stylish—all day. Dressing in a more professional manner also would be positive if the county decided to visit, or if she landed a new job. The Chicago video interview loomed three days away. She ran a nervous hand over her hair. This same combo with a blazer could work for the online meeting. If she landed an in-person session, she'd really have to go shopping. The thought was energizing. And terrifying.

Later, at work, the niggling reminder of the interview dissolved under another distraction. She caught herself swiveling in her chair every time the darn door opened. Unusual for her, she stayed at her desk through the day, finding tasks to keep her in view through the glass-fronted office. Details for the potential Liza-fest were coming together, yet as two o'clock came and went, she accepted her son wasn't going to appear. He probably decided to stick the photos in the mail.

Giving in to hunger, she logged out of her computer to head to the break room for lunch. The entry door blew open, accompanied by the usual groan of old hinges, and released a gust of chilly air. She told herself not to look but couldn't fight the impulse.

Justine blinked and bit back a gasp. Her reluctant vigil had produced him. Jackson Maddox stood on the rubber mat, stamping snowy feet. His eyes roamed toward the office and connected with hers. Her limbs froze while her heartbeat doubled. Anticipation sizzled through her body—at seeing the photos, of course. Nothing more.

She averted her gaze as Carl rose from his desk and moved toward the entrance, shooting her a wink. "Well, lookee who's here."

Willing her knees to unlock, she strolled to join the two of them and July at the front counter. Strolled, leisurely and unaffected. Nonchalant. *As if.*

In contrast to their initial meeting at the house, the visitor sported a pleasant demeanor. He finished shaking Carl's hand. "And you must be July," he guessed.

The volunteer's eyelashes fluttered as she held out her hand and he took it. "I surely am." She drew back to study him. "You resemble your mama in the shape of your face and some of your features. What a lovely woman."

"Thank you. She was." He moved on to Justine but didn't extend a handshake. "You were right, shoveling is brutal business. My muscles paid for it the rest of the day."

He also didn't offer her a greeting. But why should he. Though the others weren't aware, she acknowledged they'd moved far beyond such formalities. "Really? I felt fine. Invigorated, in fact." She strove for an airy tone, as her friends watched with too much interest. They'd love the idea of fostering a little romance. Any perceived spark between them, and they'd scheme to matchmake. To divert them, she zoomed in on the leather portfolio in Jackson's hand. "You brought the pictures."

"I dug up some good ones related to her movie and TV stints. I also have a couple of scripts you can copy. I'd like to keep the originals for now." He spread the photos on the long wooden entry counter that formerly graced a local five and dime store.

July and Carl appeared starstruck at the professional headshots, along with staged pictures and candid photos from shows she appeared in. In one glossy shot, Liza sported the same feathered hairdo from her appearance at the house. Justine swallowed hard and swooped past it to examine the scripts. They were from television shows popular in the late '70s. Handwritten notes at the side listed the cast and their roles.

Her eyes scanned for two names. Yes, Peter Nevins appeared in one. Lawrence Reynolds directed another. She flattened a hand over her heart. Jackson stared down with a solemn expression. His intensity seemed to echo her recognition. These scripts further connected Liza to two men who might be his father.

Carl broke into her racing thoughts. "These are excellent additions. We're thankful you're gifting both the originals and copies to the museum." His eyes shone as he lifted a photo of a beach scene populated with shapely actors. "Justine, why don't you show our guest where you plan to set up the special commemoration." He tugged her forward with his free hand.

"Maybe he has plans." She tried to keep her voice level, though her teeth clenched. Her friends resembled parents trying to hook up their loser daughter with a traveling salesman. Both of them beamed.

Jackson lifted a shoulder under his leather jacket. "I have a few minutes."

"Great. Follow me downstairs." With a stiff spine, she led past cases featuring dolls from different eras, personal accessories, and a rotating hat tree loaded with vintage finds. Excitement got the best of her at the bottom of the staircase, out of her coworkers' sightline. She whirled toward him. He jolted to a stop, ending up an arm's-length away. The close proximity sizzled between them—at least on her part. She stepped back but kept her voice low. "Their names are on those scripts."

"No shit, Sherlock." He walked past her.

Okay, rude Jackson was back. If he didn't want to discuss the situation, she wouldn't push. *The hell she wouldn't.* They shared in the search that night. He could always tell her to back off. "Did you try any other avenues to find out more about them?"

"I did not." He kept his back to her, stopping to examine the miniature train set, built to climb through papier mâché mountains. He flicked the switch. The locomotive whistled and began to chug around the track.

"That's your prerogative." The lights of the vintage hotel sign flashed behind him. Still unplugged. Justine rolled her eyes at the ghostly interjection. The sign flashed again. She turned away from it. "Over here is where I plan to set up the materials and clothing. Upstairs we have permanent theme rooms by era. We change things out more on the lower level but also can leave certain displays up."

She led the way to the opposite corner, where a collection of wooden children's sleds hung, fronted by mannequins in vintage winter snowsuits. "I'll move these out before Valentine's Day. We came up with the idea to do a grand unveiling and tie it in to a special fundraiser." She hesitated. "If that's all right with you?" Maybe he wouldn't want them to earn money off his mother's measure of local fame.

"Sure." He joined her as the train whistle tooted again. "As long as the event's tasteful."

Her temper spiked into sarcasm. "We're going to have a square dance hootenanny and a cake walk and a kissing booth. Good old small-town fun."

He grimaced and attempted to clear his face. "If people go for that kind of thing here."

"Not since the 1950s." She snorted and crossed her arms over her chest. "You really think LaPorte is Podunk-ville, don't you? Yes, I assure you the portrayal will be exceptionally tasteful. So wonderful that Liza herself would approve."

The sign blinked again. This time, she nearly chuckled as his face shifted to discomfort. She drove the point home. "I plan to feature one of the swimsuits and a late '60s shift on mannequins. I can hang other clothing along a large folding screen. The scripts and photos will be on that table." She indicated a carved, waist-high sofa table. "We'll also create a tasteful poster about your mother to highlight her story."

He held up a hand to stop her. "Perfect."

She tilted her head. "We should mention that her son is an accomplished screenwriter and list a few of your credits, too."

He stepped back and shoved his hands in his pockets. "This isn't about me."

"People would enjoy knowing that the creative gene runs in the family," she countered, while recognizing she shouldn't push that issue, either.

He walked away to run a hand along the massive mahogany bar. She waited a few seconds for a response and gave up the argument. "For decades, that showpiece resided at the hotel that also housed the sign over there. Now that building offers senior citizen apartments."

"Interesting. I figured it came from an old saloon. There are plenty in this town." Jackson could've been posing for a liquor ad in his tight jeans as he leaned against the polished surface, facing her. All he needed was a bottle of Irish whiskey.

She felt a flush of heat travel down her body. He caught her eyes and held them. Something zinged through the air between them. Electric and intense. He hadn't forgotten, either. She grasped the ends of the scarf around her neck and gulped, unsure what to say, or do.

He broke the spell. "About what you said earlier, I'm sure LaPorte is great for a lot of folks." One eyebrow raised to add a zing of cynicism.

Her fingers relaxed their grip on the silk. Snarky status quo restored, thank goodness.

He braced leather-clad elbows behind him on the bar. "But my mother was larger-than-life. Dramatic. Fun. Beautiful. She had bigger dreams, and she went for them. Despite Grandma's concerns." He focused beyond her, to the winter sledding scene. "Her reckless behavior led to me."

"From her letters, she had no regrets," Justine offered the comment in a gentle voice and approached his side, slowly, as if facing a skittish animal. She was much more at ease in the role of comforter. The quick flare of libido couldn't be indulged.

He ignored her attempt at empathy, still contemplative. "She never made it big personally, but she moved in crowds that did. Her second husband, Terrence, was a producer. They hosted some kickin' parties in the '90s. I was a teenager and tended to make myself scarce, after sneaking a bottle out to my friends."

"Did you run with a fast crowd, too?"

"I'm sure you won't be surprised to hear I was a rebel. I only got arrested once." His grin flared, wicked and knowing.

"I'm not even going to ask…for now."

"That's good because the story's long and I should get back to the house. I've got a ton of work to wrap things up." He straightened and rolled his shoulders back. "I can write or edit a script anywhere. Still, I didn't plan to be in LaPorte this long. There's so much old stuff accumulated in the house through the years, I don't know where to begin. Or if I should."

"Old stuff!" She interrupted, with an indignant glare. "Lovely antiques. I can't believe you aren't interested in keeping anything."

"That's just it." He tapped his boot on the floor. "I'm

out of my element. I don't know anything about values and what I should consider keeping. I'm overwhelmed by the sheer volume of my grandmother's excess. She indulged her passion through things rather than marrying again."

"What about a glass desk lamp? I recall one that was more masculine looking, and it shouldn't clash too much with your sleek décor." She stopped to envision the treasures. "Most of the furniture is probably too heavy for your style. The figurines in the sideboard would be too feminine. There were a couple of cool deco vases you might want."

Jackson threw up his hands. "I told you, I'm clueless. Why don't you come over and give me some idea into the value so I can make educated choices. The rest can go into an estate sale. Run by a company, if I can find one."

The refusal hovered on her tongue. She'd only set herself up spending time with this good-looking, irritating man. After all, he was solely interested in her knowledge of antiques and would head home at the earliest possible opportunity. Then again… Didn't she deserve to add a little zest to her existence? Even if it meant living vicariously, by admiring someone else's antiques and the remnants of "life in the fast lane." Or maybe even flirting a little? "When would you want me to come by?"

His lip lifted. "How about Sunday? That's your next day off, right?"

"Right." She was amazed that he recalled she worked every other Saturday. "I could come over after church. Unless, of course, you'd like to join me there." She laughed, anticipating his pained expression. "Just kidding. Though we have a great band at our contemporary service. How about I shoot for one o'clock?"

He looked relieved, as if the mention of a church service might have sent him running for the stairs. "If you're sure helping out again won't be an imposition. I'm feeling kind of guilty for taking more of your time and mining your expertise."

"What good is expertise that doesn't benefit others? Anyway, as pathetic as it may sound, it really will be fun for me to take a closer look at such beautiful things. If you haven't contacted an auctioneer, I could offer suggestions. I've got a friend who's a realtor, too— though I'm not trying to push your business his way."

"Any help is appreciated." He glanced at his watch. "See you on Sunday then." He turned to head back up the stairs alone.

No, she would not follow like a lap dog. The lights flashed twice from the sign. She placed her hands on her hips and faced it with a stern expression. "We have plenty of ghosts here for one museum," she hissed. "Liza Maddox better stay put in her house." As if they'd listen to her.

Especially the saucy actress.

Chapter Seventeen

On Saturday evening, Jackson wandered the quiet house, unable to settle into a task. He spent the day trying to work on a script project, annoyed at having to chip words out of his psyche. Usually, they flowed in a subconscious stream. He wasted almost as much time pacing to loosen the mental juices. Yet the block remained. Finally, he abandoned the effort to squeeze unsatisfying verbiage onto the computer screen.

Despite determination to squelch them, questions about his parentage pulled his attention. Comparing those two men didn't reveal significant differences to focus the search. Yet narrowing to two possibilities made him feel antsy and strangely cornered. Neither of the guys might be "the one," he told himself. But they were the only names he ever considered. Beyond badgering his mom, he never tried to track anyone down. The internet wasn't widely used through his teen years, when he surrendered all desire to search. To care. He didn't want to do so now, but the open door wouldn't be slammed shut easily.

To break the unproductive cycle of introspection, he decided to leave and grab a bite. He hadn't bothered to shower, or even to eat, beyond a scrambled egg. Cooking remained a rarity here, because stocking groceries indicated commitment to spending more time in the backwater.

With wallet and keys in hand, he headed into the garage, thinking he should be able to wrap the house sale plans and return to California soon. Tomorrow, he'd step closer to the goal when Justine provided input into the antiques. Not that he worried about value. Earning money from his grandmother's and mom's deaths didn't appeal, yet he doubted he could sell the house furnished with so many accumulated items.

Justine… Thoughts of their time together also intruded into his lame writing attempts. Sitting in the chair, in front of the computer where they'd searched—and kissed—tugged at his mind and body. The smooth, soft skin, sweet, yielding lips, and her curves provoked arousing memories he didn't want to indulge.

His own fault, for not being with a woman for a long time. Leaving this one, so not his type, to bounce through his thoughts. At home, he could go out and rectify the situation. More than one woman in the past year made it clear she'd welcome him in her bed. Unfortunately, he was too raw post-divorce to even pursue a physical release.

He backed out of the driveway, boosting the heat to a blast. At home, he could call a buddy and go to a hip club or jazz bar. Or sit at an oceanside eatery, enjoying the warm breeze and a gourmet meal. Here, he bundled in layers and braved a snowy chill to search out restaurants. As for a nightspot, the bars looked kind of seedy. Not that he was a snob, but he didn't want to draw attention as a stranger.

His cell jangled, pulling him out of the reverie. Seeing the number lightened his mood. "Hey there."

"Are you still in Farmfield, Indiana?" The deep voice of his best bud and writing partner floated over the line.

Jackson snorted. "Yeah, I'm still in LaPorte. What gives, Liam my-man?"

"We landed a meeting with the studio Tuesday morning on the proposed project. I need you here to help make the sell, with the reworked synopsis and draft. I have a good feeling this version's going to fly with them."

Jackson rubbed his hand through his hair. "I'll see if I can get a flight out of Chicago. Can you pick me up?"

"Sure. Text the logistics. If you can stick around a few days, we can really start fleshing this baby out."

"I'll go online now and send you the details. Unless you're going out."

Liam laughed. "Still too early here, bro. Looking forward to seeing you soon."

"Yeah. You, too." Jackson clicked off. Talk about a major change of plans, but this script was important. He believed in the concept of a group of idealistic people fighting back against a chilling dystopian society.

He pulled over into a parking lot and jumped onto a travel site to check flights. A reasonably priced one would leave O'Hare on Monday in the late morning. His mind buzzed at the opportunity. In preparation, he'd re-read the script and hone a compelling new pitch. Which would take time and creative energy. Today, the latter had eluded him. With a good night's sleep and a clear head, Sunday he would knuckle down.

Wait, they'd have to postpone Justine's intended visit. He would text her in the morning. A matter of politeness, not to interrupt her evening. No matter who she might be spending it with.

****

Justine sipped her Cosmopolitan and multi-tasked, listening to her friends talk while keeping an eye on the bar's trivia game screen. The night before, Marcy called to cajole her into going out for a drink with her and their pal, Haley.

Her bestie had called her bluff when she tried to beg off. "Come on. What else would you be doing? Sitting at home in your bathrobe eating ice cream and watching an old movie? When you could be drinking with your friends and playing trivia? We'll have a blast catching up."

Her humorous description nailed Justine's intended plans. Now the three of them sat in a semi-circular booth facing the screens at the Michigan City bar. "What's Devin doing tonight?" she asked after punching in a trivia answer. A group of lemurs formed a conspiracy. Not a conflagration.

Marcy pursed her lips at the reference to her semi-boyfriend. "Working on his Harley with the guys and drinking beer. Sometimes he's gotta hang with the dudes."

Her friends shared a side glance, unwilling to voice criticism. While cute, he was underemployed, uninspired, and took Marcy for granted. The vibrant redhead deserved much better but didn't seem to realize it yet. A talented artist, she planned to return to LaPorte to help her ailing mom after graduating from college the next year, instead of pursuing an immediate career. *We all undervalue ourselves*, Justine thought as she answered the next question. Poor Haley worked massively long hours, slaving as an accountant. "How's tax season this year? I can't believe you have the energy to go out after a grueling week of crunching numbers."

The willowy blonde lifted her margarita mug. "That's exactly why I need to escape. The job's so consuming I don't even have time to think about dating anyone." She sipped through a long straw. "Anything new on that front for you?"

Justine hesitated. The brief pause drew her friends' attention.

"What's up?" Haley demanded. "Have you met someone?"

She closed her eyes for a moment and peeked at them from under her lashes. "No. Well, kind of."

"Dish, dish, dish." Her friend clapped her hands as the waiter approached.

A knowing smile curved Marcy's lips. The day after the snow-in she texted to make sure she was okay. They kept it brief, but on the phone the night before, Justine unleashed more details. She held up a finger to forestall their excitement as the server halted at her side. "We'll share an appetizer platter."

When he left, she filled in the backstory of Jackson's initial call to the museum, the vintage clothing search, and the unseen change in weather.

"She stayed the night," Marcy interjected.

Haley's mouth flew open, her lips working soundlessly. "Is he hot?"

"That's not the point." How to describe the mercurial Jackson Maddox? "But yes. In a California cool way. At the same time, he can be so irritating. Alternating between rude and a kind of fun guy. Though I can understand his unhappiness at having to come back here." She paused and reminded herself to stay mum on the search for his father, and the letters. "With his mom and grandma both gone now, being in the house opens up beaucoup memories."

Haley mocked a yawn. "Yeah. Yeah. But did you do the nasty?"

"Of course, not." Justine couldn't help the blush heading to her cheeks, but the Cosmo had loosened her tongue. "Though he is a good kisser."

"You never told me that," Marcy yelped, her blue eyes twinkling.

"We were killing time, drinking whiskey. I think he just wanted to blow off steam."

Her friend's expression toughened. She dropped a hand over hers on the table. "Sounds a little risky. Or risqué at least. You never felt pressure, did you?"

"No. Never."

Haley hooted. "She was a willing partner. You go, girl. Will you see him again?"

"He dropped photos at the museum yesterday. I agreed to go there tomorrow to help sort through all the antiques in the house." A smile crept onto her lips, relishing the chance to share an enticing, flirty story with her buddies for once.

"We expect a full report," Marcy ordered, clearing space for the platter of fried food they anticipated. "Here's to a short, intense interlude." Yet she turned to hold her gaze. "Really, are you okay? We don't want to make light of this if the situation bothers you in any way."

"Why would it? We all have to find something to break the winter doldrums." Justine swigged the last of her drink. Between the interaction with Jackson and the pending job interview, this January proved anything but dull.

Chapter Eighteen

Despite a late night, Justine attended the Methodist church service the next morning, uplifted as usual by the contemporary music. They gathered downstairs in the massive 1920's stone building, mingling past with present. She caught up with a couple of friends afterwards and ran into her mother and father, arriving early to usher for the traditional service. She hugged them, hoping for a fast escape so she could grab lunch and compose herself for the afternoon adventure.

Unfortunately, her chatty mother held onto her arm. "I'm so glad we ran into you. I was planning to call and talk to you later."

Justine glanced at the wall clock as others milled around them. "Mmm, that's great, Mom. I'm kind of in a hurry, so yes, later's better."

Always astute, her father placed a hand on his wife's arm. "Hon, we need to grab the bulletins and get ready for the early arrivals." He winked at Justine behind her mother's head.

"I ran into Winnie Davidson yesterday," her mother bulldozed on. "You remember we're in Bunco club together, but we haven't played for a while because of the weather. Her son, Harold, is back in town from living in Milwaukee for several years. You remember Harold, don't you?"

Yes, as a shy boy with a bad complexion. The hair

on her neck tingled. The conversation was heading in a dangerous direction.

"I was telling Winnie the great things you're doing at the museum, but that no, you aren't seeing anyone. She said he's super busy as chief financial officer at the hospital, and he hasn't settled back in and connected with any old friends."

Oh no. Justine's chin drooped to her chest.

"Wouldn't it be nice if the two of you went out together? You can catch him up on news, maybe introduce him to some people and places."

Hook, line, and sinker. "Mom, we have a ton going on at work. I'm planning a Valentine's event to kick off an important new display. Not really the best time for me to date." She stumbled on the word. "Err, show someone around town. A town where he also grew up."

"Perfect. Invite him to that party. He can drive out there on his own. The event's open to the public, isn't it?"

"Yes," she gritted through clenched teeth. "But I really don't—" She sidestepped as a woman carrying a tray of cookies tried to maneuver past.

Her mother didn't budge and drilled into her with disapproving eyes. "Justine, this poor man is coming back to town and doesn't have many connections here anymore. Are you telling me you can't extend the Christian courtesy to welcome him to the museum and introduce him to some people."

The final guilt card. She cringed and shoved a fist into her coat pocket, knowing she lost the battle. Most of the time mom played easygoing and undemanding, but she also knew her weak spots. When determined to win, she whipped out every trick. While the concept of guilt rolled off her sister's back, Justine's soft heart melted. "I suppose I can be polite and introduce him to some people. As that's my job to make visitors feel welcome at the museum."

"Good." To her credit, her mother never wallowed in the victories. She played the card, achieved the desired result, and shifted to the next topic. "You've been so busy we hardly see you. How about coming over for dinner some night?"

So she could dance around light topics like losing her job and seeing a ghost during an over-nighter? "We'll compare calendars soon. By the way, are you and Dad planning to come out for the party?"

She held back a wince, envisioning them beaming as she and Harold stumbled through stilted conversation over a cup of Hawaiian punch. But better to be prepared. Please God, maybe Haley would join her for the festivities for moral support. Marcy would be interested, but Devin wouldn't be caught dead at the bougie soiree.

Her dad grinned, prodding her discomfort. "Of course, we'll come out for the evening. Don't we always support your events?"

Justine's eyes narrowed. "You sure do. Gotta go." She plunged down the now-crowded hallway, her quick pace fueled by annoyance. At the entrance, one of her mother's friends approached with another tray of cookies. She held the door, uttered a hello, and snagged two for the road.

In the car, she bit into the snickerdoodle and closed her eyes. Harold Davidson. She wasn't unkind to him but didn't encourage conversations, either. They were both shy and nerdy. How humiliating that, all these years later, her mom felt driven to try to set her up.

Later, she'd call Haley to beg for her support and vent, but for now she needed to scoot home and get ready for the afternoon with Jackson Maddox. Who most definitely was not a nerd.

She started the car to warm and dug for her phone to turn on the sound, muted for the church service. A text message popped up. Her nerves jittered at the unfamiliar number and area code. Harold, reaching out already? Or… Her finger trembled as she punched the screen.

—Last-minute studio meeting came up. Have to concentrate on prepping today and fly out to CA tomorrow. Apologies. Don't know how long I'll stay.

Short and concise. At least he apologized. Sort of. With no mention of rescheduling. Disappointment tugged as her thumbs hovered over the keyboard.

–Hope it goes well. Safe travels.

Professional. Detached. She huffed out a breath and hit send.

July would be crushed. "Those dreamy eyes," she'd uttered in a breathy voice upon learning about the second planned meet-up. "This may be a ploy to see you again." Her raised, clasped hands obscured the row of snowmen emblazoned across the day's sweater.

"Realistically, he's desperate for help," she retorted. "You two would go crazy in that house."

Carl had grasped at the opening. "Would you like me to come over and share my vast knowledge?"

"No. You'd probably lock us in the basement and pretend to lose the key. I'm not subjecting myself to obvious, appalling matchmaking."

Great. She'd done just that with her mother. Justine drove out of the parking lot, heading home for another boring afternoon alone.

Chapter Nineteen

With a wide-open Sunday afternoon, her dismay with "The Harold Situation" morphed into anxiety over the Monday video job interview. Justine wandered through the house, answering mock questions in her head. After spending time in the spacious home on Michigan Avenue, the place felt a little cramped. In under a minute, she could dash around here and pop her head into each room: kitchen / dining, living, half-bath and office down. Her bedroom, one for guests / storage, and the full bath above.

It didn't take a counselor to recognize her change of view regarding the cozy rental. She wasn't dissatisfied with the surroundings as much as her life overall. Tomorrow was a first step to changing that up. She stopped to plump the throw pillows on the couch, thinking most important, she should embody calm confidence in the interview. While their museum might be smaller in relative terms, the size allowed her to gather a wide range of experience.

At her desk in the home office, she sat for a moment to jot down key responsibilities and special assignments in case she got flustered and went blank. Though wouldn't a skype interview be less intimidating than face-to-face?

By late afternoon, her prep calmed most of the concern. Mentally stretched, she rewarded herself by running out to grab a coffee. At the new shop on one of LaPorte's main streets, she entered and sniffed the air with pleasure. The tension loosened further at inhaling fresh-ground beans, one of her favorite scents. She wove through the crowded main area where every table was filled. At the counter, she selected peanut butter and mocha. With whipped cream.

After paying, she decided to peek into the second room to see if any friends were nestled in. Lifting the lid of the takeout cup, she blew on the coffee and walked in. An older man drew her attention as he stood, book in-hand, and grabbed his coat. When he brushed past, her limbs froze at seeing another lone person, pecking away at a laptop. Jackson Maddox.

Would he think she was stalking him? Before she could back out and run, he lifted his head. His wrinkled brow gave way to a lopsided grin. "Hey. I started to go stir-crazy at the house and craved an espresso boost."

She advanced into the room, gripping the cup. "Crazy coincidence. I came for the sugar-spike as much as the caffeine. Have you accomplished your goals today?"

"Yeah. I'm stoked we can nail the pitch. I wrote this script with my friend, Liam, and we'll present together. He pours on the charm while I impress them with the meat of the story." He gestured to the opposite armchair. "Have a seat. If you want."

The opportunity to learn about the writing process intrigued her. Accepting his offer, she removed her coat and sat. "You've developed a two-pronged plan of attack. Want to practice your part on me?"

He hesitated, then closed the laptop. "Sure. Why not. You can tell me if you have questions or if I'm too vague."

She sipped, prepared to listen, and absorb. He cleared his throat. "Imagine we've finished the initial schmoozing and small talk." His gaze intensified on hers. "Brave people speak out and take action when society goes off the rails. In 2055, a handful of rebels band together below ground to build a movement to protect our freedom."

His face animated as he wove the story of the individuals, varying in age, occupation, and identity and their daring plan to rout a self-serving dictator and government. The actions would place them all in peril of death and imprisonment. He touched on their personal desires and needs, as well as their dedication to preserving a free society.

"Two will lose their lives, but surrender is unacceptable." He stopped and settled back on the cushion.

Caught up in the story, she leaned forward. "I want more. Wow, I love this. You brought that world to life for me within a few minutes."

"Imagine what we can accomplish in a two-hour film." He drank from his coffee mug.

Hers sat untouched. She took another sip, pondering. "My only question is about the personal stakes for Faron. I'm clear what motivates the others to join this risky quest and I can anticipate the hurdles and challenges they'll face. He's a little murky."

"Strengthening the stakes and conflict is critical for movies and books. I'll tweak that. Thanks for the input." He set down the empty mug and opened the computer. "That's been my day. How've you spent your free time since we didn't comb through the house?"

"Church. Trying to dodge my mom's finagling."

"Moms can be pushy. I should know. What's her angle, if you don't mind sharing? I'm always interested in scenarios that might find their way into a script." He smirked at her. "Disguised, of course."

Darn. She shouldn't have opened this door. No slick remarks or evasions offered themselves. Oh well, wouldn't hurt to vent to him. Might relieve her own dread. "This one is age-old. A former high school classmate's back in town. Mom is trying to matchmake." Mortification flushed through her. The admission didn't relieve her discomfort but increased it tenfold.

He snorted. "Ouch. That is painful. I hope he was hot."

"No. Nice. Polite. Smart. All the things a mother could love."

"Not all of them. If you'd been Liza's daughter, she would've hooked you up with someone with flash and personality. And looks. Same things she sought in men."

To escape the embarrassing dating topic, Justine leaped at the segue. "On that subject, have you followed up with more research?" She kept the question vague, though no one had entered to overhear.

He rubbed a hand across his forehead. "I'm not ready. Just narrowing down to a couple of potential candidates spun me off to a weird place. With flying back to LA for the pitch, I had to keep my head together."

Their earlier conversation had been easy and carefree. She hoped the question wouldn't shut him back down. "I totally understand. Usually I'm not the prying type, but after being involved with the search the other night, I'm curious." A grinding noise sounded from the next room, releasing another blast of fresh coffee beans.

She drew a whiff before continuing. "Please tell me if you'd rather I let the subject lie. I never want to dredge up pain for someone for my own gratification."

"That's a kind, small-town sentiment. LA loves gossip. When someone else is in the center of it, people are just glad to avoid the heat themselves." He held up a hand. "Or, if they've become irrelevant, they may stir it up to grab attention."

"I suppose you can find people like that everywhere. Luckily, I don't run in such vicious circles."

"Sometimes I wished I didn't." He thrust his legs forward, crossing them at the ankles. "But I don't regret the choice to pursue screenwriting. At least the profession is behind-the-scenes most of the time."

"Sometimes a vocation chooses you. With my love of history, for instance, museum work is a perfect fit." The reminder struck her. For the past half hour, she'd forgotten the momentous interview the next day. "I'll leave you to wrap up and wish you the best—wait, do they say 'break a leg' for these meetings, or only for auditions and performances?"

"Good luck is a safe bet."

She threw him a thumbs up and as she stood, her purse tumbled from the chair to the floor, dumping the phone and mini-wallet. What a clunky exit. She tried to stem the embarrassment and knelt to collect items while he gathered her coat. He held it aloft, apparently to help. An unexpected gentlemanly action. She resettled the purse on the chair and stuck her arms in the sleeves. When she swiveled her head to thank him, he hovered right behind her, his face a whisper away. She couldn't move, pinned by the memory of heated kisses.

Those searing blue eyes held her. He remembered,

too. Her lips trembled and she backed up before doing something foolish and rash, like latching them onto his. "I'll get you more coffee, if you're staying."

"I'm done here. Time to head back."

The comment, appropriate in the moment, also reinforced his oft-stated intentions. LaPorte was a blip on the map. He belonged in LA.

"Safe travels. Nail your pitch." She fled without taking time to zip her coat.

****

Over the evening hours, Justine tried to concentrate on her interview. Yet she couldn't avoid rehashing the interaction. A bolder woman would have initiated the kiss when the opportunity presented. For the sensation alone. Why not leave him—and herself—with a titillating, unexpected action? A spicy move she could relay to her awed friends.

Not her. Justine might think such thoughts after the fact, but never act on them. She burrowed into the crocheted afghan and accepted she couldn't separate emotion from desire. While they ramped up the heat at the house, their final comments to each other carried an air of cold finality. Maybe he could kiss and forget, but she harbored such memories.

No more introspection. The caffeine buzz was long gone. She felt drained again and trudged up the stairs to get ready for bed.

The next morning, the interview dominated her world. She nibbled a piece of toast and went over the responses in her mind one last time. Her usual quick routine expanded to an hour getting ready, including dabbing concealer on faint, undereye shadows.

Fifteen minutes before eleven, she booted up the

computer. Five minutes till show-time, she launched the skype program. Where she sat in a waiting room, wondering if they were observing her. With a slight smile pasted on her face, she stared ahead. Thank goodness they couldn't see her knees bouncing below the wool skirt. As the appointed hour ticked by, another person joined her onscreen.

A torso filled the view. The image distorted as the woman adjusted the camera to reveal a face. Red lipstick and a pert nose, topped by chic, chopped black hair. "Ah, there you are. And here I am." Bracelets jangled on her wrist as she tilted the screen again. "I'm Samantha Chan, director of the Drysdale Museum. Thank you for meeting with me today…" Her eyes dropped briefly, "Justine."

"Thank you so much for the opportunity." Good. Her voice came out calm and level. "The museum is quite lovely. I've enjoyed my visits there."

The woman's dark eyes flashed with intensity. "When were you here last? Since my hiring last summer, we've made rather extensive changes."

"More than a year ago, for the traveling Edwardian clothing exhibit. I especially love the transition to the slim skirts pre-World War One." She browsed for three hours, lost in the wonder of the garments, until Marcy and Haley dragged her away to a wine bar.

"Yes. I've heard it was an exceptional collection." Samantha tapped a manicured finger on her chin. "Though we're veering away from such displays in the future. Less emphasis on clothing and more on the family's innovations." Her eyes dropped again, as though perusing something below eye level. "You have expertise in vintage fashion. This curating position is broad-based." She peered up. "I assume you've also worked with other collections."

"Oh, yes." Justine launched into an overview of her role, stressing the variety of tasks. She exuded positive enthusiasm, though her confidence quivered at the director's words. The woman was no longer smiling.

She leaped for a quick, convincing wrap-up. "Our gun collection is one of the largest in the world. Most of the visitors mention coming for that, or for the Belle Gunness atrocity."

The director's nose wrinkled. "One of the most prolific female serial killers, dating back to the early 1900s. I must say I'm glad our founding family is known for more beneficial causes than guns and murder." She tilted her head. "I visited the LaPorte Museum's web site. How many people do you typically see in a year?"

Five years ago, she could've stated the numbers with pride. The stats had fallen. Justine swallowed hard and relayed the true figure.

"I'm surprised," Samantha's dark brows arched. "We see double that figure."

"In Chicago, which is a popular tourist destination." The words sounded defensive. She hastened to add a gentler spin. "We're focusing on new special events and promotions to draw in people of all ages. Awareness of our existence is half the battle." Her foot, encased in a gray knee sock and a house slipper, tapped silently against the desk chair. "For Valentine's Day we'll unveil an exhibit around Liza Maddox, a LaPortean who made movie and television appearances."

The video image remained passive. "I've not heard of her."

"She was friends with some big names in Hollywood and acted with them. In small roles, of course." To hold the woman's interest, she tossed out the signatures inscribed on Liza's posters. The director appeared more engaged. "Plus, she worked with well-known directors such as Lawrence Reynolds and actors including Peter Nevins."

Justine ground to a halt, feeling heat rise through her body at mentioning the names. Not that she'd ever reveal the possible true connection. But really. What a blabbermouth. Just to further herself.

Samantha straightened. "Lawrence was recognized for his artistry in several influential films. Now that is interesting. Did you know he lives in Chicago now? I met him when he attended one of our galas."

"I wasn't aware of where he lived." Justine's eyes widened at the unexpected proximity. Looking beyond Jackson, she realized the connection could be beneficial to their museum. They had to pursue every advantage to protect themselves now. "If you have any contact information, we'd really appreciate it. Maybe he'd recall her and want to visit here or donate a related item."

The director nodded. "I'll see what I can do. He was quite approachable." She finally warmed enough to smile. "I like people who take initiative."

"Excellent. Thank you so much." Her mind raced at the new idea. "We'd be thrilled to reach out to such a stellar contact."

And maybe narrow down the mystery.

Chapter Twenty

She barely maneuvered to her desk Tuesday before Carl appeared alongside. July followed in a vest with woodland animals schussing across a slope of sparkly snow. A skunk skied behind a raccoon, followed by a rabbit holding its nose. Justine tried to keep a straight face but couldn't. Her lips quirked up.

Before her friends could ask, she headed off the questions. "Jackson cancelled. He got called back to California for a meeting." She continued to focus on the computer screen, scrolling through her email.

Carl perched on the corner of the desk, frowning. "He stood you up? I thought he was begging for help."

His co-interrogator chimed in. "When are you rescheduled?"

"We didn't. He might not come back, just contract with an auctioneer to take everything on." Her heart twinged a bit. Only because she'd miss the opportunity to dig into the antiques in the house. Nothing more.

July patted her on the shoulder. "That would be so disappointing."

"This is not a big deal." She let a cranky edge slide into the response and rolled her chair back. "Please know that I haven't told my family about meeting him and being stranded overnight, because they'd react the same way. My parents plan to come to the Valentine's Day party. I'm sure I'll say something to them by then. But just in case, keep all this confidential. Mom's already on a crazy matchmaking tangent." Darn, she intended to keep that choice tidbit to herself. Along with Jackson's parentage mystery.

Carl straightened his glasses. "Uh uh, you can't leave us hanging. What gives?"

They'd find out sooner or later. In blunt words, she revealed the Harold scheme.

Her boss rose and headed across the room to a bookshelf of school yearbooks. "He was in your class?"

"Please don't."

He ignored her and pulled out a slim, recognizable volume. She'd written articles and snapped photos as part of the 1998 staff. Justine cupped her hands to her cheeks and waited in mortification. His peal of laughter drove July straight to his side. Heads bent together, they perused the page.

"Oh man," he wheezed through a chortle. "I bet he had a tough time. What a geek."

"Pot meet kettle," Justine deadpanned.

July peered up with a woeful expression. "He has good bone structure."

"Beyond the acne. We were both gawky adolescents."

"Were you friends?"

"No. I've probably only spoken to him a couple of times."

"To please your mamas, just be polite, introduce him around a bit, and stay busy." The volunteer shut the book with a snap and reshelved it.

Their boss approached, now solemn. "We'll make sure you aren't alone with him long."

"Thanks." Justine appreciated the support, knowing

they'd come through for her. "I'm going to use Hayley as a buffer and twist her arm to come. She owes me for a horrendous blind date set-up a couple of years ago."

She called her friend later that day to ensure she didn't have other plans for the evening of the event. "I apologize for calling during tax season, but I desperately need your help."

"What's up? My head's spinning with numbers." Yet her voice sounded calm and casual.

"Please reassure me you're free the Saturday night before Valentine's Day to attend our party. My mom cooked up a scheme to foist her friend's son on me."

"For real? That sucks."

"You went to a Catholic high school, so you wouldn't know him. But he was the king of the bowls: Quiz Bowl, Spell Bowl, Math Bowl, you name it. Oh, sorry." She called to cajole her CPA friend into doing her a major favor, not belittle her love of mathematics. "I don't think math itself is nerdy."

"No numbers offense taken," Haley snorted out a laugh. "Lucky for you, I'm footloose and fancy free. I'll be delighted to be your date for the evening. By the way, what does that say about our own nerdy status?"

Justine rolled her eyes. "I don't even want to ponder that. I'm just really, really thankful. Consider this payment rendered for the flop blind date set-up."

"Yeaahh. I do owe you for that one. How about we go to LaPorte Little Theatre and borrow a couple of knockout vintage dresses?"

"Great idea. Can you do tomorrow night? They're rehearsing the upcoming show, and the doors will be open. I'll buy you a glass of wine afterwards."

After agreeing to the logistics, Justine hung up,

satisfied she'd gathered enough friendly allies to run interference that evening.

****

The next day, a trio of volunteers would arrive at the museum to help her nail down details for the event. In addition to the Harold fiasco, the potential of inviting Lawrence Reynolds tugged at her conscience. Did she dare? And why not? Jackson would never even know. Unless she told him. She would carefully think this one through.

Also, nothing prohibited her from sleuthing. If she dug deeper into both men's histories, she might find other details to help raise one possibility above the other. Again, she'd have to decide whether to share any findings with Jackson. From yesterday's conversation, he wasn't keen to follow the trail himself. For her she could categorize it as historical research—background to support the Liza display.

Her thoughts bounced between those considerations to wondering if she'd hear back from Samantha Chan. The director indicated they were taking time with the hiring process, as the retiring curator gave plenty of notice and planned to train a successor. Without her prompting, the woman also promised to reach out to Reynolds to ask if he'd be open to sharing his contact information with the LaPorte museum. If he was Jackson's father, hearing Liza's name should jog plenty of memories. Talk about stirring a hornet's nest.

Justine decided to remain mum on the possibility a famous director could pop in or donate an item. They'd proceed with planning a tasteful event either way. By some miracle, if he did confirm, the publicity could drive record numbers to visit. She hesitated in front of the printer where she ran off her meeting agendas. With the county budget situation, such a coup would position the museum as positive and innovative. Perhaps saving it from deep cutbacks.

But if she left the job, they might not fill her position, burdening Carl and the rest of the staff with her workload. Too many factors she couldn't control. She picked up the copies and aligned them in her hands. Well, she'd know soon enough, if Samantha reached out to set up a second interview. The director had ended their session by relaying that chosen applicants would advance to in-person meetings with members of their board hiring committee.

A shiver skittered through her at the thought of facing a group grilling. Justine pursed her lips and grabbed her full coffee mug to head into the meeting, trying to clear her mind. Really, wrangling their own volunteers here could be just as difficult. She entered the community room and squinted into the light pouring through the row of windows. A visitor had left sheets of scrap paper from where he hunkered down at a table to gather stats from history books and records. She cleared it off, plunked down her mug, and settled in a folding chair to wait for the committee members.

Her fingers clenched in her lap when Camilla MacKenzie arrived first. Justine steeled herself for plenty of opinions and criticism, a pattern established through the woman's years of board service. *Thanks, Carl, for reminding me I shouldn't breach protocol and ignore her as the sitting president.* No wonder he preferred to delegate much of the committee work to her.

The woman sailed in, a wool cloak billowing around her thin frame in a black and white houndstooth pattern.

Her quilted handbag thumped onto the table. "We haven't held a decent public event for too long. Let's make this one memorable." Foregoing any form of greeting, she swirled off the cloak and settled in the chair at the head of the table. She didn't remove the cloche hat perched atop her white pageboy.

"Good morning." Justine forced her lips to curve upward. "I'll be happy if we match the success of our adult prom where folks dug out everything from 1950s tulle to overblown '80s satin."

The volunteer donned a pair of aqua-rimmed readers to glance at the agenda. "I remember when the hoopskirts dictated the traffic patterns in the narrow aisles during the Civil War-era ball. We could've used a traffic cop."

Two new arrivals entered, diverting Justine's slow burn. "Hi, Wilson. Nice smiley-face bow tie. And Faith, thanks for giving us an hour here before your volunteer shift out front." Her grin was natural; she enjoyed these people.

Their newest board member sat and smoothed her streaked blonde hair. "I love meeting new people. Joining the board has given me a fun outlet in my early retirement."

"Could we get the meeting started, please." Camilla raised her voice. "I have another appointment this afternoon. What are the concepts for the Liza Maddox grand reveal?"

Three pairs of eyes swung to Justine. Her "concepts" were still a tad hazy, but she mustered enthusiasm. "Liza's son provided great photographs from her heyday. An 'on the beach' motif seems fitting since she appeared in a couple of those movies, and we have 1960's swimsuits and minidresses."

Faith held up her hands, palms out. "How about a sign: 'LaPorte's Cinema Sweetheart.' That would make a great overall theme for the evening. Will her son attend?"

The question sent a quiver of apprehension through her. "He lives in California. I doubt he'll be able to adjust his schedule."

Camilla scowled. "It certainly would be nice if he could rouse himself to join us in honoring his mother. Especially since he provided the items. I'll discuss it with Carl."

Please don't. Justine shouted the word in her mind and looked down to hide her annoyance. "If there are no other questions or suggestions for now, why don't we discuss refreshments." Not caring enough to weigh in, she doodled on her notepad while appearing attuned to the hash-out over plain punch versus the addition of raspberry sherbet. If they spiked the punch with vodka, the guests would be really happy.

Camilla tapped her pen on the table in a rapid staccato. "We should be especially cost conscious now with the county's budget threats. We don't want to attract any more of their negative scrutiny."

"More?" Justine's stomach clenched. "Have you heard rumors? Carl said the last meeting was contentious, but they didn't single us out."

"Scuttlebutt." The woman glanced toward the open doorway and gestured with an imperious finger for Wilson to close the double doors. He jumped to obey. She lowered her voice when he returned. "My friend works in one of the government offices. Word is, outrageous suggestions are being tossed around. Non-essential services are all under the microscope." She huffed out an agitated breath. "We all know arts and culture is the soul of a community, but in a crisis, they're the first to go."

The other two members exchanged worried glances. Justine lifted her chin and attempted to sound positive, as renewed concern also pumped up her adrenaline. "The event is doubly important, not only to show we can raise funds, but to provide quality entertainment and historical education. We should brainstorm sponsorship possibilities."

Or invite famous guests to make an unforgettable splash...

Faith interrupted Justine's fast-derailing thoughts by rolling off a list of local businesses. "I'll contact these once we have sponsorship levels established."

The others added to the list and declared they'd reach out to the remaining board members to assist with approaches and other details. Relieved and warmed by the support, Justine felt her shoulders loosen as she jotted each suggestion. These people were passionate about the museum, too—even the snooty president.

Camilla stashed her pen in the quilted carryall. "Everyone has their assignments and timelines. We'll meet again next week, same day and time if that's amenable. Justine, send out a reminder."

"Of course." She made a note to jog her memory.

The houndstooth cape swirled around the volunteer's shoulders as she swept out of the room without a goodbye. Justine looked up to catch Faith's wink.

Wilson leaned toward her. "She means well. You do a great job for us here. Don't ever forget that, especially when you're dealing with a cranky board member."

The comment restored her mood. "I appreciate you both. All of the volunteers. Thanks so much for your dedication. Now I'd best get back to work implementing all our great plans."

She left the room and increased her pace to a swift walk, hoping to roust out the dark chocolate bar she'd hidden in the breakroom cabinet. Emergency chocolate could take the edge off challenging meetings.

Relieved at discovering her stash intact, she sank into a chair and envisioned the possibility of Jackson Maddox and Lawrence Reynolds meeting there, for the first time. Her mind sank to the worst possible scenarios. Accusations. Punches. Curses. The event would be memorable for sure. Infamous, even.

And her mother had guilted her into inviting Harold Davidson. With a chunk of chocolate melting on her tongue, she bolted toward the door to allay her fears by immersing herself in tasks. On the lower level, she slowed to scope out the area designated for the new Liza exhibit.

"Why do you let that woman push you around like that?"

Justine's heart catapulted and she whirled toward the voice. Liza Maddox perched on the wooden bar a few feet away, legs crossed at the knees above white patent leather boots. She wore a splashy lime green and blue flowered frock. The same dress would be used in the exhibit.

"How can you be here?" Justine plastered her hand to her chest and glanced around all corners of the room to ensure they were alone. "You scared me half to death."

"My things are here. Don't try to deflect me. I can't believe you let her get away with being such a bully."

"As the board president, she's our boss." Justine began to approach her. She caught a whiff of perfume, and the sensory smack froze her steps. She wrapped her arms around her torso and rocked back. "Sometimes one has to put up with bullshit in a job."

Liza swung her legs in a lazy rhythm. "I suppose most women aren't as fearless as me. I wish my mother had sat on some of these committees. She'd have reset their priorities in record time."

"They have the best intentions. Our volunteers are the lifeblood of the museum. Including Camilla, despite her often-irritating ways." She straightened her spine and dropped her arms to her sides. "Besides, you weren't so fearless in dealing with your baby daddy."

The black eyebrows arched. "Low blows aren't your style. Why don't you want to ask my son to the party?"

Whoa, a sneaky subject change. *I don't have to answer. I don't even have to acknowledge this…apparition.* Justine shifted her gaze to the stairway but couldn't make herself leave. If Liza hung around—Heaven forbid—she'd keep trying to ferret out the "relationship" details. "As we say these days, it's complicated. Especially if Lawrence Reynolds by some miracle ends up coming."

The swinging legs halted. Liza's face shifted to a blank, passive expression. "Whatever would he be doing here?"

"He directed you. Right? Turns out he lives in Chicago now and I spoke with someone recently who might be able to connect us up. Wouldn't that be incredible?" She watched her closely.

The face didn't change, but a hand fluttered in her lap. "I doubt he'd even remember me."

Justine stepped closer, bolstering herself for a two-sided, pointed inquisition. "You're a better actress than I'd have thought."

The image flickered and faded.

"Chicken." Justine found herself staring at her own reflection in the mirror behind the bar, unsure if she was addressing Liza, or herself.

Chapter Twenty-One

Liza, May 1980

Liza paced the floor of the budget motel room, alternately snuggling and bouncing a fussy Jackson in hopes he would settle. Jewel had suggested he might be teething, and she'd bought him a rubber ring to chew on. Sometimes the diversion helped, but today he spat it out multiple times. The baby was good natured, but definitely could show a stubborn streak.

Of all days, why couldn't he show a docile side when he was about to meet his father? Though in truth, Liza figured his daddy would respect the early show of strength from his first male offspring.

Her own weakness had seeped through, spending a half hour deciding between a dozen tiny baby outfits. A zip-front jacket won out, with pants covered in baseballs and bats. The powder-blue brought out his eyes—the startling shade that captivated her when she met his father.

Since the brief glimpse at the hospital, they hadn't dared meet. Over the past six months, he called three times and sent a trio of discreet envelopes of cash. Each phone conversation passed too quickly, hushed and furtive. She knew his risk in being caught.

Her heart soared a week ago, when he whispered, "I want to see him. Please. Can we meet at the Palmetto

Motel on Grant Boulevard at noon next Thursday?"

To avoid a trail, she booked the room. The next envelope would cover the extra expense.

Liza dressed with care, too, full aware with the baby in the room there'd be no intimacy. A feisty little part of her couldn't help playing up her figure, which she worked hard to regain through dieting and exercise. In contrast, his demanding wife had a paunch after the birth of their three daughters.

She peered at the bedside alarm clock. Ten minutes late. Jackson sniffled and rubbed chubby fists against his cheeks, his weight growing heavy in her arms. No way would she lay him on the flowered spread covering the mattress. The place provided discretion, not ambiance or cleanliness. His face began to crumple. "Oh, my sweet, sweetheart." She paced across the worn brown carpet rubbing his back.

Two sharp taps sounded at the door. The baby's head shot up and he wailed. "Shhh, shhh," she soothed. "Daddy's here."

Unfamiliar nerves knotted her insides as she checked the peephole and unbolted the door. She snuck a finger inside the baby's mouth for him to chew on. Thankfully, he quieted as the visitor entered and quickly pushed the door shut.

While she'd undergone transformations over fifteen months, he looked the same: tall, lean, with handsome, patrician features. For several moments they stared at each other, the child seeming oblivious. A burst of emotion left her speechless. Yearning. They couldn't be together, but she also couldn't extinguish the intensity of the feelings. Hadn't really tried. She still loved him, still desired him, and knew he felt the same.

His gaze stripped her bare, but neither of them spoke. Liza dropped her eyes first and shifted to bring their baby's features into his full view. Would he see himself in them? He moved forward and reached out a tentative hand. Jackson lifted his head from her chest.

"He's beautiful." The whispered words sounded hoarse. Her heart fluttered at seeing the tears film his eyes. He cradled a broad palm over the thatch of brown hair, fingering the silky strands.

A shaft of pain and love knifed through her, twisting in her gut. Her legs and arms trembled. "Would you like to hold him?"

"More than anything." A tear rolled down his cheek as she shifted the boy to his chest.

With a finger, she captured the wetness and brought it to her lips, tasting salt and regret.

Chapter Twenty-Two

Jackson braced his crossed forearms on the high-top table, watching his buddy throw darts across the room. He'd talked him into grabbing a brew at a neighborhood hangout, instead of trolling the trendy wine bar he favored. A hoot erupted, and Liam, the victor, clapped a hand on the shoulder of the man he bested.

Meandering back to their dark corner, he pumped his fists in the air, flexing muscles under his polo shirt. "Woohoo. Undefeated in three matches. Take a turn, bro."

Jackson nudged the mug of beer toward him. "No, thanks. I'd embarrass myself."

"Understandable." His friend plopped onto the stool and lifted his drink. "To my wins, and our presentation. I gotta thank you again for flying out here to strengthen our pitch."

"Now we wait for the word. I hate this part."

"But you love the work. I have a feeling we're going to land this. The angsty, finding-yourself-drama sells, and we relay it through kick-ass characters in a cool, dystopian universe. Add in the dark humor—your specialty—and we have a winner." He clinked glasses and drank deep, emptying a third of the pale ale. After swiping a finger over his lips, a grin tugged at his mouth. "While we wait, I do believe a fine-looking lady over by the bar has her eyes on you." He waggled his brows.

"Definitely worth your time."

Jackson ducked his head and fought the natural impulse to turn and stare. "What are you jabbering about?"

"A delish brunette is casting glances your way. I hoped they were for me, but she skimmed right past when I aimed for eye contact. You want to send over a drink?"

Despite himself, he was intrigued. "What's she drinking?"

"From the color, I'd wager a Cosmo. Probably something sexy, like pomegranate." Liam's smile widened. "Hold on. I believe she's taking the initiative."

Silky fabric brushed against Jackson's forearm. His eyes traveled up a form-fitting red top to glossy lips, a pert sculpted nose, and dark-lashed navy eyes. "Is this chair taken?" The voice channeled Marilyn Monroe.

Liam stood to pull it out. "Waiting for you."

"Thanks." She sat and swiveled her body toward Jackson. "My friend is running late, and I felt so conspicuous standing there alone. I appreciate you taking pity on me. My name's Mindy." She held out a small hand, tipped with silver nails.

"Jackson Maddox." Her skin was cool and soft, and her smile transmitted a clear message of interest. She held onto his fingers a few moments then offered a quick shake to his companion.

"Liam Emsworth. Are you a native?"

Shiny hair bounced over her shoulders as she shook her head. "I moved out here three years ago from Wyoming to break into acting."

"How's that working out for you?"

"At the moment I'm working as a receptionist at an

insurance agency. I've been in a couple of commercials. Do you work in the business?"

Ah, the infamous question. Jackson didn't want to come off as a dick or uninterested, so he interjected, "We're screenwriters. Not connected to the casting end." If the girl was looking for a job, the conversation would end quickly.

She laughed. "Don't worry, I'm not scoping for work. You two looked like nice guys and I didn't want to give off the wrong vibe at the bar."

He found that he believed her and felt his shoulders relax. "You chose us because we looked safe and boring."

"I didn't say *that.*" Her words were interrupted by a loud feminine voice, angling in from behind his head.

"Min, I'm so sorry. I got caught up finishing a project for one of the partners." They all peered up at the statuesque woman in a black sleeveless dress, with a cap of tight, dark curls. "Hi, I'm Tanisha. I need a drink. Fast."

"Happy to oblige. I'm Liam, and I'm good for the next round." He stood and pulled out the empty chair.

She dropped into it while Jackson added his welcome. Without saying a word to each other, he read the quick telepathic message transmitted between the women. Liam lifted his hand to call the waiter and caught Jackson's eye for their own buddy-to-buddy signal. Let the games begin.

Which meant he needed to polish up his dormant conversation skills. At least he wouldn't feel as rusty at polite chitchat as he had with Justine. Being snowed in forced them to make nice, but they didn't lean flirtatious. Except for that incendiary kiss. And the little sizzle of electricity in the coffee shop Sunday.

What was he doing, inviting her to the house again? He did desire help in wading through all the stuff. But it wasn't right to fan the flame that burst between them.

"Jackson. Hey, do you want another brew?" Liam's raised brows urged him to tune back in, to the attractive woman sitting to his right.

A woman who lived in the area and understood his world. He could stay here and have another drink and banter with fun company or return alone to his quiet loft. "Another beer plus a shot of whiskey." He met Mindy's eyes.

Her lips curved. "Make that two shots."

Chapter Twenty-Three

Her cell rang after work Wednesday night as Justine finished a plate of leftover spaghetti. The number on the screen didn't register, or the area code. A punch of nerves jabbed her midsection. Not Jackson Maddox, she remembered the LA prefix. Maybe Samantha Chan? Better answer, just in case. She clutched the phone and carried it into the living room. "Hello. This is Justine."

"Hello. This is Harold Davidson. My mom told me you'd been ambushed."

A mix of guilt and dismay gripped her system. "I, uh, I wouldn't say…yeah, I guess that's the word." She made her way to the armchair and attempted a small laugh, which came out forced and unnatural. "My mom mentioned something about how you were back living here and might enjoy the museum's upcoming event."

In contrast, his chuckle held a true lilt of humor. "I'm so sorry. I wanted you to know I had no prior knowledge of their machinations."

"That's a relief?" She wasn't sure how to proceed after his blunt admission. The vise of anxiety around her chest began to loosen. "Look, you're under no obligation at all to attend. I'll be busy working and—"

"I'm into supporting the museum." He hesitated. "Actually, I called to suggest we get together prior to the event."

The pressure returned, working its way up her

throat. "Before?" She barely squeaked out the word.

"The symphony has a fundraising concert a week from this Saturday. The hospital bought a table. I wondered if you'd like to go."

Oh my, a very public outing. Hundreds of people would attend. Would see them together. Her nose crinkled with concern. Yet the evening also would provide an opportunity to hobnob with folks she could invite to the museum's dance. She certainly didn't have a better offer. Mustering her courage—and hoping his skin had improved—she made a decision. "I'd enjoy that."

****

A half hour later she burst into the "green room" at LaPorte Little Theatre and stopped dead. Makeup containers, wigs perched on foam heads, and props from past and present shows littered the long counter. As she stared at a papier mâché turkey, her fingers itched to dive in and start organizing.

"Hey, girl." Haley's voice interrupted her distressed perusal. "From the furrowed forehead, I bet you're thinking the costume loft better be more organized."

"Exactly." Justine forced herself to ignore the clutter and wrapped her in a quick hug. "Let's go up and find two fabulous frocks." She pulled back but held onto her friend's arms. "Get this, though. Harold thwarted our mothers' meet-cute conniving."

"He's not coming to the event? Well, you're still gonna be stuck with me. I have no social life."

"Worse. He called tonight and invited me to go to the symphony concert. With dinner first." She disengaged in expectation of the explosion.

"Whaaat? And you said yes? You didn't deploy

your well-honed bob and weave skills?" Haley mimicked shifty movements with her hands.

"Sneak attack. I wasn't prepared." She tightened the scarf at her neck. "To be fair, he sounded nice. And equally appalled at the motherly intervention. Plus, sitting up front at the hospital's table provides an opportunity to highlight our event. Success is critical."

"A nice, contained event at the museum is one thing. Flaunting your date at the Civic Auditorium with a nerdy guy is downright martyrdom."

"As if I'd ever flaunt." Yet the conversation spiked her unease. She shook her head. "I don't see how I could back out now. Let's head up to the loft." Any random cast member could walk in on the conversation. She scooted through the narrow room and up the back stairs.

Haley poked her from behind in the shoulder blade. "Have you heard back from Chicago?"

"No, and maybe I won't. If they pass, I at least hope they send a letter or text, so I don't hang in agonizing limbo." Her best friends were in the loop about the interview. Generally, she shared all aspects of her life. Though some recent situations demanded secrecy: Jackson's father search, the slight possibility Lawrence Reynolds might come to the museum, and Liza's appearances. Those might never be revealed.

They entered the costume loft, which remained in decent order. After shedding their coats, Justine placed them on a chair stacked with harvest-gold drapes. "This color screams 1970s appliances," she joked to lighten the mood. Through the half-wall, open to the stage below, a smattering of voices echoed. Rehearsal hadn't started.

Haley stepped next to her and muttered, "You'll land a second interview. Don't sweat it." Coming straight from work, she looked interview-ready herself in a polished, rust-tone suit.

Justine smoothed a hand down her Chicago Cubs championship sweatshirt, thinking they'd witnessed the best and worst of each other's fashion since bonding over Popple toys in Kindergarten. "For tonight, I'd rather avoid the topic," she whispered. "You know I prefer the ostrich approach."

"Does that mean I can't quiz you on Jackson Maddox?"

"Nope. He's not even relegated to limbo. I texted you and Marcy that he canceled. We had a brief run-in at the coffee shop yesterday. He flies out tomorrow, probably for good." She dove her hands into a rack of costumes, attempting to act nonchalant.

Her friend's eyes softened. "Made for a good story."

"Imagine his toney clique laughing themselves breathless. If he even bothers to talk about it." She yanked a dress out of the cluster. "What's exciting about being forced to host a boring yokel? Just because you don't have a snow shovel."

"You're not boring. You're one of the smartest, creative people I know." Haley planted her fists on her hips. "Plus, sweet and kind."

"We're overlooked, under-appreciated gems here in LaPorte, for sure." She couldn't help cracking a grin. "Let's find something to wear so we can move on to whine and wine." She pulled out additional gowns. "See if any of these beauties interest you. Some are true vintage. Others were sewn for certain roles."

Together, they discussed the choices and narrowed them down. "These four dresses are probably late '90s," she estimated.

Haley measured the royal blue velvet against her waist. "Love this color." She stripped out of her jacket and tugged the gown over her head.

Justine eased up the side zipper, which nearly closed over her turtleneck. "Perfect. You look like a princess." She picked up the pink lace and held it to her chest.

"Huh uh. We're not going matronly." Her friend wrested the dress away and shoved it back onto the rack. Take a walk on the wild side and try the red."

She mock-glared but obeyed, removing the sweatshirt to reveal a cotton camisole. The rustling fabric slid over her head, slick and cool to the touch. A back zipper tightened the fabric around her. She gaped down at the exposed cleavage—not much, not tacky, but more than she ever dared.

"You look hot, girl. Check it out in the mirror."

They turned together, taking in the reflections. Justine twirled, flaring the skirt around her feet. "Correction. We look hot. Look out LaPorte, these ladies are aiming to make some history." No, she didn't have to remain in a boring life loop. She could rewrite her script at any time.

Chapter Twenty-Four

The next morning, Justine alternately kicked herself for agreeing to the date with Harold and wondered when or if she'd hear from Samantha Chan. Or Jackson Maddox. She'd nearly written them both off when the director's number flashed on her cell. Anticipation and dread twisted through her. The phone rang twice while she peeked around the basement. She was alone but didn't dare use the speaker.

The woman's cultured tone filled her ear. "I imagine you've been wondering about the outcome of our process. My apologies. Finding a full day to meet with a busy hiring committee is challenging.

Justine held her breath and walked to a far corner.

"The good news is we're conducting initial in-person interviews a week from today and would like to schedule with you at three."

Justine's mouth fell open with surprise and elation. "Thank you. I'm very honored to be considered."

"I suggest you bring your portfolio." Samantha rattled off more details. "Please arrive a half hour early. We look forward to meeting you. Oh, and I talked to Lawrence Reynolds."

She gripped her cell as the emotions surged again, fluttering butterflies in her system. "We so appreciate that. Does he remember Liza Maddox?"

"Yes. When I shared about your efforts to commemorate her, I admit he hesitated. After all, that was decades ago. He agreed to pass along his email."

No phone number, but he would consider their information or requests. Justine rushed to her nearby notebook to jot the email address. "Thank you so much for reaching out to him. Any support by Mr. Reynolds would be a highlight of the event."

"I'm always happy to assist another museum. And we look forward to meeting you in person." With a reminder on the interview logistics, Samantha clicked off.

"Woohoo!" Justine pumped an arm in the air and bounced on her toes. My gosh, she'd made the cut—and a path had opened to contact the director. She glanced around, half-expecting to see Liza lurking. There was no sign or scent of her.

What a puzzle. She felt a little contrite for pursuing Reynolds with a hidden background agenda. But her loyalty to the museum ranked above the Maddox' family secrets. Reaching out to him didn't mean she'd uncover any information, anyway.

The call with Samantha had added to her own secretive agenda. She'd have to take at least a half day off that Thursday to travel more than an hour into Chicago. Her heart stuttered, recognizing Carl should now hear the truth. With their strong relationship, she felt confident he'd support her, or at least understand the motivation. If the county decided to chop jobs, she wouldn't wait, dumb and complacent, for the axe.

The request to bring a "portfolio" tugged at her. Marcy no doubt would lend her artistic flair to such a project. Mounting the stairs, she experienced a renewed twinge at approaching Carl. They'd bonded over the years, with no judgments and no topics off-limits. Until she started holding back. She clasped her hands together and approached his desk, where he faced the computer with a mangled pencil between his lips.

"Can we talk in the community room?" Their glass-walled office provided full exposure to the working volunteers and handful of roaming visitors.

He pulled out the pencil and his face crinkled. "About your hot-to-trot new friend? Does he want to move up the date?"

She narrowed her eyes. "Every time I think the word 'date' my insides quiver. Rendezvous sounds worse. Consider it a meet-up. And no, that's not my news."

He rolled back the chair. "You're making me nervous."

"Yeah. Me, too."

They made their way to the larger room, where he closed the door and sat across the table. Unable to sit still, she fidgeted with her fingers on the table. "I love working here. You know that."

"Of course. We're a talented team." His face softened. "Spit it out. I don't bite. Hard."

"You're a great leader." Darn, she should've practiced the delivery. She steepled her fingers under her chin.

His brows furrowed. "You're leaving us."

"No. Not yet anyway." The words loosened, spilling out the Chicago opportunity. "I am interviewing because of the county's financial predicament."

He smacked a palm against the table. "I hate that the situation's come to this. Losing good talent. But I totally understand. We can't predict what will happen here."

She stared past him through the window, to the bleak winter landscape outside. "Not only that, but I'm in a rut, too. The work is great, but outside of here, my hours are as lifeless as our artifacts. I need to push myself, and my potential."

He covered his hand with hers. "Indeed, you do. I'll support your directions, always. Best of luck and keep me updated. If you want them to call me, I'll give an awesome reference."

Her tensed shoulders relaxed as they segued into a few details for the upcoming event. When she shared about a certain famous director's willingness to connect, Carl could barely stay seated. "Wow. Well done. We need to reel him in as soon as possible for the publicity."

"Would you prefer to be the one to email him?" She respected the chain of command, though with the ulterior motive, she burned to be the direct link.

"No. You found him." He pushed back the chair and stood. "The coup could be your parting shot. Exit on a super high note."

The idea of "exiting" still rattled her senses. After leaving the room, Justine took a quick break to clear her head then sat at her computer to compose a draft email. Before she could marshal her thoughts, her cell dinged with a text. A new shiver of concern skimmed along her skin at the irony of reaching out to the director at the same time Jackson messaged her. Her foot tapped under the desk as she read.

—Project's moving forward. Staying here to work with my partner on script. Will let you know decision on handling house contents.

Terse and concise. She didn't expect the disappointment tangling in her belly as she replied.

—Congrats on the big win! Alert me if you need help later at house.

Minutes passed. He didn't respond back. Heck, he wasn't obligated to update her at all. Resigned, she shook out her fingers and typed an introductory email to a man who might be his father. Jackson wouldn't return to LaPorte again. He'd never know she reached out to Lawrence Reynolds. Or that she talked to his mother.

No need to hold back. After she wrapped this task, she'd delve further into the director as well as Peter Nevin's past.

Chapter Twenty-Five

Liza, February 1988

Liza held her breath across the kitchen table as Jackson tipped glitter over a glue-covered, construction-paper heart. Tongue between his teeth, he sprinkled the art project and showered a crimson cloud onto the newspaper beneath.

She sighed in silent relief when he set the container aside. At age eight, the boy exhibited a strong, determined temperament, adamant to master things himself. Which translated to huge messes. This time she intervened, to protect her tile floor. The cleaner wouldn't arrive for five days. Her own energy was tapped with filming a sitcom appearance, plus cooking, entertaining, and driving Jackson to early-morning tennis lessons.

Tenting the edges of the newspaper, she formed a rough funnel. "Honey, please hold the vial and keep the end of the paper steady." When they accomplished the task, she ruffled his hair. "You did a wonderful job. Who are you going to give this to? A girlfriend at school?"

"Yuk. No." He looked up with those big blue eyes that always tugged at her. "Maybe grandma. But I can make more. Do you think my dad would like one?"

"I'm sure Roger would love that."

Jackson pouted. "I mean my real dad."

The paper crumpled in her hands. When they

married, she and Roger agreed to hold off on the prickly subject till he could process the information. That was her excuse, anyway. The child was mature enough to understand they didn't marry until he was two. She bought time to form an answer, refolding the newsprint for recycling. He also was sensitive. How would he handle realizing her husband could've adopted him? And chose not to.

"Last night you asked why you have a different last name. Where did that question come from?" The buzzing doorbell had interrupted the conversation, with guests arriving for the evening. She'd hoped he would forget.

He picked up the child-sized scissors, opening and closing them. "I heard you through the door last night when I got up to get a drink." His lower lip jutted again, defying her to lie to him.

She couldn't. Not again. Her eyes lasered on his. The words would alter his life forever. "Your biological father and I loved each other very much." Her throat started to constrict. She grabbed the nearby glass of water and gulped it down. Jackson stared, silent, solemn, waiting. She suddenly envisioned him as a too-serious adult. "He and I knew we couldn't be together, no matter how much we loved each other. And you." The words pierced her, after all these years.

"Why not?" He slammed down the scissors, voicing the question she feared most.

Career sabotage. Gossip. Infidelity. Concepts much too distasteful to dump on a child. She still wrestled with the guilt of her careless actions. "There were too many…complications. I promised to keep the secret because we didn't want to hurt his career."

"What about hurting you and me? Why won't you

tell me anything about him?" Jackson's mouth began to quiver. "Does he hate kids?"

No. He adored his acknowledged children. Her stoic resolve crumbled. She slid out of the chair to kneel beside him, enfolding him in her arms. Tears silvered on his hair as she rested her cheek there. "I'm so sorry to hurt you," she whispered. "I'd do anything to protect you from pain, but I have to keep my word."

His slim body jerked out of her arms. Off-balance, she steadied her hands on his chair. He grabbed the art project and ripped it in half, releasing a shimmer of glittering red. Before she could stand, he ran out of the room. She didn't have the guts to follow.

Chapter Twenty-Six

Channeling the flattering color of the Valentine's gown, Justine chose a similar red hue for the Saturday date with Harold. No more monotone colors. A first step to revamping her life, which meant she'd have to go shopping to supplement her wardrobe. Her knees shook—as much at that thought as pondering the "date"—as she tugged on warm black tights. The wool pencil skirt ended above her knees. She gulped calming breaths and donned a matching scarlet turtleneck and a black jacket threaded with silver.

The nerves built in her chest as she wielded a curling iron to smooth her hair into waves, adding hairspray to fight frizz from the snow flurries. Why in the world had she agreed to such a public outing with a man she'd prefer not to meet? She stared at her reflection in the bathroom mirror and winced, kicked by guilt stemming from her family's Christian upbringing.

Harold probably turned into a fine man. Not his fault that her life had swung into turmoil, including the buried longing to be with someone mysterious and exciting. Like Jackson Maddox.

Who wouldn't be returning to town unless necessity dragged him. Meanwhile, her burst of internet snooping brought her no closer to solving his paternity. Both of the men were married for years to blonde spouses and raised children. Their careers flourished for decades. Photos mirrored physical characteristics to Jackson: a similar range of hair and eye color and a slim build. Instead of theirs, his face leaped to her mind. In the coffee shop when he helped with her coat, he loomed so near she smelled coffee on his breath.

She yanked out the curling iron cord and rummaged through her sparse makeup, feeling her cheeks burn without a touch of blush. Darn him for invading her psyche, and to his mom for butting in. Interesting, the ghost hadn't appeared since their discussion about Lawrence. Justine chose a spicy red lipstick and murmured toward the mirror, "Oh Ms. Maddox, did you hear us talking about the email response from your director friend? Noncommittal, but he didn't tell us no." She rolled the color onto her lips and put it away, chuckling at the dig.

The laughter caught in her throat, replaced by unease. Liza said she could appear at the museum because "my things are here." The green satin robe, a taffeta party dress, and a beaded cashmere sweater hung in the closet in her own bedroom. Justine whirled to check behind the shower curtain. Empty, thank goodness. Feeling a tad foolish, she tiptoed into the bedroom and approached the closet. The doorbell pealed from the living room. She jumped and yelped with alarm.

No Liza, but Harold had arrived. She'd rather face the ghost but couldn't keep him standing in the cold. Her tall boots were waiting downstairs. In stocking feet, she trotted down to open the door. The lock clicked open as she drew a shaky lung-full of air. A tall man stood on the top step in a long dark coat, holding a cellophane-wrapped bouquet.

"Oh, thank you." Her eyes traveled up to his face.

"Umm, come in. Come in."

"Justine. Great to see you again." Harold stepped past with an easy smile. His complexion had cleared. The once-gawky body filled out to broad shoulders. Longer, straight brown hair gave way to a closer crop. A pleasant, nice-looking guy.

Relief surged through her. "Nice to see you, too. Please, sit a moment. I have to grab my boots and coat and put these in a vase."

He pulled off his leather gloves but didn't choose a seat. "You've got a fun vibe in here." He gestured to her trio of framed vintage fashion prints and the fringed shawl thrown over the back of the sofa.

Pleased, she dug in the corner curio cabinet and chose a cut-glass vase for the sweet pink roses. "Thanks. I'm into cozy and antiques. I'll take care of these and be right back."

When she returned wearing her black boots, he stood in front of her one original watercolor painting. "My friend Marcy is a wonderful artist. She's finishing a fine arts degree in Chicago." Justine moved next to him. "I love impressionist garden scenes. This was a birthday surprise."

"She's good. I'll keep her in mind for when I move into my own place and maybe commission a piece."

"Are you renting?"

He paused. His neck reddened above the wool collar. "I'm living with my mom. Not my first choice, but she's ecstatic to have me for a couple of months while they finish work on my condo." He turned away from the artwork. "New construction, over by the lake."

"Can't beat a lake view." His apparent discomfort at admitting he lived with Winnie was rather endearing.

He flashed a row of white teeth. "Here, let me help you with your coat."

Minutes later, they arrived at the Italian restaurant downtown. The conversation had continued smoothly in the car, easing her earlier tension. Yet when they were led to a high-backed wooden booth, she appreciated not sitting at a central table. People tended to know each other in LaPorte. Some reveled in the latest gossip.

They ordered glasses of wine and the getting-to-know-you talk chugged along. Justine had dipped a bite of sourdough bread in herbed oil when he leaned forward with a tentative grin. "I probably shouldn't go there so soon, but we both know I had a crush on you in high school."

He did? The wedge of bread slid onto her plate. She hardly remembered him, except for the sad recollection he surpassed her own geekiness. A smidgen of memory began to surface. "You hung out in the library when I was an aide, junior year." She fumbled for her wineglass. "Actually, wow. I, uh, didn't know."

He snickered. "You probably would have run in the other direction. I mainly watched you from afar. Not like a stalker or anything," he hurried to correct. "Didn't you notice what a voracious reader I was?"

The oversized swallow of wine warmed her. "My own nose was always buried in a book. I was way too shy to encourage any boy." A simple, truthful-sounding explanation that wouldn't bruise his ego.

He raised his glass. "Here's to growing up, coming into your own, and taking second chances."

Another upfront statement. Justine drank, too, and realized her mom and Winnie didn't have to press this man to call her. He probably welcomed the introduction.

Such an idea would have alarmed her before. To her amazement, they were having fun. Why not explore the possibility of second chances?

An hour later, she indulged a slight happy buzz as they mounted the steps of the eighty-year-old Civic Auditorium. Inside, they wove their way toward the raised stage. Dozens of light strings twinkled above, suspended from the two-story ceiling. Dressed in winter finery, people of all ages visited, sitting at about twenty decorated tables. Dozens more perched in balcony seats ringing the perimeter.

At the hospital's table, Harold introduced the two middle-aged couples, noting the wives were on the management team with him. She exchanged greetings and tried to commit their names to memory. He helped her off with her coat, adding, "Justine is the assistant director at the county museum."

One of the husbands rubbed his bearded chin. "I've never visited. Suppose we should stop in some day."

The comment presented the perfect opening to plug their upcoming festivities. "We're holding our own special fundraising event the Saturday before Valentine's Day. You could visit all the rooms, dance to a string quartet, and be the first to see our new Liza Maddox display." She wished she had actual tickets to sell, but that might appear too pushy.

The man perked up. "Now that would be worth seeing. Did you—" He broke off and stared past her shoulder. "Martin, we're hearing about a fun time coming up at the museum. You and Delores want to join us again?"

Justine looked up, prepared to wait till the newcomers had settled to continue her pitch. Her teeth chomped painfully on her tongue. Martin Collier of the County Board budget committee stood at her elbow.

He settled in the open chair beside her. "We got wind of a special fundraiser. Any initiative is appreciated at this point. If the night is successful." Gray hair curled around his prominent ears as he unwound his scarf past them. The words sounded promising, yet his lips thinned.

Of all the luck, to sit with one of the people examining the museum under a microscope. The evening would demand all her social skills. She pasted on a bright expression. "We're definitely headed for an excellent event. Our awesome volunteers and staff have gathered sponsorships and silent auction items."

He tilted his head. "What's the money earmarked for?"

The thought hadn't crossed their minds to specify an exact cause. Justine's pasta-filled stomach lurched while she frantically considered plausible ideas. Admitting to their own growing anxiety wouldn't be wise, or their focused intent to appear innovative rather than a money-losing venture.

"Preservation," Harold piped in. "Artifacts require special handling, cases, lighting. One less expense to the county."

She lifted grateful eyes to his. "Yes, our patrons and the community are eager to support maintaining and protecting our collection." A touch of dizziness swayed through her at being grilled and unprepared. "We're trying to lure a really special guest to join us to generate even more interest in the evening."

Martin's wife leaned around him. "Who? Liza herself?" She giggled and the others joined in.

Justine had turned to stone in her seat. How could

she have blurted such a hint? No, she would not give Lawrence's name. Let them all buy tickets and come out. If he decided to show, their minds would be blown. Darn, the incentive for encouraging him to attend had just increased tenfold.

She was saved from an answer by the symphony conductor bounding onto the stage above them. Hands clenched tight in her lap, she joined the others in tuning in to the energetic introduction. If they pressed her at intermission, she'd remain vague and mysterious about the *special guest*.

With the lights dimmed, her concerns dwindled. She immersed herself in the romance-themed pops tunes. If Martin wasn't next to her, she'd sway along in her seat. After an hour, she blinked back into reality. The lights came up. The audience thundered applause. When the clapping died down, Harold stood, caught her eye, and pulled out her chair. She gratefully followed him back through the maze of tables toward the lobby.

He halted midway to whisper, "Hope you didn't mind my intercession before the concert. You seemed a little dazed at Martin's probe."

"You're right. With the budget crisis, I prefer a low profile." She laid a hand on his arm. "You chose the perfect bail-out. I'll buy you a glass of wine as a thank you."

"Only if you'll allow me to get us a plate of those chocolate-covered strawberries." His head dipped lower. "Between us, Martin's kind of cocky. The hospital has to make nice with the county, too."

With mere inches between them, she smelled his simple, clean aftershave. Close up, a few tiny acne marks were visible. Yet she no longer cared about his past appearance. Harold was nice, kind, funny. Good company. Too bad they didn't meet before all the interview, possible move, and Jackson-Liza drama slammed into her. Now she felt compelled to be cautious.

Their camaraderie grew when the concert ended, with sharing favorite music genres on the car ride home. He switched on a country station, while she confessed a preference for light, upbeat pop. "Next time we'll listen to yours," he promised.

A second date, before the museum party? All right, they'd had a fun, comfortable evening with no pressure. Why not enjoy the companionship while she waited for the interview process to wrap, and for Jackson to reveal his intentions. Regarding the house. Nothing more.

She unbuckled her seatbelt as he parked in her driveway, comparing the smooth, cultured gathering to the rocky, boozy, secret-laced night with Jackson Maddox. To use a food analogy, homemade chocolate pudding compared to flaming baked Alaska. Heat suffused her chest at the comparison. She had to get that man out of her head. Thinking of him just held her back.

Harold again leaped out to open her car door. His gloved hand gripped her elbow as they walked up the slick sidewalk. The nerves she subdued hours before fluttered back as snowflakes began to drift around their heads. Before mounting the steps, they tilted up their heads to survey the sky. A few stars twinkled, seen through the lacy fall of white.

His palm slid down to grip hers. "I'm glad we did this tonight. The museum event won't be so awkward. If you still want me to come."

"Of course." She meant the words. "I'm glad, too. I had a great time."

"The only thing missing was a dance floor to practice our moves."

"You like to dance?" Most men she knew had to be dragged into the activity. She swiped her glove across a wet drop that splatted her cheek.

White flakes settled on his hair. "Waltzing. Swing. Cha cha. Fox trot. The quartet's bound to play one of them."

She lifted onto her toes and kissed him. When she lowered, a grin split his face. "I'll take that as a yes and call you this week." He didn't wait for the answer and loped down the sidewalk.

Her cheeks tingled. Her lips didn't. The kiss had been sweet but unremarkable. He didn't pull her in for another one. No push. No passion.

She unlocked the door while he waited to enter his car, ensuring she got safely inside. With a brief wave, she entered and leaned her back against the wall in the dark. Apparently, she'd have to try harder to erase J. Maddox's devouring kiss from her memories.

Chapter Twenty-Seven

On Monday morning, Marcy and Haley stood guard at the door of an upscale local hair salon. As if she'd try to bolt and run. Justine gave her name to the receptionist, distracted by the reflecting mirrors and the pink color scheme. When the woman walked away, she narrowed her eyes at her meddling friends. "Are you really going to stay here the whole time and watch? Don't you have class? And work?"

Marcy flexed her fingers together. "My first class is at noon today. Haley's working so many hours she can go in a little late. I referred you to Evan. I should stay and say hello to him."

"Your curl wizard."

"Wait till you see what he can do with your waves. What's it been? Six months since your last cut? Long enough you didn't know your stylist moved and closed her in-house salon."

A young woman entered. Haley sidestepped to let her pass. "You want to look your best for the upcoming meeting in Chicago. With a cut that'll complement the magenta suit you borrowed from me."

"Point made," Justine grumbled. "I just don't want Harold to think I ran out for a makeover right after meeting him. He might get the wrong impression."

"Why? You said you liked him." Haley sidled closer. "Did you pick up on a red flag or something?

"No. He's a perfect gentleman. Easygoing, polite."

"Boooring," Marcy hooted. "Or is it just in comparison to another hotter man you met recently?"

"Absolutely not." Darn her friend's dead-on intuitive nature.

"You must be Justine?" They all swiveled toward the male voice. "I'm Evan. Great to meet you. Marcy, you look funky awesome, as usual." A shock of dark hair topped his full, trimmed beard and warm brown eyes.

Justine regathered her manners. "I appreciate you fitting me in. Please, work your magic."

At work the next day, the enthusiastic reception to her new hairdo matched that of her friends. July walked around her, examining the cut. "Mmhmm. Now we can see that pretty face."

"Evan lopped off four inches and added layers." Free from the extra weight, her waves were more defined and bounced below her shoulders. Thinned bangs were pushed off to the left side of her forehead.

Carl nodded agreement. "A trendy, urban cut. I like."

Urban. As in Chicago. They weren't telling anyone else about her interview status, but the comment seemed to signal his continued support. In the meantime, she would fill them in on the disturbing conversation with Martin Collier. "If you two have a minute, I also should share a less pleasant topic." She summarized the back and forth from Saturday night, concluding, "The pressure's really on us to convince Lawrence Reynolds to attend. And to nail down his confirmation soon so we can publicize."

Carl tapped a finger on his chin. "Or how about Jackson Maddox? Camilla jumped me to intervene and ask him. I told her you had the situation covered."

Did everyone have to keep bringing up his name? She rolled her eyes. "He isn't interested in our event. He dumped the clothes and gave us the photos. I highly doubt he'll return, even to sell the house and contents."

July stopped tidying the stacks of papers on the worktable. "Has he contacted you again?"

"A brief text." Justine dug her fingers into the pockets of her long cardigan. "His project is gathering steam. Before you ask, he didn't mention coming back or rescheduling for me to assist at the house."

"Oh, honey. How disappointing." The volunteer's face drooped for an instant. "But I almost forgot to ask how your date went?" Her eyes lit with interest again.

Longing to escape the interrogation, Justine repeated the vague summary she shared with her friends.

Carl settled into his desk chair. "A nerd no more. Some of us do improve over time. I'm glad you had fun."

"Yes, and he asked me to go out again before our event." Her gaze darted between the two of them. "Enough small talk. I have loads to do over the next three weeks. How long do you think I should wait before reaching out again to nudge Lawrence Reynolds?"

****

Thursday afternoon Justine smoothed the skirt of Haley's suit as she waited in the Drysdale Museum's administrative offices. From her previous visit, she recalled the former family home's walnut woodwork carried throughout the three floors. Stained-glass windows and multiple fireplaces boasted Victorian-age opulence. Outside, the red-brick façade featured jutting turrets.

She tried not to fidget, waiting for the assistant to

return, yet her nerves sizzled. *Calm down*, she mentally counseled. *You have a job. You aren't desperate.*

The woman returned and instructed to follow her. "The conference room is in the third-floor ballroom. The room's subdivided for smaller meeting spaces. Partitions can be removed for large gatherings." Her heels clicked on the steps at a quick pace.

Justine gripped her new leather portfolio and held onto the railing with her free hand. Too soon, they reached the upper level. Her guide knocked on a double French door and entered. Four people spread out along the ornate, carved table, including the director. Justine lifted her chin and smiled at each in turn, willing her lips to hold steady.

Samantha Chan rose, exuding polish and power in a chic black pantsuit. "Welcome. Please come in and join us." She indicated the open chair next to her and made the introductions. After they sat, questions began to fly.

Having rehearsed answers to possible queries, her confidence built as she relayed her background and skills. A man introduced as Nathan Rosen rolled a gold pen between his fingers. "LaPorte's a relatively small community. Tell us about your special events experience. We have a reputation for providing outstanding public and private festivities, in addition to our exhibits."

She tried to gauge their expressions while she shared highlights of their annual vintage car shows, plus the Civil War encampment and ball. "I have photos, including some of the displays I've coordinated." The woman to her left opened the portfolio when Justine offered it to her.

Samantha interjected. "You were telling me about

an upcoming fundraiser. How are the details proceeding? Did you reach Lawrence Reynolds?"

"I did." A tinge of nerves returned to edge through her system. "He wasn't able to commit yet but is considering the possibility." She turned to the others. "Mr. Reynolds directed a movie with the late hometown actress who's the focus of our new showcase. At the unveiling next month, we hope he might attend or provide support through a signed item. The connection would be a big draw, especially in-person, as we're raising funds for our preservation efforts." When she presented that idea, Carl and the planning committee approved.

The leather book reached Nathan, but he didn't open her work samples. "I've always found Lawrence to be generous and open to helping nonprofit causes. We're having lunch later this week. Tell me more about your plans."

She clutched her hands together under the table and gathered her powers of persuasion. Her employment status, whether here or at home, might be secured by this one crucial pitch.

Chapter Twenty-Eight

At a meeting two weeks later, the LaPorte Museum committee plowed through final event details. With the importance of the festivities, Carl joined in. Seated across the table, he sent Justine a slight, commiserating wink. A tiny movement anyone else might read as a twitch. His mood had veered from upbeat to melancholy ever since she ran into their shared office, elated at the invitation to return to the Drysdale for a full-board, final interview.

Camilla again ran the meeting, ignoring the printed agenda to consult her notebook. "Any update in status with Lawrence Reynolds?"

Justine curbed a desire to smirk back at her boss. "In his second email, he said he can't commit to attending due to the weather and his health. However, he did send us a very special gift." An easel stood nearby with a framed item facing away from them. With pride at the accomplishment, she stood to reveal the valuable contribution.

Wilson clapped his hands. "A signed movie poster is pure gold. I saw that murder mystery at the theater when it came out. I assume Liza Maddox was in the film."

"We searched online to confirm. She spoke several lines in a party scene as a flirtatious guest. I'll indicate that on the accompanying note card."

Justine had pondered the quick offer of the poster. Perhaps Reynolds was prompted by Nathan's outreach, but how did he recall a bit actor after more than three decades? He also buried another telling question within the email: *"Are any family members able to attend the ceremony?"* She debated and finally crafted a careful response, saying Jackson was invited but busy pursuing his screenwriting career. The man didn't follow up on the issue.

With the gift in their possession, even the prickly board president appeared impressed. "If the director can't come, this is a wonderful addition. And we still may land a celebrity guest." She peered around the table, waiting for someone to ask the question.

Carl took the bait. "Who might that be?"

"Why Jackson Maddox, of course." She turned her back on the easel. "I know you sent him an invitation, but I felt we should extend a more personal outreach. I found a phone number on a web page linked to his screenwriting partnership and left a message. He got back to me last night."

Apprehension twisted in Justine's chest. "You talked to him?"

"He called after eleven p.m. our time. So no, not directly." The woman fiddled with her wedding ring and avoided her eyes. "The message was quite nice, thanking me for the contact."

"He didn't commit to coming?" Darn, her voice trembled. They hopefully would attribute it to her investment in the event's success.

"No. He referenced his busy schedule but did say he'd consider the opportunity."

Carl rubbed his neck. "If Reynolds can't attend,

Jackson provides the splash we need to make this a talked-about, memorable occasion."

The board president leaned toward him. "Neither have outright refused. I've attempted to raise excitement and ticket sales by saying both have been invited and are considering attending."

Justine slumped lower in her chair. Technically, the tactic could work. A little fudging, not an outright lie. A flash of color drew her attention to the corner. Liza appeared, standing with pursed lips before fading away.

No one else in the room responded. Not one flinch or yelp. She blinked hard and tried to refocus on the meeting. The details swam in her ears. What had piqued the ghost enough to pop into a public gathering? The concept of two special guests colliding? She wasn't alone there. But at this point, no proof existed of any deeper connection, let alone paternity. With her interview and this critical event pending, Justine hadn't resumed research into the two possible father candidates. Maybe she should dive into the internet one last time.

A half-hour later, with the meeting wrapped, she settled at her computer to try a new tack. She knew about a film project Nevins and Reynolds were connected in at the time of Jackson's early November birth. But what were they doing around the time of conception? She started with the director, analyzing the biographical outline of his life, including a dated order of his works.

No new projects were listed for early February of that year. He probably was in post-production for the December release, coordinating with the editors, sound engineers, and other technicians.

For Nevins, the bio was longer, with guest appearances on TV shows and supporting actor stints in films peppered between leads. When she zoned into the chosen timeframe, her lips fell open.

"Hey, Justine." She jolted at Carl's voice, not having heard him enter. By reflex, she minimized the screen as the reflection of his image neared on her computer screen.

He stopped, arms crossed over his chest. "Since Camilla's been spreading the word, how should we post teasers on Facebook about the event, hinting at the possible special guests without people expecting to see them?"

"Tricky, but we can do it. Let's brainstorm." Even trickier would be the two men attending together. She rolled back in her chair, assuring herself neither man would bother to come to LaPorte. She couldn't help wondering how many times Liza faked her way through challenging social encounters. According to the letters, she ran into Jackson's father at a gathering. In their rarefied world, they probably collided more than once.

Chapter Twenty-Nine

Liza, July 1995

Terrence's martinis were lethal tonight. Liza clutched the empty glass and ignored her throbbing temple. Smiling and bobbing, she wove through their open-concept living room. The alcohol buzz helped her endure the shoulder-to-shoulder crush of people and conversation, to avoid coughing as expensive perfumes and Cuban cigars filled her sinuses.

The roar of voices heightened, giddy at the successful opening. The movie appealed to critics and the public, alike. Now the film must earn back the investment by Terrence and his co-producers. For tonight, though, they were high rollers. His partners celebrated with the actors, director, and high-level crew members. A smattering of A-listers also hobnobbed, testament to her husband's current status.

While the guests laughed, drank, and gossiped, they were one wrong move, one snarky rumor, away from toppling to second string. She wondered how many of these overdressed movers and shakers would wake up hungover, or in someone else's bed.

Liza paused to trade air kisses with the film's leading lady, dressed in a form-fitting halter dress. "Exceptional work, darling." Usually, she distanced herself from that viper tongue, especially during the time she was pregnant. Laying low kept questions at bay.

She moved on, forcing her lips to curve, and acknowledged other long-time friends and acquaintances. Instead of loosening her up, the vodka seemed to have disrupted her ability to play the glowing, carefree hostess. Tonight, she viewed the guests through a distanced, clinical lens, evaluating their standing. The editor to her right slurred his words. Top of his game, but everyone feared he was sliding down into the bottle. She touched his shoulder and kept her tone light. "Make sure you come to tell me goodbye before you leave." They'd discreetly confiscate his keys and find him a ride home.

She extracted herself from the clique of crew members and checked around for her husband. No longer at the bar mixing drinks, he perched on the arm of the sofa, leaning into the supporting actress sitting below him. Her stomach tightened. She wouldn't embarrass herself in skimming up to remind him of her presence. As long as he didn't disappear with someone, she'd stay cool. The price paid for a third marriage to provide financial stability for her and her beloved, frustrating son.

Her temple throbbed again. Beyond the throng of people, the moonlit ocean beckoned through a wall of windows leading to the pool. Maybe she could slip away and—

An arm snagged her around the waist, pulling her close. She looked into the face of the main supporting actor. The pat smile warmed her. Years ago, they'd been close. Gossip-worthy close. The hot attraction soured, finally, when she discovered his true nature. Nothing and no one came before his ambition.

Today, the wags bet on the handsome, blue-eyed devil as an Oscar shoe-in. Deserved, actually. He buried his cocky personality beneath a humble, quirky, loveable nerd. *Superman meet Clark Kent*, Liza thought, aware his hand caressed down her exposed back to land on her butt. Her role tonight was to beguile and befriend. She'd learned to overlook small indignities.

The trio of famous men pulled her into their private circle, all shooting admiring glances. Nearing fifty, her long, black hair swung loose around her curvy body, embraced by a coral silk dress.

The actor added a familiar squeeze to her fanny. "So, loveliest-of-ladies, you think this one's gonna be a big hit?"

She saluted him with her empty glass. "Every sign points that way."

The hint didn't go unnoticed. Another of the film's producers wrapped a hand around her upraised wrist. "Looks like you need a celebratory refill. Let me clear the way to the bar." He swept out an arm for her to move in front of him.

Liza sent him a grateful look. The guy was one of the few happily married, decent men she knew. In this crazy, competitive world, she appreciated his uncomplicated friendship.

"Make way for the hostess," he proclaimed. The crowd obligingly parted. They slid through, arm in arm.

****

Jackson scowled, watching from the top of the dark staircase. His mother hadn't achieved the fame level of many of the guests, but her presence always created a splash. He wondered if she regretted giving up acting when she married that a-hole. Probably not. She loved soaking up little slices of limelight, rubbing shoulders with the Hollywood guns.

Everyone who was anyone came to their parties—with agendas. Greeted by a well-stocked bar and a few lines of blow, men turned into fools drooling over her. With most women, he could read the growing, competitive calculation in their eyes.

He hunched forward on the step, also wondering if his biological father mingled in the mob scene. Though he hated going there, when people gathered in the fancy-schmancy house, he found himself watching his mom. Did she favor one man more than others? But, no, she was a butterfly, floating with a fake smile, never landing for long.

He snorted, cocooned above in the darkness. Damn it, if he had his license, he'd have left long before the poseurs arrived. But he was a few months short and trapped for the evening, with his buddy grounded for drinking. His friend didn't rat him out that night, and Jackson breezed back in without getting caught. He suspected Liza knew about some of his escapades but avoided the fight.

Tonight, after an early, command-performance entrance, he snuck off for a long, solitary walk on the beach. Their waterfront location rocked, even if the homelife sucked. From his hiding place, he watched his mom and the producer grab martinis from the bar. That guy, he semi-trusted. A couple of times they had intelligent conversations about the industry. He seemed to be into his kind, funny wife. Still, that didn't mean he hadn't shagged his mom sixteen years ago. His gut kicked. They were headed out the French doors toward the pool, lit by a line of flaring tiki torches.

His eyes scanned the living room. Terrence was hanging on another woman. No surprise.

Jackson grabbed the moment. He sauntered down the stairs, projecting an air of confidence as he stepped up to the bar. "I'll take a Miller."

The dude didn't look much older than him. He complied without a second look, pouring the contents of the bottle into a glass.

"Thanks, man." Without acknowledging anyone in the crowd, Jackson carried the beer upstairs to his bedroom. He'd plug in his earphones and jam to U2 and the Stones until the racket calmed. If the night followed the usual pattern, a few stragglers would hang around until the early hours or pass out. His lips twisted as he kicked his door shut behind him.

Chapter Thirty

Liam nudged Jackson's elbow as they stood in their joint office space in his loft. "J-man, your all-nighter was worth the loss of sleep. The polish is buffed to a high shine. I'd say we're ready to present the final script." He waggled his brows. "Sure hope Mindy wasn't miffed at having the bed to herself."

Jackson yawned and stretched. "She doesn't stay over. We're casual."

"Does she know that?"

He hesitated and grimaced. "She should. I haven't made any promises or been very attentive with our project demands." He walked away from their connecting desks. "Stop pulling my chain. Just cause her friend isn't into you."

"Can't account for taste. But we'll both have more blessed free time soon. Want to blow off some steam with a ski trip to Colorado?" Liam joined him at the picture window. Through the bright sunshine, they squinted down three stories to the busy LA street.

"I'd love to. But I haven't wrapped my mom's house and estate stuff. I need to make some decisions and contacts." He swiveled away from the view. "A local museum back there is honoring her with a display this weekend."

"Impressive." His partner perched on the edge of his desk. "You're not going?"

"You know our relationship was complicated. I provided them with materials and clothing. But attending…"

Liam laid a hand on his arm. "You know how much she loved you. I'd use the term doted. When you let her."

"Which was rare. Shit." Jackson buried his head in his hands. "How can I write about all these deep emotions, but when it comes to dealing with them personally, I freeze."

"A defense mechanism built to handle your father's desertion," Liam inserted a touch of humor, mimicking a Sigmund Freud accent.

The ploy drew the desired wry grin. "I have to let go of the angst sometime, don't I?"

"Seriously, I think you'll feel much lighter coming to terms with your feelings. Owning them."

"I'm sure Justine would agree with you." The words slipped out. He'd only shared a few hazy details about their snow-bound entanglement. Yet the woman knew more about him than Mindy after those few intense hours.

"The frumpy gal from the museum?"

"She's not frumpy." The defensive comment sprang out. Digging him into a hole.

As anticipated, the admission drew a long, searching look. "That why you're keeping Miss Mindy at arms-length?"

"You and I have been way too busy to deal with women. Especially one hundreds of miles away." In truth, he'd been writing and revising non-stop. Yet he'd never divulge how the small-town girl crept into his mind in the rare off moments. Somehow, her touch of naivete laced with caring insights and intelligence hooked his attention. Leaving him even more unsure whether he ever wanted to return to LaPorte, Indiana. To move ahead, he had to accept his past and put it behind him.

But could he do it long-distance? Or would he have to exorcise the ghosts within the house in person—and take a chance on reaching out to the men who might have sired him?

Chapter Thirty-One

The morning of the event, Justine worked a few hours before returning home to rest and get ready. She returned to the museum before five, carrying her long dress. The public would start arriving within a couple of hours. She peered up at the darkening sky, thankful snippy weather hadn't derailed the party. The town did glow brighter, though, when a dust of snow fell, as if the angels had sifted powdered sugar over the landscape.

Inside the break room, July sat in her long, black skirt, stocking feet propped on a chair. "I'm resting up for a busy night, honey. We sold ticket number one-fifty today and I'm sure there'll be walk-ins."

Justine tugged off her coat and hung it with the dress, encased in a clothing bag. "Martin Collier didn't buy yet, did he? I'm hoping he forgot about our discussion. We don't need the additional pressure tonight."

"The mayor and his wife are on the list, but no county officials." The volunteer rubbed her hands together. "With that income, plus the sponsorships and the silent auction, we'll make a nice profit. How could the county folks not be impressed?"

"Faith did an incredible job soliciting sponsors and items and wrangling the board to gather more. I assume they're excited to learn more about Liza. People love a Hollywood connection."

"Word spread about our possible famous special guest." The older woman chuckled. "Leave it to Camilla to flash fire a rumor. If you or Carl do the program introduction, you'll have to be prepared to tap dance if neither of those gentlemen shows."

Heat flushed over Justine's skin, and she toyed with the sleeve of her sweater. "Carl's allowing me the honor. I'm definitely not expecting them and will make a huge to-do over the signed poster and the scripts."

"Bait and switch." July slid her feet to the floor. "Guess we'd best float around and ensure we've covered all the other details before Ms. Camilla arrives to rearrange them."

They wandered upstairs and down discussing logistics and double-checking the descriptive flyers next to each silent auction item. Justine reminded herself to place a bid on the goodie basket from the new coffee shop while July preferred the massage-mani-pedi package. Across the room in the lower level, they straightened the draped fabric that covered the new showcase. A ploy to prolong the suspense.

Liza hadn't reappeared after popping into the committee meeting. Justine hoped she wouldn't manifest tonight to distract her. She tried to peg the ghost's demeanor from the brief glimpse in the community room and landed on "perturbed." The same could be said of her own state of mind when she contemplated the thought of Lawrence and Jackson colliding. But as the day ticked on, her worries lessened. Her thoughts were consumed with the success of the evening.

Carl arrived when they returned upstairs, wearing a dapper charcoal suit with a red and black plaid vest. After complimenting his attire, Justine excused herself to get dressed in the back storage room. The slick crimson fabric caressed her skin. She contorted her arm but couldn't quite maneuver the last couple of inches of zipper at her back. When she ventured out to seek July's assistance, a man wearing a homburg hat entered through the front doors.

Her heart plunged into overdrive until she recognized Martin Collier, with his wife. He headed straight toward her. "I hope you don't mind us coming early. We wanted to make sure we got tickets and could see the place without a throng." He pulled off his leather gloves. "Everyone is buzzing about a famous director attending."

Carl beelined out of their office. He thrust his hand forward to shake. "Martin. So pleased you two could come. We invited both Lawrence Reynolds and Liza Maddox' son. Neither was able to confirm, but they donated exceptional items."

The man returned the handshake. "Disappointing to hear they may not show after all the hype. But if you make money, the night's a win in my book. Mind if we look around?"

"Please do." The museum director maintained a pleasant expression. "Just don't peek behind the drapes of the Liza exhibit. To heighten the surprise." The couple sauntered off. He watched and swiped a hand over his perspiring forehead. "We used to be able to avoid the political ping-pong."

"Before budget-mania set in." Justine picked up her skirts to head off again. "I'm doubly determined to make a success of the evening."

"So you can share it next week with the full Drysdale Museum board? Congrats again on being chosen for the final round." His face sobered further. "I'm going to miss you. We all will."

She fanned a nervous hand in front of her face. "I haven't landed the job yet. Maybe they're bringing me back to illuminate the superior skills of their number one choice."

He grasped her hand to still the movement. "You never give yourself enough credit. You're a great asset here and as a person, too. Now scat and get to work."

Within the hour, dozens more arrived. She whirled around, settling the string quartet, welcoming guests, and overseeing refreshment arrangements in the community room. Sweeping onto the main museum floor, she spied a tall man with broad shoulders. Harold caught her glance and waved. She headed in his direction, pleased to see him, but totally level from an emotional standpoint. No thumping heart or sweating palms. So much for Valentine's passion. She reminded herself to be patient. The earth didn't need to move. They also had fun at the second date for a movie and milkshake.

Behind him, garlands of hearts in shades of pink, red, and silver festooned the rails of the museum's central staircase. The steps led up to the classic car collection, popular for photo ops. To his left, visitors gathered around a display featuring vintage Valentines. Justine's eyes shot to the ceiling in a silent prayer. His mother was among them. *Please, don't let the other guests catch wind of the matchmaking intentions.*

Winnie took her arm. Despite a six-inch height difference, she locked steps to reach her son together. "Justine, you're pretty as a Victorian photograph. Harold tells me you've gotten together already." She giggled— a girlish sound belying her graying hair. "Sweet that you couldn't wait till tonight to see each other again after all those years since high school."

Justine paused, grasping for a polite response to the over-enthusiastic explanation. She didn't have to when a familiar voice floated past her. "Hi. Honey."

Great. Her mother and Winnie probably timed their arrivals to coo over their linked offspring. "Sweetie, you look beautiful tonight." Her mother appraised her as if she was judging a brood mare.

Her father remained silent, spit-shined in a navy suit and a red and white tie. As an electrician, he only "fancied himself up" when her mom laid down the law. Justine's foot tapped a nervous rhythm at the ambush.

To her amazement, Winnie gestured toward the community room. "I'd like some refreshments before they get picked over. Would you two join me?" Her gaze lasered on her parents. They murmured assent and followed.

Ah. They were providing them "alone time." Justine's eyes narrowed at the obvious tactic, until she caught the sly curve of Harold's lips. He watched the trio disappear beyond the doorway. "This is the highlight of their week. Remember, I foiled their plot to throw us together tonight."

"Or did you spring their trap yourself by calling me in advance?" She snickered, releasing the tension. "I'm happy they're happy."

"And so am I. To be with you." He offered his arm in the well-fitted gray suit.

She felt a blush creep onto her cheeks. "How about we go downstairs, out of the parental spotlight? The quartet is playing. I can take a few minutes to wander and show you around."

"Fill me in on this place. Later, we can brush off our dance moves."

They descended to the lower level while Justine shared details of how, four years prior, they moved nearly eighty thousand items several miles to the new location. "Over ten intense months we wrapped, labeled, and transported artifacts such as the Rumely Oil Pull Tractor and eight hundred and fifty pieces of the W.A. Jones gun collection. Quite a process."

"Fascinating."

His face reflected interest. Perhaps he appreciated history as much as she did. Her spirits rose as the music swirled around them. Dozens of folding chairs ringed around the room, leaving a space for a dance floor to the side. She hoped he was a decent dancer. They'd be on full display there. A flash of blue caught her eye. Haley exited the staircase, swiveling past the clusters of visitors sitting or standing to chat. She waved and cut toward them.

"Hold on. That's one of my best friends." Justine made introductions when she reached them, adding, "Haley is an accountant."

He snickered. "I pity you at this time of the year."

They veered into career chat. Justine half-listened while she studied the growing crowd. Everyone appeared happy and engaged, even Martin and his wife. The grandfather clock nearby indicated a half hour till the formal dedication ceremony.

The music slowed. Harold tilted his head and reached for her elbow. "They're playing a waltz. Will you excuse us? I want to impress Justine with my technique."

She swallowed hard. "Are you sure? No one else is dancing." As an employee, should she encourage others by going first? Or would she be judged as showy by a county board member?

"Somebody has to break the ice." Her partner didn't offer a chance to refuse, leading her into the open area with a hand on her back.

Really, who cared at this point? Landing the interview in Chicago emboldened her. She placed a hand at his waist and the other on his shoulder.

His eyes twinkled down at her. "You have to hold my hand so I can lead." He grasped the palm resting at his waist and lifted it out to their sides. "Ready? Here we go." They were off and moving, slowly at first as she found her footing, then faster and more confidently.

Harold provided a strong lead, his hand warm and smooth over hers. He didn't try to talk, just spun her out into a wider arc to cover the dance space. Under his guidance she felt graceful. Free. A happy laugh bubbled up, celebrating the committee's work in creating a memorable evening. Even if she didn't land the new job, they might earn a reprieve from the budget axe. Harold twirled her again, flaring the long skirt.

Her heart clutched in her chest as she stumbled for the first time.

Jackson Maddox stood framed in the entryway. She bit down hard on her lower lip, swung and lost sight of him. A box step later, she double-checked. Yep, he remained in the same position, watching them.

His face was inscrutable as she met his eyes before the next fluid turn. She should stop and welcome him, as a guest of honor, but couldn't just halt their dance mid-step. "Harold, I need—" Jackson turned and walked to the opposite corner, next to the draped display where July stood in conversation with another volunteer. She squeezed her partner's hand. "Jackson Maddox is here. I should fill him in on the program. He didn't tell us he planned to attend."

Harold slowed to a stop and frowned. "The tall, cool guy with the attitude who just came in?"

"That would be him. I'm sorry. Umm, you can come meet him. Or…Haley," she raised her voice and beckoned, "come and dance. I have to prep Jackson Maddox before the ceremony."

"Where?" Haley's gaze roamed around the room. "Ohhh. The hottie with July. Go do your work thing."

"Thanks." She swiped her damp palms together and wove toward the corner, trying not to hyperventilate. July appeared perfectly content entertaining the newcomer. And someone else noticed his arrival. Martin and his wife beat her to his side. They were introducing themselves as she sidled up.

She took advantage of the moment to calm herself. Her cheeks felt hot, which could be attributed to dancing. But the trembling hands would give her away. She tucked them behind her back. When the handshakes ended, she interjected. "Jackson, we're all so pleased you could join us." Her voice held remarkably steady.

His blue eyes swung to pierce her. "I got the reminder message from your board chair but wasn't sure if I'd be able to make it. We submitted the final script Wednesday. I decided to try to wrap things here before the next project phase kicks in."

Of course. He needed to sell the house and the contents. Surely a driving force behind the unexpected visit. Still, she couldn't help the tingly sensations sparking along her nerve endings. "Yes, we had to postpone our appraisal session."

"I can still use the help."

July beamed beside him. "Good idea. She'll fix you right up."

He lifted a brow, as if catching an unintended innuendo in the homey expression. Justine's knees weakened. He did look hot in the silver-gray suit and black, button-down shirt. No tie.

The volunteer checked her watch. "My goodness, in a few minutes the program will begin. We should let you two confer." With a firm grip, she took Martin's arm to lead the couple away.

Alone, they eyed each other for a long moment. Snippets of memory from their time at the house and the coffee shop filtered into her consciousness. Justine shook her head, partly to dislodge them. "Wow. I can't believe you're subjecting yourself to our small-town festivities. On behalf of the museum, we're pleased you're here."

He flipped his hands palms up. "My writing partner guilted me."

Something more lurked behind the casual comment. Intrigued, she waited and stared, crossing her arms at her waist. "Guilt drove you here?"

He looked away. "My mom would want me here. Liam also made me think. Damn him. I'm not doing myself any favors by keeping up all these walls."

"A healthy attitude. He sounds like a good friend." To ward off more painful thoughts, she adopted a light tone. "You look good cleaned up. But that suit's more California than LaPorte."

"I'd hope so. I'll probably wear it for our next premiere, if we keep moving ahead." He stepped closer and reached up to curl a wave of her hair around his finger. "And vintage becomes you. New hairstyle?"

Her breath caught at the close contact. The intimate gesture. In a room full of people, she felt very much alone with Jackson Maddox. She didn't pull away. "My friends guilted me into it."

His eyes pinned her with intensity. "They do have our best interests at heart."

With the chattering of the crowd, she dipped her head closer to hear the comment. She didn't pick up a scent of aftershave, just a fragrance impression that her senses read and remembered as "pure man." A jolt of electricity seemed to zing between them. A crazy impulse gripped her to sniff his neck. Then lick it.

She pulled back, catching sight of Harold and Haley now standing at the edge of the dance floor, facing their way. The close stance with Jackson couldn't look good. She'd have some fast-talking to do later, with both of them. Her view of the couple was blocked by Carl exiting the staircase. Her boss halted and looked behind him. A distinguished older gentleman joined him and surveyed the room. She gasped and covered her mouth with her hand.

Jackson swiveled to determine the cause. His shoulders stiffened; fists clenched at his sides. He spun back, eyes shooting blue fire. "What the hell. Did you set me up?" His voice grated low and furious.

"No. I, we—"

He stalked away from her.

"Jackson, please wait." The whispered plea drowned below the crowd noise. Down deep, she knew he'd ignore it. She started to follow. No. People might notice the dissension. His angry outburst was muted. He wouldn't hold back a second time. With so much riding on the evening, she didn't dare draw negative attention.

In addition to the stairs, the museum had an elevator. Rooted to the spot, she watched him skirt far around Carl and Reynolds to reach it. The doors opened. He stepped in just as the grandfather clock struck the first of eight chimes.

She spied Carl approaching with the newcomer and her whole body iced over.

"Justine, Mr. Reynolds has arrived," her boss said. "Was that Jackson Maddox?"

Chapter Thirty-Two

"Mr. Reynolds, we are beyond thrilled you could join us." Justine thrust out her hand to shake his, searching her reeling mind for a plausible explanation for Jackson's exit. Her discomfort swelled to panic as Martin joined them.

"Yes," she continued, "that was Jackson. He just, uh, got an emergency call. From his partner. They have to rewrite a scene tonight on deadline." She attempted a smile to erase his doubting expression. "Too bad he didn't see you come in, so the two of you could meet. We know you understand the demands of Hollywood. Oh, but you also should meet Mr. Martin Collier, one of our County Board members." Overwhelmed at her worst fears materializing, she tossed the conversational ball, clutching her hands at her waist.

The usually dour politician beamed. "Sir, your coming is a highlight of the night. I'd like to add my thanks on behalf of the county. It would be an honor to introduce you to my wife later."

"Of course." Yet the older man focused back to Justine. He was nearly as tall as Jackson, and lean, with white hair over strong features. While showing age through a network of tan lines, his face reflected the attractiveness of his early photos. "When Samantha and Nathan extolled the value of your efforts, I decided if the weather cooperated, I'd try to attend. I remember Liza fondly." The blue eyes held hers, probing.

"Our goal is to keep Liza's memory alive for generations." A queasy sensation rolled through her. *He wonders how much I know.* With those familial eyes and now seeing the strong similarity in build and facial structure, her gut confirmed the parental connection. She didn't reveal the recognition. He might see it as manipulation to bring him here.

Oblivious to the undertones, Carl intervened. "To respect that you have a long drive home, we'll begin the brief recognition program. Your arrival was perfect timing."

Perfect. She winced at the incongruity of the word.

Her boss shot her a concerned glance. "I'll make an announcement and call everyone down here. We can't beat standing-room-only attendance. Right, Martin?" Carl shifted past them to the wall intercom system, which could broadcast throughout the museum.

While their guest stepped away to observe the surrounding crowd, Martin whispered in her ear. "Jackson Maddox appeared upset. Was he unhappy with the event?"

She cringed from his hot breath on her neck. "No. Of course not. He believed their script project was sealed. The concerning, last-minute request sent him flying off." The lies flowed easier. "He apologized profusely."

She maintained eye contact, trying to project the essence of innocence. Jackson's defection still rocked her. Any fallout could be handled later. They'd pulled off a win tonight with the packed event and the guest appearances. Time to capitalize on the coup. "If you'll excuse me." She raised her voice. "Mr. Reynolds, you'll be seated up front."

When he rejoined them, she launched into final details to prepare the esteemed director for the ceremony. The other anxieties niggling in her mind were shoved forcefully away. Martin slunk off to claim his seat. On the outskirts of the growing crowd, she glimpsed Harold and Haley chatting. In the upheaval, she forgot all about him. Thank goodness for her wonderful friend. For now, she avoided his eye.

Within a few minutes, all the guests assembled, filling seats and wedging into available open spaces. Camilla flounced into the room and sped toward the reserved front row. Having appointed herself the refreshment matron, she must've missed Lawrence Reynolds' understated entrance. The woman would be seething at losing the opportunity to be the first to fawn over him.

Carl moved to the stand microphone and tapped it. The voices trickled off when he announced, "Welcome everyone." As planned, he thanked the board members, volunteers, and sponsors for supporting the festivities. "We are also proud to host a very special guest tonight, award-winning director Lawrence Reynolds, who currently lives in Chicago." With his knowledge of movie trivia, Carl rolled off names of some of his most recognizable films. "Mr. Reynolds also directed Liza Maddox in *The Sensational Sinclairs* and a television episode of *Taxi*. We are beyond excited that he graciously donated a signed movie poster for our collection. Please join me in thanking him for the great generosity."

He gestured for the honoree to stand. The crowd thundered applause, which Lawrence acknowledged with a nod and smile. The director had declined the offer to make comments. Interestingly, he'd offered to help reveal the display.

Carl waited for the clapping to die down. "My invaluable Assistant Director, Justine Saunders, headed this special project and curated the content. I welcome her now to share brief background on Liza Maddox."

Another round of polite claps ensued. Gathering her courage, she stepped to the podium and peered at the sea of faces—many of them familiar. "As you're aware, Liza was born here to a grand home on Michigan Avenue. Sadly, her father died when she was a child of eight. Her mother, Margaret, never remarried and was known for her work in the schools and supporting local volunteer efforts. Through high school, Liza achieved honors acting in all the plays. Yearbook entries note her sassy personality and beauty."

Justine glanced at the note card she placed on the podium earlier. "Soon after graduation, she sought the adventure of heading to Hollywood, where she enjoyed acting in many memorable movies and television shows. We've compiled a full listing of them for the exhibit. While she never achieved stardom, she surely reveled in the life. She was married three times, with the last two—Roger Abernathy and producer Terrence Cooper—opening her to mingle in Hollywood's upper echelons."

She paused, noting the audience's rapt attention. In preparation for the evening, she rehearsed several times. The practice should've loosened the band of tension that gripped her. Lawrence Reynolds' presence only heightened the discomfort. She couldn't look at him, afraid of faltering. "Most important in her life, she raised a son named Jackson. Tonight's presentation resulted when he called us to offer the donation of clothing and other items. He joined us here earlier, before unfortunately being called away to handle an emergency work request," she improvised. "Some of you may be aware he's a talented screenwriter, who penned the critically acclaimed movie, *Winter Frost*."

Murmurs passed through the crowd. Justine lifted her voice. "If you've seen it, the scenario focuses on the challenging relationship between a woman and her mother. Which resembles the dynamic between Liza and Margaret, two strong-willed, loyal, resilient women." Despite her resolve, her eyes were drawn now to Lawrence where he sat in the front row. He appeared composed, yet contemplative.

She refocused, nearing the end of her remarks. "Liza returned to LaPorte a year ago to care for her ailing mother. After Margaret's death, she stayed in town, in the house where she grew up. Those LaPorte roots must have called to her. In October of last year, she unexpectedly passed away, too. Much too young to lose such a vibrant personality." The reality of the statement jarred her. If they'd actually met, they might have become friends bonding over vintage fashion and creativity. Aside from the stalky situation with her son, she came off as fun and witty. Justine veered from her planned comments, adding, "I hope some of you had the chance to meet, and to know her. Her bold nature opened her to many adventures in life. We should all live so large."

"And now, with the help of our esteemed guest, and board president Camilla MacKenzie, we'll reveal the exhibit." Relief loosened her stiff shoulders. She reached the corner display, and together with Lawrence and the volunteer, carefully removed the fabric drapes. The audience burst into applause at the costumes and the "LaPorte's Cinema Sweetheart" banner, produced to resemble a movie marquee.

Carl returned to the mic. "Please everyone, stay and visit, dance, eat, and don't forget to bid on the silent auction items to support our ongoing preservation efforts. Thank you again for joining us. Watch our web site and Facebook page for future events."

As people made their way toward them, Camilla cornered Lawrence. Justine sidled away from the swarm of people who approached to view the items—and the visitor—up close. The adrenaline of the crazy evening drained away, leaving her limbs and mind feeling heavy. Disconnected. She longed to kick off her shoes, climb into her jammies, and hide under the covers. Maybe Jackson had done the same.

Ha. She suspected his retreat involved the rest of the Irish whiskey. A ranting text might be lurking on her phone even now.

Her face scrunched at the thought, and the realization she should get back to Harold and Haley and relieve her friend of the "babysitting." Standing in the path of the elevator, they couldn't have missed Jackson's irate departure. She'd have to feed them the same lie. Preparing herself to face them, she froze in her heels. Lawrence Reynolds disengaged from the admirers, tossing brief comments to outliers but heading straight toward her. His flat expression seemed to resonate with reserve, compared to the previous affability. Tension wrapped around her chest and squeezed.

Would he go off on her now, or press her about Jackson? For more privacy, she backed up a couple steps to wait behind a local chapel replica, replete with mechanized choir members.

The older man reached her side. She tried not to tremble, from the fatigue of hiding the truth. Their eyes held for a few moments before he broke into a small smile. "Nicely done, my dear. Indeed, I can't stay, with the drive back to Chicago, but I would like to speak with you on the phone. Soon."

About Liza. And her son. The unsaid words hummed between them. If he pressed for information, she feared she'd fold. Her throat constricted. "Of course. At your convenience. Again, we're so thankful for your attendance tonight. My cell number was in the initial email I sent you."

A group of people began to gather, others clamoring to meet him and ask questions. Grateful for the interruption, she drew a deep breath and fled. Maybe he just wanted to thank her and would ignore the "situation" as he'd done for three decades. Highly doubtful. But she had to get through the evening and couldn't afford to twist herself up further. Jackson's angry departure already had ripped through her composure and chipped her heart. Should she try calling him, too, or send a pleading, mea culpa text?

She must tread carefully. Poor handling on her part could implode any effort to bring them together. Not to mention, Reynolds might complain to Nathan that he'd been manipulated to come tonight. Such a comment would tank her interview with the Drysdale Museum. At least she had the respite of additional hours to concoct an explanation.

She scanned the crowd for her friends and rubbed her temple, where a throb of headache erupted. Across the room, a fuchsia splash drew her attention. *No. Not tonight.* Liza leaned against the prototype of a 1960's electric car, the exact shape and color of a Meyer lemon. In her ruffled formal, she could've posed for an advertisement, except for the slump to her elegant shoulders.

With an internal groan, Justine paced toward her. She spotted Harold and Haley and waggled her fingers, mouthing, "Be right back." *Please, don't let them be mad at me, too.* She should stop and make nice. Yet she couldn't resist exchanging a couple of testy sentences with the renegade spirit. Who knew when—or if—she'd appear again.

When she turned back, the image faded. Despite her annoyance, Justine's heart tugged at the woebegone expression on the pale face.

Chapter Thirty-Three

The pealing phone woke Jackson Sunday morning. He rolled on the mattress and squinted at the time. Ten on the nose. The name on the screen bolted him upright. For some reason, he created a contact to add Justine's name to her cell number. As if he intended to use it again. With a groggy moan he debated sending her to voicemail. Staying up till four, cursing and drinking, didn't lessen his upset. He could swallow his anger and slink back to California with no contact. Or blast her with it now.

He jabbed the phone. "Yeah?" The best he could muster.

Silence. Did she hang up?

Before he could click off, her voice floated into the overheated room. "This is Justine. I wanted to explain to you…about last night." Her words quavered, arousing a slight pang of compassion.

He steeled himself against turning soft and propped his bare back against the headboard. "I'm not in the best mood to listen. Were you trying to force a reunion? You could've clued me in." He didn't try to sugarcoat the irritation.

"I swear I had no idea he was coming." Her tone strengthened. "We connected to him by a fluke through a museum in Chicago. If I had any inkling he'd show, I would've warned you. Though you didn't bother to

RSVP either."

He raised a brow. Even on the defensive, she zinged him. He actually believed her, yet the frustration remained. "Did he see me?" Is that why he answered her call today, to find out if they'd zeroed in on his paternity? Bile churned in his gut, only partly from the alcohol.

Her sigh cut over the line. "He did. Along with everyone else. I made a lame excuse for your running out and said too bad you hadn't noticed him entering. Or surely you would have stayed to greet him."

Sarcasm. He'd mastered the art himself. "How did he react?"

"He wants to talk to me on the phone. Maybe just to repeat a thank you for the awesome unveiling he *stayed* to enjoy." She paused. "Or maybe because he's ready to share his secrets. I'm sorry if I overstepped, but the other day I delved into him and Nevins again. The actor lived in England to film a weekly live program right after their film together wrapped."

The info took a moment to settle in his fuzzy brain. "How did we miss that?"

"Maybe the factoid couldn't penetrate our liquor haze that night at the house."

Yeah, he remembered. A buzz of whiskey and desire. "You're saying Nevins likely wasn't in the US early in 1979, when I would have been conceived?"

"Exactly. The situation doesn't provide one hundred percent clarity but helps lean that direction. As for Lawrence Reynolds, what do you want me to say if he asks a leading question—such as whether you know his identity?" Her tone softened.

His gut rolled again. Jackson thrust a hand through his hair and remained silent. Seconds ticked by. A renewed surge of anger drove him to throw back the covers and stand. "Tell him I suspected as much, but too many years have passed for us to form a relationship. I bet he still wants to hide his dirty secret bastard. And then you can tell him to go to hell."

"Look, I totally understand, but that's not the vibe I got. I really just called to apologize for how everything turned messy." She sounded a tad frantic. "To make it up to you, let me help with the house stuff. You don't have to deal with me if you don't want to. Just leave a key somewhere. I'll send you a detailed email with my recommendations."

Punishing her wouldn't accomplish anything. His attitude today had been insufferable enough. And he did need help. Jackson picked his discarded jeans off the floor and pondered. "I'll be here for a week to get everything wrapped. If you can come over tomorrow, we'll dig in."

****

Having braved one difficult conversation, Justine touched base with Haley. Harold hadn't called. In reality, she didn't expect him to. Or blame him. She barely talked with them after being spooked by the sad Liza appearance. "Did he seem upset that I didn't hang out more with you two?" She propped the cell on the counter and bustled around her kitchen, grabbing ingredients to bake peanut butter cookies in a peace offering to Jackson. Unless he had a peanut allergy. She paused with the jar in her hand. If he couldn't eat them, her co-workers would.

Haley's voice pulled her back. "He's a super mellow guy. I only saw him react once, when Jackson fondled your hair." Her tone teased.

"He didn't fondle." She slapped a spatula against her palm. "Be serious. I wanted to check the temperature before diving back in. Do you think he'll call me again?"

"Do you want him to?"

"What's with the mean girl attitude?"

"Don't blow me off. Last night I observed a spark between you and Mr. California that didn't seem to exist with our local friend."

"You weren't even standing close to us."

"If I had been, my fingers would've singed when I touched you." Haley snickered. "I'm probably jealous. You have two guys after you. I'm stuck crunching numbers, as usual."

"Please. I called you to talk about Harold. No way is Jackson Maddox interested in me."

"His actions say otherwise. I know the logistics are difficult, but anything's possible."

Justine glared at the phone before retrieving the flour canister. "He'll leave here as soon as he can straighten everything out. I'm going over tomorrow to help with the cataloguing. Only so he can skip town faster."

"Really? Well, if you do decide to cast off one of these fine fellows, remember your poor lovelorn friend. Harold's a great catch around here."

The wistful comment stopped her in the middle of the kitchen, clutching the flour to her chest. "I know. I like him. I do. Life's just messy with the interview process and all. At least the event's out of the way. Even Martin Collier can't complain about the turnout and the funds we raised."

A shriek ripped out of her mouth. Liza Maddox perched on a kitchen chair. Justine's grip loosened. She juggled to hold the canister and lost. Luckily, it was rubbery plastic with a tight, sealed lid. It hit the floor with a thud, bounced, and rolled.

"Justine, what's wrong?" Her friend's voice shifted to panic.

"Nothing," she panted out, hand plastered against her chest. "I dropped the flour. Gotta go. Bye." She clicked off the speakerphone while shooting the intruder the evil eye. "I definitely didn't invite you here."

Liza steepled her red-tipped fingernails. "I don't buy what you told your lovely friend. You do think my son's interested."

"You can't read my mind, can you?" Justine reared back.

"No, sweetie. I wish I could. But I do agree with her. The other gentleman's pleasant enough but doesn't have much pizzazz."

She crossed her arms over her chest and returned Liza's steady gaze. "Harold's very sweet, obviously interested, and happy living here."

Her companion pointed a sharp fingernail. "Once you have a taste of something more, you'll find it harder to settle. Take a tip from one who knows and has regrets. The ultimate road not traveled." Her face sobered.

Justine allowed a twinge of empathy. The ghostly visitor might be here to nudge her into embracing her own new path. Not necessarily a romantic one.

Liza crossed her legs, clad in a grass-green jumpsuit. "Going back to Harold, did you feel the same delicious spark when you two kissed?" Her expression lightened and the slender shoulders shook with mirth. "Oh my. If you could see your face."

"Your offspring must get his mood swings from

you. But he's not so nosy. Why are you here today?" She stared her down.

The spirit didn't flinch. "You have some of my clothing. I'm glad you kept the gold taffeta dress. The style looks darling on you."

"Not how are you here. Why?" Determined to finish her cookies despite the interruption, Justine moved closer to crack an egg on the table. A tad too hard. The yolk gushed out. "Crud. I only have enough to make the recipe." She held the bowl over the edge and maneuvered the slippery residue into it.

Liza wrinkled her nose and shifted her legs farther away. "So this is what some people resort to when they live alone."

"The table's clean. Why would you care anyway? You can't eat them."

"Oooh, how mean." She grimaced again, under the swish of dark bangs. "Perhaps I earned it by sneaking up on you, but I enjoy our encounters. I have no idea how long we'll be able to continue. Though as you can guess, I've always pushed the edges of propriety."

"So I gathered." She cracked the second and third eggs more carefully and added them to the bowl. "Me, I've always walked the proper, boring path." Her head shot up. "Wait, maybe I should see a therapist or something. Maybe this really is my subconscious taking over and I'm experiencing a psychotic break." Her voice rose in genuine concern.

"Get hold of yourself," Liza commanded. "I may be a curious, unexplained phenomenon, but I'm very much here with you and not a figment in your mind."

"Says the figment." But she felt calmer. "Sorry to freak out. I never expected to see you here."

"I also came because I think Jackson should try to connect with his father and you can support him through it." The frosty gray eyes shot out a hopeful appeal.

Justine planted her hands on her hips. Why did everyone try to read more into this relationship than truly existed? "If he makes that decision, I'll support it. If he even cares what I think or decides to tell me about it." Emboldened, she narrowed the space between them. "The main issue is we don't know for certain who his father is. We're centering on your director friend. Care to elaborate?" She stressed the words to try to coax a confession.

Liza's face fell. "On my honor, I can't tell you. Just know I always had the best intentions. I'm terribly regretful at how we've all suffered." Her form began to shift. The jumpsuit paled to a key-lime green. She spread her hands on her thighs, as if to stabilize the fading image. "Anyway, I'm so glad you like to bake cookies. I neglected those homey duties." The words grew faint, as if spoken from the depths of a well. "What I wouldn't give for a bite of a fresh peanut butter…"

Justine stared at the empty chair, registering a mix of awe and dread. What a convoluted mess. How did she end up being the chosen one to pursue Liza's ambitions? And why wouldn't she share the scoop on her baby daddy now? Would breaking the promise land her in hell?

The thought chilled her. How wild that she could even consider such a concept. For now, she'd try to save her sanity and refocus on baking the cookies. Hopefully they'd also soothe the soul of the lonely, bereft boy, as well as the sexy man Jackson grew into.

Chapter Thirty-Four

By the next afternoon, baking for Jackson made her feel juvenile and ridiculous. She stood on the stoop in the biting cold and decided to rush the packet back to her car. The homey gesture smacked of small-town sentimentality he wouldn't appreciate. Warmth seeped through the plastic bag to her gloved palms as she turned to trot away. The scent of delectable peanut butter filled her nose, making her stomach rumble.

The front door opened. Busted. Her lips twisted. The only other option was to toss them in a bush. She spun to face him, unable to overcome a lifetime of Midwest frugality and opposition to littering. As Jackson ushered her in, she swallowed hard and presented the gift.

His frown morphed into pleasure. "I smell peanut butter."

"Weekend baking binge." *With your mother*.

He lifted the clear plastic to his nose and drew a deep sniff. "My favorite. But where're the kisses?"

Her heart stuttered before she grasped that he meant chocolate. "I didn't have any." She chucked off her coat, suddenly overheated.

His exaggerated mock pout reminded her of an impish boy. "I still appreciate these. Besides my grandma, I don't recall anyone's ever made me cookies."

Including his mother. The remembered confession made her sad for all they'd missed out on together. She disguised the pity with sass and hung her coat on the nearby rack. "Don't people bake in California?"

"Yeah, in the sun."

She chuckled, intent on maintaining his mellow mood. Though she suspected he continued to ponder and brood over Lawrence Reynolds' visit. Better to avoid that hot topic today and focus on the lovely antiques. She gestured toward the living room. "How about we start in here?" As they walked, her eyes dropped to his butt. The worn jeans fit him closely. The blue, long-sleeved T-shirt brought out the color of his eyes.

Lawrence's eyes. Off limits.

Inside the room where they read the letters, she gravitated toward two carved side chairs. "These are Chippendale-style. Not terribly old, but a fine pair." The table lamp she admired on her first visit drew her eye. When she pulled the cord, light shimmered through the glass-domed top. She turned over the base and the shade. "I love this. The piece is marked Handel, a less expensive contemporary of Tiffany. If you wanted to keep anything, it would make a statement in your loft."

"Possible. This may have been handed down from my great grandparents." His finger traced the stamped name, stopping short of where her thumb gripped the rim.

In close proximity, she smelled the clean scent of his shampoo and marveled at the thickness of his lashes behind the dark frames. When he looked up, she didn't bolt but stood mesmerized, a shaft of heat tickling her torso. Despite their resistance, she knew something simmered between them. Something immediate and primal. A depth she hadn't discovered with Harold.

She dragged her eyes away at the traitorous thought

and murmured, "On to the dining room." Leading him out, she felt his eyes on her backside, same as she'd eyeballed his. Or at least she hoped he was checking out her best-fitting skinny jeans.

They didn't speak, which enhanced the sexy vibe. He lounged in a straight chair and watched while she inspected various figurines and vases, silently estimating their value. Finally, she offered a concise overview. While she could spend hours immersed in the treasures, she figured he'd soon grow bored.

When she closed the cabinet doors, he stretched and yawned. "Are you dating that guy you were dancing with?"

Her pulse bounced at the totally unexpected question. She smoothed her palms down her sweater. "You mean Harold?"

"No. I mean Joe, the old-guy janitor who was sweeping the floor." Humor lifted his lips. "Sorry if I'm being intrusive, but July said Saturday was kind of a set-up. Was that the situation you said your mom pushed you into?"

Oh, July, you well-meaning, meddling... "Yep. He returned to town recently. Our parents decided we should get reacquainted." Ouch, the admission painted her as a desperate woman tied tight to her parents. "Thankfully, he's changed a lot over the years." Justine covered her lips with her fingers over the unkind comment.

Jackson smirked. "He wasn't a prize in high school?"

"Neither was I, but he had some complexion issues. I really didn't know him well." *I had a big crush on you* floated through her brain. "He's a really great guy. Smart, funny. Polite."

"A real Boy Scout. So you're dating him."

"Twice before we saw each other Saturday." She crossed her arms over her chest, suddenly annoyed. "Why the third degree?"

"You looked happy." He rapped his fist on the dining room table. "What do you think about this set?"

Darn him for keeping her off-kilter. As if he gave a hoot about her dating status. He must enjoy teasing the country mouse. She gritted her teeth and pulled out chairs to disappear under the table to find the maker's tag. The moment also allowed her to regain composure. With a terse statement she estimated the value, slid back out, and stalked down the hall.

Silence resumed, without the sexy undertones. Without waiting for him, she entered the hallway leading to Liza's bedroom. Justine ventured into the room with clenched fists, half-expecting to see the mischievous spirit. The drapes were still drawn, casting a pall in the dim light. She ignored the wild thought to go over and throw them open, to brighten the "shrine."

While the actress wasn't apparent, she might be lurking unseen. The thought made her shiver. *Don't even*, she sent up a mental message.

He joined her and headed to the movie posters, removing one from the wall. "I'm going to take these for now." His voice was all-business. "Maybe I'll donate them at a later date."

"Great. Then we'd have a quartet—" Her words faltered. In her perturbed state, she'd stumbled into the forbidden territory. Please let him ignore her gaffe.

He stopped and tilted his head. "You have another poster?"

She wouldn't lie. With her luck, Camilla would send

him the newspaper clipping describing the event. "From…Mr. Reynolds."

His spine straightened. "What did he give you?"

Her stomach twisted and she bit back a groan. "A signed poster from a movie Liza was in."

In two large stomps he was in her face. "How did he even remember a bit actress like her from decades ago?"

She backed up a quivering step. "I wondered the same thing."

He swiped a hand through his hair and paced away. When he pivoted, his set jaw radiated anger. "We weren't wrong in narrowing down to him. Am I going off the rails, or do you agree?"

"The circumstantial evidence is pretty strong." She spoke carefully. Quietly.

The thunder seemed to leave him. He dropped to sit on the bed. "Do you think he suspects that we know?"

"I'll know more when I talk to him. If he calls."

"If this was a script, I'd define it as a crossroads moment." He collapsed back on the bed, his eyes glued to the ceiling. "I'd been able to distance myself from the issue for decades until the drunken web search after we found the letters."

She perched on the corner of the duvet, not wanting to interrupt the breakthrough line of thought. His face remained stony and disturbed. "Maybe I should take the upper hand and call him first. I've told myself I've been controlling the situation, but all along he's gotten what he wanted." His tone came out flat and lifeless. "I did what you said and let everything stew around in my mind after I left here. I know in my gut if I don't try to make contact to confirm or disprove his paternity, not knowing will haunt me later. I don't want anything from him," he stressed, "but the truth."

Moved by the honest revelation, she laid her hand over his.

He rolled onto his side but didn't dislodge their connection. "Do you have his number?"

"Yes."

"Can we use your phone? If he has your number, we could catch him off guard."

Was he going to place the call now? From her phone? She thrust out a long breath. Much as she wanted to support him, she didn't want to get caught between the two of them with the museum interview pending this week. Yet she'd promised Liza. If she was lurking unseen, she must be jubilant. Maybe this moment would be enough to allow her to cross over.

Justine dug the cell out of her cardigan pocket. She found the number in the notes program and handed the cell to him.

He sat bolt upright. "Not yet. Call me a coward, but I need a little more time. Do you want to go out and grab an early dinner?"

Now he wanted to eat? Her head swam with the whip-quick transition. No, he wanted to procrastinate. A tactic she was sadly familiar with. She returned the phone to her pocket. "Sure." Despite the complications, the draw was too appealing. Toward him, and to solving the mystery.

Giving up on the antiques, she followed his quick progress to shove into their coats and boots. He led the way through the kitchen to the detached double garage. Inside was a sporty red convertible.

"Liza's car." He patted the hard top. "I might have to keep this baby."

"You'd be a fool not to. And your mama didn't raise no fools." She mimicked one of July's favorite quips.

"That, I'm not so sure of. Jump in." He sobered and maneuvered his frame into the compact car.

She wondered what the evening would hold. Did he want to be distracted, or to dive deeper into his feelings about his parentage? She'd let him lead where he wanted. After he maneuvered onto the street, he gunned the engine and raised his voice over the roar. "Tell me where to go. I'm in the mood to drive. This baby responds to hard and fast handling." He winked, acknowledging the innuendo.

Her head spun again with the quicksilver mood change. That's when Jackson Maddox was most dangerous, Justine realized. A woman could find herself vulnerable to the charm when he chose to shut down the cynicism. Heck, any woman would find him alluring, while convincing / deluding herself she'd be the one to tame him.

She wasn't about to try, but she needed to blow off steam, too. "Let's ditch this state."

A half hour later they crossed the Michigan border. In New Buffalo, she directed him to a favorite, The Stray Dog. She loved the campy motto that hung above them at the entrance: "Come. Sit. Stay."

After they settled into a booth and ordered drinks, he slumped against the wooden bench. "This feels like I'm living in one of my screenplays. The kind of drama my mother would have thrived on." He toyed with the bundle of silverware wrapped in a paper napkin, fixing his gaze on it.

Justine's forehead wrinkled. "I remember being touched by your theme in *Winter Frost*. Years before, the younger woman debated whether to have or keep her baby. But you know, none of Liza's letters stated that your father definitively urged her to…" She hesitated to choose a more descriptive term.

"Abort me. No need to beat around the bush." He rolled the silverware aside. "That certainly would have been the easiest solution for both of them. Though that can backfire, too. Just ask my ex-wife."

Her head shot up. "Dare I ask?"

The waiter arrived with their drinks. Her mind buzzed, waiting for the response, stunned at the admission.

After swigging his beer, Jackson pinned her with a stare. "I've shocked you. Which I suppose was my intent. Dealing with all this crap again is making me pretty edgy."

She could practically feel his nervous energy jittering across the table. "You can't just drop a bomb and go on to talk about the weather. Tell me about your ex."

"I'm gonna be sorry I opened my mouth. Or maybe you will." His lips twisted. "Desiree resembled my dear mother in many ways. Dramatic. Demanding. Beautiful. She took delight in slowing de-balling me."

She remained silent, fingers tight around her glass.

"After about a year of not-so-wedded bliss, she set out to seduce one of my friends. Not that she had to try very hard. For her, she wanted a fling, an ego boost, some hot sex on the side. It threw a real crimp in her plans when she got pregnant, because she'd never had interest in marring her toned body with a baby." He slapped his palms down onto the table. "Sorry, this isn't polite dinner talk."

His tone remained flat, but revisiting the pain had to sting. Justine steeled herself for the resolution. "Go on."

He checked to ensure the waiter wasn't approaching. "I wouldn't have suspected anything if she hadn't started hemorrhaging. We had a few friends over. Suddenly, she's doubled over. I'm frantic, and while we're waiting for the paramedics, my drunken friend has an attack of loose lips and conscience. He pushes me out of the way to bend down to her and asks if she's miscarrying."

"You didn't even know she was pregnant," Justine guessed.

"Nope. She's scared shitless and shrieks, 'You idiot. I got rid of it!' Oblivious as I'd been before, that cued me in pretty fast." He paused again to drink. "Call me a grudge-master, but we didn't last long."

"I appreciate you telling me. That seriously sucked."

"I can't believe I'm spilling so much. Maybe because I'm far from home in an alternate reality." He met her eyes across the table, his gleaming with intensity.

"I'm a sympathetic stranger who isn't making judgments."

"You aren't a stranger." He rubbed a hand across his jaw. "Somehow you exert a calming influence on me, which is no easy feat."

While he shook her to the core. A shiver rolled through her at the thought. How had she left herself vulnerable to becoming emotionally ensnared? Within a week he'd be back in California; She'd never hear from him again.

Their food arrived, interrupting her bleak musings. She had to force herself to chew a few bites as they segued to more mundane conversation. The bombshell admission also rocked her. No wonder he came off jaded and defensive. The most important people in his life hid secrets. Some had even betrayed him.

With a to-go box on her lap, twenty minutes later they were zooming back to LaPorte. She peered out the window as they entered the town limits, without registering the strip of businesses and fast-food restaurants that trailed into a maze of quiet residential streets.

At the house, Jackson eased the car into the garage and twisted to face her. "I think I'm ready to call him now."

Her eyebrows rose. Their restaurant conversation pushed the idea clear out of her mind. "Okay."

"Will you come back in?" He sounded like an uncertain boy. "I need your Zen effect to get through this."

Chapter Thirty-Five

With anxiety pulsing under his skin, Jackson waited for her answer. He could make the call alone; he didn't want to. This woman had been by his side from the discovery of the letters through the computer search. Reynold's appearance at the museum event further connected the three of them. He didn't exactly believe in "fate," but somehow, the linkage continued.

She pursed her lips but didn't hesitate. "Of course, I'll come in. You're going to use my phone."

"Yeah. Great." His system swirled with an edgy mix of determination, nerves, and dread. In the living room, he placed her phone between them on the couch. He flexed his fingers, unready to make the call. Even if he and Lawrence Reynolds didn't reconnect beyond this moment, he'd be reshaped by it. He should take a few minutes to plan his approach—

His finger jabbed the call button. The phone rang. Once, twice, three times. The sound of an answering voice shot dizzying electricity through his nerve endings. "Hello." The man's tone sounded refined, leaning toward reserve.

Jackson paused long enough that the man repeated the greeting as a question. "Hello?"

"Is this Lawrence Reynolds?" He projected toward the speakerphone, not daring to pick it up.

"Yes. Who is this?"

A deep breath… "My name is Jackson Maddox."

Now the pause hovered on the other end, suspending time and reality for a string of charged seconds. He heard an exhalation of air. "Jackson. I've expected this call. She finally told you."

The confirmation, so soon, increased the dizzy sensation. "No. Liza never told me anything." Justine grasped his hand, which he'd begun clenching and unclenching.

"Then how…" The question hung unfinished.

His heart had never rocketed so hard. He fought to stay dispassionate by grounding in the facts. "We found letters here at the house in Indiana. Nothing concrete, but with a few clues and ingenuity, the wonders of the internet help you dig up loads of interesting info."

Another pause. Of course, he must be weighing each word. Jackson squeezed his companion's hand as Reynolds began again. "My sincere condolences on her passing. Liza and I re-established contact after she moved to live with your grandmother. When I hadn't heard from her in some time and couldn't reach her on the phone or the computer, I discovered her obituary." He spoke more rapidly, as if trying to make his points before the call could sever. "Jackson, I'm an old man now. I am heartily sorry for the way I handled this whole situation. I let fear and selfish ambition blind me to the path I should have taken. The outcome wasn't fair to you, or to Liza."

"I don't need your apologies." He couldn't help the ice that coated the words. He'd lived with the cold reality for too many years. "I ceased to care long ago. But she deserved better."

"You're right." Lawrence's voice quavered. "You

may not believe me, but I'm glad you found me now. I watched you growing up, and I've watched your career. You're a good and talented man and you deserved to know the truth. Yet even when I knew Liza was gone, I believed I'd forfeited the right to contact you and disrupt your life."

Still holding onto Justine's fingers, Jackson closed his eyes. The man might sound sincere, yet he couldn't blindly trust him. "Then let's leave it that I finally, foolishly, sought confirmation of the identity of my sperm donor."

"Please don't misunderstand." Lawrence's voice pitched with new urgency, as if to reach through the phone to bind him there. "I'm glad you've taken the initiative. Before you hang up, please consider getting together so we can talk in person."

Jackson sought Justine's counsel. His eyes searched hers, questioning.

"It's your call," she whispered, reminding him of his power in the situation.

"Is someone else there?" Apparently, the old man had sharp ears.

Jackson paused. "You met my friend Justine at the museum the other night. She found the letters when we were going through the closets here."

"You're still in Indiana?"

"For now."

"Although I know I have no right to ask, I'd really appreciate the opportunity to meet you. Bring her along if you want."

No, he did not get to call the shots. "I'll think about it." Jackson severed the connection and dropped his head into his hands, regretting the demented impulse to connect. "Damn it!" He thrust himself off the couch to pace with long, agitated strides. "I don't know what I expected, but getting together for tea and crumpets wasn't on the agenda."

He knew the truth. That was enough.

Justine tucked her knees up and wrapped her arms around them. She followed his progress back and forth across the rug. "He didn't try to deny it."

"And he could have. Without a DNA test, I have no proof." He stopped in front of her. "Do you think I should meet him?"

She lifted her chin to peer up. "What do you need going forward? Is the confirmation enough? Or do you want to spit in his eye?"

He couldn't help the snort of humor. "I can be a rude ass, but even I wouldn't accost an old man." He dropped onto the couch beside her. The idea of meeting face-to-face didn't thrill him. He might weaken again, though. Somehow, he sensed his mother would have wanted him to. Which was nuts, considering she hid his identity. "I don't know how to process this yet. Not sure I even want to. But if I go off half-cocked again and decide to visit him, will you go with?"

Man, she did not have a poker face. He watched her expression flux and pressed his advantage. "Like it or not, you're a catalyst in all this."

"I suppose I am. If you make that decision, I'll at least ride with you. I promised—" She clamped her lips together, eyes wide.

"You promised?" he prompted.

She unfurled her legs and leapt off the couch herself, avoiding his gaze. "I promised to help you get everything ready here so you could return home. If that includes meeting Lawrence Reynolds, I'll support the visit." She grabbed her phone. "But I have to work early tomorrow so I should scoot."

He frowned at the abrupt departure. Yet why wouldn't she want to leave? He put her through the wringer again with his drama tonight. While she shrugged into her coat, he donned his own, determined to be polite for once and escort her to the car.

Outside, she held the rail to descend the snowy steps and started down the short sidewalk. At her car she stopped, head tilted up. He barely caught himself from plowing into her and followed the direction of her gaze. His breath caught at the expanse of glittering stars. The moon shimmered an opalescent white, as barren black trees stretched sharp tentacles skyward. "No wonder I've been acting out of character. Full moon," he joked.

She giggled. Moonlight drew planes of shadow across her face, illuminating the slight smile. Drawing him in. As if the world was turning in slow motion, he lifted an ungloved hand to trace her lips. She trembled under the touch.

His breath formed puffs of steam as he narrowed the distance between them and muttered, "I swore to myself I wasn't going to do this, especially with Harold in the picture, but I'm feeling amazingly reckless tonight." His lips lowered to graze hers. When she didn't protest, he whispered them around the corners of her mouth.

Her eyes fluttered closed. Emboldened, his tongue toured the soft contours of her lips. Heat coursed through his body, erasing the biting cold. Mittened palms clutched at his back as he eased her body against the car. He tightened his arms around her as their lips melded together.

She moaned when he eased away. But instead of retreating, his fingers slid down the zipper of her bulky coat. He pulled it open, plunged his arms around her waist, and pulled her tighter against him, relishing the joining of their bodies as their mouths moved in a sweet synchronicity of teeth, tongue, and lips. His body urged to carry her inside, but a thread of rational sanity ruled. He didn't use women as a distraction.

He kissed her eyelids, her cheeks, before separating from her quivering body. With shaking fingers, he re-zipped her coat and leaned his forehead against hers. "Blame it on the moon," he whispered, reaching for the car door.

Her eyes were lidded above a well-kissed mouth. She stepped away, appearing a little dazed. Their eyes held for a moment before she stepped inside the car and backed down the driveway.

Awash with sensation and emotion, he squinted against the headlights and raised a hand.

****

Justine's head still spun when she pulled into her own garage minutes later. Other parts of her also tingled. The kisses packed the wallop of four tequila shots, leaving her off-balance and horny. Beyond the physical response, she couldn't quite wrangle her emotional reaction. Was he playing with her? Distracting himself from his own distress? Or…was he interested? After all, this was the second hot make-out session.

Her phone rang as she stepped inside the house, before she narrowed to a choice. She jumped in alarm and checked the number, hoping Lawrence wasn't calling back.

Worse. Harold's name flashed on the screen. Well,

not worse. She just wasn't prepared to talk to him in her current state. She could always ghost him.

Their mothers would kill her. And she did like the guy. "Hello."

"Hey, Justine." His voice sounded tired. "Sorry. Work is insane. I hope everything slowed down for you after the event. Which was great, by the way."

"Thanks. I'm glad you could come, and that Haley kept you company. I'm really sorry I didn't have much time to chat." She settled in the padded armchair in the living room and tugged off her boots.

"I get it. That's why I suggested we get together a couple of times beforehand."

"Yes, the symphony was wonderful." Cripes, were they just going to rehash their brief history?

"I wish we'd gotten the chance to meet Mr. Reynolds and Jackson Maddox. Too bad the son couldn't stick around. I imagine he found it all a little lame."

Now she had to lie. "In reality, he was very complimentary. As I said, a work emergency dragged him away. I'm sure you can sympathize."

"No slap intended. He looked a little detached and bored when he first came in. I guess he warmed up after you went over there."

The comment dangled between them. Was he fishing for something? Haley said he reacted to Jackson touching her hair. She thought the comment was a joke, and tonight, lacked the energy to second-guess. Her soothing skills also were exhausted. Yet she didn't want to sabotage a possible relationship with Harold before it even took hold. "He appreciated seeing a familiar face. You grew up here. He was surrounded by strangers. The man is not an extrovert."

"I suppose I can see that." His acceptance rang as grudging. "Do you want to get together this weekend?"

Her body flushed with heat in the bulky coat. She unzipped it while her mind rolled with an image: Jackson performing the same motion—in a much sexier fashion. "Frankly, you sound whipped. How about we touch base later in the week to see how you're holding up. I have a couple of important things to tackle myself." She hadn't told him about the Thursday interview. Now, a possibility lurked that she might accompany Jackson to Chicago. She extracted her arms from the coat.

"Good idea," he agreed. "I'll call or text. Sleep well."

Wow, he clicked off fast. Relieved, she sank into the chair and waved her hand around her face to stir a breeze. Her eyes closed. Maybe she'd take a long, soothing bath.

"Are you going to string that poor man along?"

Justine bolted upright and groaned. "Do you have a full wardrobe up there in Heaven? Or limbo—wherever you're at?"

Liza reclined on Justine's couch in a slinky black, floor-length halter dress. She smoothed her hands down the cut-out sides. "Only a few favorites. Don't digress. You are leading him on when you're obviously into my son."

"Were you at the house, too?" Justine's nails bit into the chair arms. "For the phone call and—"

"The kissy-face. The snow melted into a puddle around you two. Not that I watched for long. I'm a bit of a voyeur apparently, but it does feel icky to watch you and my son."

"Speaking of digressing." Justine gritted her teeth. "I'm tired. Let's keep this concise. You heard Jackson call his father. I agreed to go with him if he wants to meet him. Are you pleased?"

To her surprise, the gray eyes shimmered with tears. "What Lawrence said, how he reacted, was unexpected and lovely. I do hope they'll meet."

"I can't push him. I won't." Justine stood. "This may be the only closure you all will get."

Liza swiped a finger under her eyes. "If it is, I'll have to accept that. But I don't know if that will be enough for me to…move on."

Despite a wrench of sympathy, she held firm. "Well, you can't keep ambushing me. If you stay, there'll have to be limits." She stepped toward the couch to tower over the apparition, arms crossed. "Restrict yourself to your house and the museum."

"You'd welcome me there?" The voice sounded hopeful.

"As if I have a choice."

Chapter Thirty-Six

Liza, September 2005

Liza paced the entry hall of the home she'd undoubtedly have to vacate after the divorce. While she waited for Jackson—running late again—she mentally calculated the value of the artwork flanking both walls. Collected over sixteen years, the diversity reflected their growing divide. While his tastes grew bolder, wilder, experimental, hers tamed to soothing landscapes.

Terrence probably would fight her for the one piece she wanted, an impressionist rendering of the Hollywood Walk of Fame. She paused and ran her fingers across the frame, trying to call up fond memories to submerge her fatigue and sadness. While she never harbored grand illusions of joining the stars, for many years she had treasured this golden world, floating among the famous.

Crowds, parties, and nightlife no longer interested her. She didn't socialize much these days and spent most of her time here, casual and barefoot, on the beach or by the pool. Her arches ached already in the heels, but she wanted to look her best. Perhaps she should give them a rest while she waited.

The front door opened, flooding sunshine and heat into the foyer. Her son entered in dark sunglasses, hair tousled from the wind. As usual, her heart swelled. She glimpsed his black convertible outside as he paused, seeming startled to catch her lurking there.

"Hello, Mother. You're looking fashionable." He didn't move to embrace her. He avoided hugs after his eighth birthday. After she and Roger split. She finally gave up the strained attempts.

She faked a bright smile. "Sweetheart, I appreciate you carving out time for me today." They hadn't connected, either by phone or in-person, for two months before she reached out to set up the lunch. She felt a bit guilty at the lapse, but he shared in the blame. Her heels clicked as she approached him, hoping he'd contain his tendency to push her buttons. Conversations too often spun out of control—on a wave of recriminations about his mysterious paternity, or Terrence's drinking, or her squabbles with his grandmother. Avoiding contact was an easy out. For both of them.

Instead of sitting and talking privately here, as she planned, his late arrival jeopardized their country club reservation. The car would have to do. She certainly wouldn't divulge the reason for the meeting in a public venue. "We should go to secure the table."

Perhaps she should have served them lunch, but she preferred to drop the news quickly and move on to benign, pleasant conversation. Being alone could open the door to rehash old wounds, and she didn't have the energy to dodge, explain, or justify.

The sweltering sun led her to dig out her oversized white sunglasses. Her nerves jittered while they settled in the low-slung car, top down. She grasped the armrest but stayed silent as he gunned the engine down the long driveway. They maneuvered along the quiet, residential street flanked by McMansions and pristine expanses of green lawn. Actually, she wouldn't miss the haughty atmosphere. Let Terrence have the house.

She couldn't put off the news any longer. Speaking over the blaring music, she dove in. "I invited you to lunch to tell you in-person that we're getting a divorce." The sun blinded her for a moment as she lifted her chin, striving to keep her voice level. "His drinking is shifting to drugging. Plus, he's got a sweet young thing on the side who thinks he can make her career. I've had enough."

He kept his gaze on the road and flipped off the music. "You won't get any arguments from me. I can't believe you've held on for so many years." He shifted gears to approach a stop sign. "The dude's always been an ass. I know he treated you okay for a few years, but he's been way out of line since his last film flopped."

While she agreed, the comment stung. She swung to face him, not wanting to fight, but to make him, finally, understand. "Overall, he was good to us. I knew how bereft you were when Roger and I split. We got together partly because I wanted to give you the same level of lifestyle, and a family." His lips twisted yet she persevered. "He didn't always know the best way to connect with you, but he did try." She held back her whipping hair with one hand when he pressed the accelerator again. "Believe me, I won't spend any more time defending his atrocious behavior."

To her surprise, he didn't respond. Within two minutes, they rolled up to the club entrance. The guard tipped his hat and waved them through the iron gate. Probably the last time she'd ever enter here without someone else adding her to the guest list. Jackson parked and looked around to ensure no one would overhear. "Do you think he'll fight you? I can't imagine him parting with any of his assets, especially when the job offers are sparse."

She wondered the same thing. "Surely Terrence will appreciate the opportunity to openly show off his nymph of a girlfriend." Her bravado cracked. Love was long gone between them, humiliation remained. "He's gotten bolder. This one seems to have captivated him. The others were flings." She opened the visor mirror and wiped an invisible smudge from her lip, avoiding his scrutiny. "Our lawyers will hash out the details. I don't want to take him to the cleaners. I just desire to live decently. After all, I gave up my own career after I married him."

She looked over the top of the sunglasses, daring him to shoot off a comment about her limited "career." For once her son held his tongue. She grasped the door handle. "Today I'll put on the performance of my life. Let's go in for a celebratory lunch."

Chapter Thirty-Seven

Attempting to move past the Maddox drama to focus on her own, Justine drove to Haley's to borrow another interview suit. She wasn't willing to invest in one with no promise she'd wear it again.

Marcy joined them to consult, though her fashion choices leaned way left of conservative. "Don't you have anything that doesn't scream 'accountant'? Maybe a pattern or something?" She flopped on the bed with a glass of wine and grimaced.

Their friend stepped out of the closet with another armload. "One time I went wild and dipped into plaid." She placed the pile between them and dug through the padded hangers.

Justine perched on the mattress and tried to tune in. Her mind didn't cooperate, pondering why Jackson hadn't called about driving into Chicago. He likely decided to avoid an emotional, wrenching father-son reunion. Or maybe he decided to go without her. The thought gnawed at her. *Blame it on the moon.* Had she lost her freakin' mind?

"Earth to Justine." Haley snapped her fingers. "How about this? Jazzy yet responsible." The burgundy plaid jacket nipped in at the waist above a pleated skirt. "Try it on."

"A daring choice," she teased back, stripping off her pants but keeping her turtleneck on.

Marcy sat up. "I like. Something that shows off your figure for once. Though from what I hear, your Valentine's dress sizzled. Enough to grab the attention of two available men."

She stuck her arms into the jacket while heading toward the full-length door mirror. The skirt skimmed a few inches above the knee. Respectable, but a little kicky. "Harold is more fizzle than sizzle at the moment. And Jackson. Obviously, there's no future, but geez, the guy can kiss."

Haley squealed behind her. "Did you two lock lips again?"

The Reader's Digest version of that evening rolled out as Justine admired the suit in the mirror. "I helped him with the house contents. He was grateful." She unbuttoned the jacket. "You're right. I like this."

"Don't try to blow us off. Plenty of clients are grateful for my services. They don't try to kiss me."

Justine shimmied out of the skirt. "It's kind of like an alternate reality sets in. We both know this won't go anywhere."

"Why not?" Marcy demanded. "People do long-distance all the time."

"Don't talk crazy. Harold is the nice, solid, local choice."

Haley held up a finger. "Wait. Do you feel the same way about them both? Does Harold rev your motor?"

She squeezed her eyes tight. "Truthfully. No. He's more sympatico for you." Seeing her friend's fleeting, hopeful expression cemented her resolve. "I'll have to think of a way to finagle you two together, without it seeming like a dump."

"I'm not asking you to do that." Haley planted her

hands on her hips.

"Shh." She waved a hand to shush the weak complaint. "For too long I've let others dictate a direction for my life. My parents wanted me to attend an Indiana school to save money, so I did. And while I do love it, I took a local job because everyone begged me to stick around and not live in a big, unsafe city. Now our parents want Harold and me to fall madly in love and settle down with four kids and a dog." She grabbed her wineglass and swigged half the contents. "He and I don't have that much spark. You two, however, might."

A round of slow claps swung her toward Marcy, who kept her hands clasped together. "Bravo, girl. Here's to our new, fearless friend. You're going to nail the interview with that confidence. If another opportunity arises to kiss the crap out of Jackson Maddox, I say you grab it, too. Along with his butt."

Chapter Thirty-Eight

Jackson sprawled on the couch and stared at his phone. He already made the hardest decision—to meet with Lawrence Reynolds—so why did he hesitate to call the woman who set the train in motion? She'd be a welcome buffer between them. Yet he couldn't deny the chemistry that ignited when they kissed.

His body stirred in response to the memory. Damn it, he could get sex at home. Without the charged emotional connection. He scrubbed a hand through his hair, reminding himself nothing more would come of this. Despite the time nearing ten, he punched her number. If she was in bed, he'd leave a message.

"Jackson?" Her voice sounded soft, but alert.

He straightened. "Sorry for calling late. I decided tonight to take him up on the offer and go to Chicago. You may be tied up, but I need to go before my flight on Saturday." Best to get to the point quickly.

"Wow. Okay." She hesitated. "I'm assuming tomorrow's out on short notice. Thursday, I have the day off already, for an afternoon interview in the city."

"Interview?" She caught his attention with the revelation.

"For a curator position. Not in a major museum, but a wonderful one based in a family's Victorian mansion."

Her voice lilted and he sensed pride behind the statement. "Congratulations. I didn't know you were looking."

A sigh filtered across the air. "The county has serious financial concerns. It seemed a fine time to polish my resume while they continue to debate how to slash the budget."

"You're smart to be proactive. What time is the gig?"

"At one with the full board of directors. They're down to two candidates."

The upbeat note in her voice dissipated. He understood; a final interview presented big pressure. A plan began to formulate. "What if I drive and wait around while you interview, then we swing on to meet with him?" He waited, anxiety tapping through his fingers on the couch cushion. She might prefer to be alone in those important lead-up hours.

"Hmm. That saves me tackling the madhouse traffic. I'm always edgy with everybody zipping between lanes."

"I'm used to the insanity of LA freeways." His fingers relaxed. Her presence might help keep his temper in check, with other drivers on the road, and with Reynolds. "I'll tell him we either meet Thursday at four, or not at all."

****

Thursday morning, he pulled up to her cottage-sized house, jogged out into the cold and rang the bell. Seconds passed and the door opened. He took in the smart, fitted suit, tamed hair, and careful makeup. Another three-sixty turn from the slumpy outfit she wore when they met, and the killer red Valentine's dress. "You look great. Corporate but approachable."

Her lips turned up. "Perfect. Step in and I'll grab my

coat."

He took in the cozy room, painted a basic cream but accentuated with bright artwork and oversized throw pillows. A far cry from his own stark loft. When she bent to grab a long wool coat, his eyes traveled from the high heels to the skirt, ending about four inches above the knee.

She caught him staring. "Do I have a run in my tights?" A hint of color flushed her cheeks.

"Nope. Just haven't seen your legs before." *Suave, Jackson. Real smooth.* He mentally rammed a palm against his forehead. "We better head out into the wilds of Chicago traffic." To make up for his cloddish behavior, he helped her into the coat before they hurried out the door.

The car's map program guided them through town and onto the interstate. After a few minutes, he loosened up to discuss his progress with the house. "The auctioneer seemed pretty eager to land the work, but I felt good about him. Your realtor friend thinks the house could take longer to sell due to the economy."

"People around here love estate sales. Did you set a date?"

He moved into the left lane to pass a lumbering semi. "Not yet. We're working out the logistics. I'd rather not make another trip, but I may have to."

"Let me know if I can help." The car had heated finally. She shifted to pull out of the coat.

"You might be busy training for a new job."

"Maybe." She sent him a side glance. "If I land the opportunity, my life will change drastically. Which I definitely need. I've been happy here in my proverbial rut. No doubt, it's time to branch out and experiment."

"I admire that." He decided to share a realization from the night before, reached while nursing a whiskey during the sleepless night. "I guess my mom did the same thing. I've never given her credit for taking such a leap. If she hadn't left, some milder version of me might be lurking around LaPorte, too."

She lifted a brow. "That would be tragic. Instead, you're a moody screenwriter in chic California."

"Ouch." He winced, keeping his eyes on the road as the traffic picked up. "I apologize for dissing your hometown. Some folks might think sitting in front of a computer alone is lame, creating characters and writing fictitious dialogue for people you've never met. But that's the work I love, and I could do it anywhere. Why not in eternal sunshine?"

"I'd miss the change of seasons, but winter, not so much." Justine peered out the side window at the flat, barren fields dusted with snow. "As for your work, the screenplay is critical to an excellent movie. A strong director brings that vision to life. Was Lawrence Reynolds considered a top director in his day?"

His fist clenched at the reminder of why they were traveling together. "He had a gift for pursuing interesting camera angles, making the most of the scenery and locales. Also, bringing the best out of his actors. He wasn't well-known as current geniuses like Spielberg, but he was recognized beyond the trade. Most important, the work's held up." He slowed to roll into a toll plaza. "When he met Liza, he took a huge risk to get involved at a pivot-point in his career. With a possessive wife and her powerful, connected father, getting her pregnant must've really rocked his world."

"He admitted to making a poor choice at the time,"

she reminded.

He retrieved his credit card from the terminal and drove on. "Part of me understands why he didn't chuck it all to marry her. But the kid who grew up without a father can't quite get past it. I never forgave my mother for the whole situation, either. Having an affair is never the way to go. I saw that amplified in my own farce of a marriage."

"I hope today brings you needed closure. You have a chance to get answers, politeness be damned. Not that you'll be unpleasant," she dropped a warning tap on his shoulder, "but he opened this door. You should walk out with the satisfaction you need, as well."

****

How strange, Justine thought. They barely knew each other yet felt free to share such powerful feelings. He certainly brought them out in her. His upbringing and the calamity of the failed marriage coaxed out an urge to soothe. When he was playful, she was beyond charmed. Yet his initial impatience and distance annoyed the heck out of her. She suspected he usually kept himself tightly reined. Few would glimpse all these personality facets.

She recrossed her legs and smoothed the skirt pleats, sneaking a peek at his profile. He probably regarded her as an unpaid therapist. A safe space to unleash feelings, far from home, without any true bonds between them.

She wanted more.

The admission sizzled through her. No, no, no. Dangerous territory. Yet this depth of feeling was leading her to toss away a chance with Harold. After dipping into real passion, mundane wouldn't suffice in her life anymore.

Hard reality gripped and grounded her. She couldn't

indulge it with Jackson, but someday, another person would generate the same excitement. Shared by both parties.

Her spirits drooped, and she regretted accepting his offer to drive. She should be building herself up, prepping for the interview, not pining over an impossible dream. Since their conversation about his father dwindled off, she opened her portfolio and studied it for inspiration. A new page highlighted the Liza unveiling. In the largest photo, Lawrence Reynolds talked with Carl next to the donated poster. A reminder to Samantha and Nathan of her ingenuity in working with them to snag a renowned director to their rural county museum. They didn't have to know the other factors influencing his decision.

She startled when Jackson chortled. "You were right. These drivers come to play." A panel truck zipped in front of them and skimmed through two more lanes to exit.

Her hand wrapped around the armrest. "That's why I don't drive here. We're almost at the museum turnoff, thank goodness."

"Are you ready to face the inquisition?"

"My main concern is they'll see me as an unsophisticated country girl who can't keep pace up here."

"You've made it through two interviews. Take a little credit for your accomplishments. You've even impressed me."

Really? She tilted her head back on the headrest. "You're right, and I know that. Projecting confidence isn't my strongest suit. I'm usually comfortable behind the scenes, setting up displays." Yet she didn't stumble through her Liza program introduction, in front of dozens of people, in nerve-wracking circumstances. She would call on that level of moxie today to impress the full board.

Chapter Thirty-Nine

The Drysdale board consisted of ten members dressed in tailored suits and designer wear. After Samantha Chan led the way into the meeting room, Justine greeted those she'd met and introduced herself to others. Points for taking initiative, appearing at-ease even as her knees shook.

The executive director sat her in the open chair at the end of the table and took the adjacent seat. "As you know, Justine comes to us from a general historical museum in Northwest Indiana. Larger in size, but smaller in annual attendance."

The board chair picked up the top sheet of paper in front of her. "We have your resume. Please elaborate on the 'you' between these lines."

An interesting turn of phrase. Justine added color to the details, focusing on her love of history and the opportunities for growth and learning over a broad spectrum of duties at their facility. She concluded with thanks for the collaborative effort to bring the renowned director to their recent event.

Nathan Rosen interjected. "Lawrence was impressed with the professionalism he witnessed. From your display talents and introduction that evening, to the overall vastness of the collection."

"We're pleased he enjoyed the experience. His appearance definitely thrilled our guests." Justine held her surprise that he'd bothered to report back in a glowing fashion. A payback for her intervention, opening the door to unite him with his son?

****

In the car two hours later, she literally shook the tension from her body, bouncing on the seat and flipping her fingers. Jackson shot her a side glance. "Were you that keyed up for them? Wish I could channel some of that enthusiasm for the next leg of our adventure."

"I was quite proper and charming," she teased. "The grilling wasn't as scary as I'd expected. Like our volunteers, they care about the place and recognize the curator is an important role." Her speech slowed as the energy level wound down. "The man who knows Lawrence well said he gave a positive report about the experience in LaPorte. The testimony scored points." Or so she hoped. While the interaction was positive overall, she sure couldn't predict how they'd proceed.

"Interesting. He can take a stand. When he chooses to." He avoided her gaze.

She didn't mean to rub it in, just to share the kindness. Jackson would meet with his father, but the prickly defense mechanism remained in full force. To defuse the stiffness in the air, she rambled about the interview process. His hands relaxed on the wheel. He both listened and concentrated on the heavy traffic.

Soon they stood at Reynold's door. Early, but she suspected Jackson preferred to catch him off-guard. Her spine stiffened as it had at the beginning of the interview. Please, let them remain civil. She didn't have enough adrenaline left to play referee. She peered at the two-story, modern façade, fronted by pale brick and walls of windows. The man had transferred his California lifestyle to an affluent Chicago suburb. "More your style than mine," she muttered, sneaking a glance at her companion's clenched jaw.

He merely rang the doorbell again. She took his free hand and squeezed in solidarity.

The door opened. She nearly yelped at the increased pressure of his grip before Jackson loosened the spasm. Thankful for the protective glove, she slid her hand back.

Lawrence Reynolds appeared elegant, even in black slacks and a cardigan over a pressed shirt. But she detected a stiffness in his posture and gestures as he welcomed, "Good afternoon. Come in, come in." The height of politeness, he didn't comment on their early arrival.

No one spoke as they handed over their coats, and he hung them in a closet. He returned to extend his right hand. "I'm glad you came." He seemed confident, but careful.

"Sir." Jackson mirrored the same air of caution and reticence. He ignored the handshake. "You remember Justine. She's been kind enough to help me wrap things in LaPorte."

The older man lowered his hand without a change of expression. "I enjoyed my time at your event. Thank you for making the trip today. Please, let's get acquainted." He led through a hallway with a glass ceiling and turned into a gathering room. Sleek leather sofas flanked a fireplace tiled in dramatic black and white. An expanse of manicured lawn loomed beyond the picture windows. He gestured for them to be seated. "Would anyone like coffee, a soda, or brandy?"

Both shook their heads. "No, thank you," she murmured. "I thought maybe I could go out for a walk to give you two a chance to talk."

He took in her skirt and high heels. "That's kind of you, but with the cold outside, I'd suggest you wait in my library down the hall. You can browse through books or a magazine."

Eager to allow them to get to know each other, Justine stood. "Thanks. I'm sure I can find it."

****

Jackson felt as if his security blanket had been whisked away. "I'd prefer you stay," he blurted. He didn't want to face the old man alone. Anxiety spiked along his veins, steeling him for the confrontation. She shot a questioning look between the two of them.

Reynolds gestured to the sofa. "Of course."

They all sat silently, taking the other's measure. If he spoke first, Jackson feared spewing three decades worth of anger and abandonment. After agreeing to connect, something—perhaps an inner urging from his mother—compelled him to at least remain civil. For the moment.

The man finally locked eyes and broke the stalemate. "I've anticipated this day for thirty-two years, but one can never really be prepared." His face sagged, exaggerating the network of tan lines. "I don't blame you for not trusting me. After all, what have I done to earn it? Still, there are important facts I wish to share today. One is that I truly did love your mother." He leaned forward, clasping his hands tightly over his knee. "She loved me, too, even when I chose to hide our secret."

The immediate confession rocked Jackson. Trite words couldn't erase the pain that knifed into his chest, banding tight around his heart. He focused on his breathing, kept up his guard, and chose not to respond.

The man's lips twisted. "Obviously, I wasn't man enough to give up my…lifestyle…and my dream of being a respected director. I felt I had the vision for making films. A calling. I was driven to pursue that, above all else."

Jackson well understood, and shared, the compulsion. Yet the explanation didn't absolve the selfish actions. "Our lives suffered for your obsession." He fought to keep his voice tight and controlled. On his right, Justine stared down at her lap. Probably wishing she was back in the hotbox of the interview. Anywhere but this tense, insufferable stand-off.

Their host's head also bowed low. "My actions were indefensible. I chose my career over love and my son. You have no idea how I've regretted my cowardice."

"You kowtowed to your father-in-law's power to kill your career, left me a bastard, and my mother open prey for smarmy assholes." He started to spring to his feet. A warm, calming hand dropped onto his forearm, anchoring him.

The older man winced. "You don't mince words, and I don't blame you. I'm not trying to defend myself, but as the old cliché goes, times were much different. I already had three daughters. My wife wouldn't have hesitated to rip them from me. She'd also have gone for blood with your mother." He stared toward the window, as if looking back into the cloudy past. "Hollywood is vicious. You should know. Liza believed she was tough, but she couldn't have handled the shunning and the gossip. Which also would have followed you." He pushed to his feet. "I need a drink." Silence loomed while he retreated to a built-in wet bar.

Jackson slumped on the couch, unsure how much

longer he could last. Frustration threatened to fray his temper. He should gather Justine and make their goodbyes. She removed her hand from his arm and mouthed, "You okay?"

Before he could answer, a half-full tumbler of amber liquid hovered before him. He swallowed back the contents as the man handed a glass to his companion. His eyes closed as the fire singed his throat. He could sit here and wallow in anger and self-pity. Or he could rise above the emotional fallout to gather information. The storyteller in him yearned for more backstory. "How did you two meet?"

Reynolds had returned to his seat. His somber expression lightened. "At a party. One of those big studio affairs after our movie opened. Bored and halfway into my third Manhattan, I spied a gorgeous woman heading toward me at the bar and remembered her from the party scene. Liza had this slinky, sensual way of walking. When she smiled, I was the only man in the room. We started to talk. Between her beauty, wit, and the bourbon, I was hooked." He paused to sip his brandy. "I got her number. She knew I was married, and who to. She didn't want to make trouble for me, but damned if either one of us could help it. We saw each other for dinner a couple of times on the sly and progressed from there. Four months later she found out she was pregnant."

Despite asking for details, Jackson couldn't suppress his sarcasm. "Guess that was a blow."

He frowned. "I loved her. I also had a jealous wife, three young girls, and a domineering ass of a father-in-law who not only controlled his studio but would've gleefully killed my career with his cronies." Reynolds broke eye contact. "Selfishly, I believed the easiest thing for both of us was for her to put an end to the pregnancy. She did think about it, on my urging, but not for long." He caught his gaze again. "It wasn't the way she was brought up. She was going to have the baby and keep it. No, I wasn't thrilled at the time. But I helped her financially as much as I could, without being noticeable."

Jackson found himself curiously removed, as if the events happened to someone else. Imploded another child's life. He considered getting up to pour another drink but didn't. A clear head was necessary to safely navigate Chicago traffic.

Reynolds asked, "Shall I continue?" Hearing no response, he finished his drink. "All right. Before we met, after her first painful experience with marriage, Liza decided she wasn't the type to settle down and have babies. She was too nonconformist and freewheeling. When she married Roger Abernathy, I was jealous, but happy to see her in a solid relationship. For your sake and hers. Though frankly, he bored her."

Jackson felt the need to defend the one man in his life who tried to provide a loving father figure. "Roger was a good and decent man. I think their marriage dissolved because it couldn't survive her insistence on keeping your name secret. His ego couldn't take living up to an unknown demi-God."

His host's lip quirked at the term. "You very well could be right. What were your thoughts on Terrence Cooper?"

"The guy's a major dick. She stayed with him much longer than she should have, attempting to provide me with a stable 'family.' Terry's drinking and whoring undermined any potential for stability."

Reynolds settled the empty glass on an end table. "I'm truly sorry to hear that. The few times we connected over the years, she never let on about problems between them."

"Yeah, well, she was an actress." Jackson's nerves quivered despite the calm tone of the conversation. He let his eyes roam the room; he hadn't paid attention to the surroundings. His attention focused on a grouping of silver-framed photos on a shelf. Family photos. His half-sisters. A burn of emotion—part anger, part envy—rolled through him.

"Yes. Those are my daughters and grandchildren." The man's voice pitched low and careful, as if handling a powder keg. "The oldest, Deirdre, lives in the city with her husband and their twins. When her mother died, she urged me to move closer. I had no qualms about leaving California. The lifestyle ceased to woo me in retirement. And you," he shifted the conversation, "have done well for yourself in the industry. *Winter Frost* was quite an achievement. Am I wrong, or did the story mirror aspects of the relationship between Liza and your grandmother?"

"It did." But he hadn't come to talk about himself. Jackson diverted to another concerning track. "You said you had contact with my mother after she moved to Indiana?"

"Liza and I had infrequent contact through the years. She sent me condolences on my wife's passing. When I moved here, I touched base. She came to visit a couple of times and we emailed and spoke on the phone occasionally." He held up a palm. "Before you ask, they were just cordial visits. Too much transpired for us to pursue anything more."

The thought of them even considering reconnecting

as a couple, combined with the cozy family pictures, revved up his suppressed resentment. "One more thing." Jackson spat out the words. "Why in hell wouldn't you release her from the promise to protect you after all those years?"

Reynolds hesitated. His hand worked the cuff of his sweater, the first tell of nerves. "Not that it was needed, Jackson, but I did voice my permission."

"What the hell." A mix of disbelief and rage pushed him to his feet. "I think I've heard enough. Both of you have screwed with my life for too long." He took two steps to tower over the older man. "Don't worry, this meeting will remain our secret. I didn't come here to open a connection, to meet half-siblings, or to claim a share of the inheritance." He didn't look her direction, commanding, "Justine, let's go."

Reynolds appeared to shrink in his seat under the barrage. He didn't fight back.

Chapter Forty

Justine flinched as Jackson gunned the accelerator before zooming around a slow-moving minivan. He'd barely spoken since they left Lawrence Reynolds' home, almost dragging her out of the house. She'd tossed a goodbye to the older man as she shoved into her coat, her heart sinking at the sadness etched on his face. And the mulishness evident in her companion's clenched fists and jaw.

Tamping her curiosity, she stayed quiet to let Jackson process his feelings. But if bottling them up was going to get them killed on the freeway, he'd damn well better talk. "Please slow down and talk about what's got your shorts in such a bunch. Or better yet, we can stop for coffee somewhere, and I'll drive."

His eyes narrowed, but their speed decreased. "Let's see," he muttered. "Cliff Notes version. He loved my mom and regrets his cowardly actions. They talked and even met a couple times after he moved here. And boom, he urged her to tell me the truth."

Justine swung toward him. "Understandable. Hearing that knocked you off balance."

"I was furious. Until I got out the door and remembered she begged me to fly out for Thanksgiving this year." His knuckles tightened on the wheel. "I think she wanted to tell me in person."

Oh no. "To soften the news and answer your

questions face-to-face." Remorse must be chewing him up. For ripping into Lawrence and robbing her of the opportunity to finally confess.

His head jerked in acknowledgement. "My schedule was packed. I didn't commit. She died before Halloween."

She cupped her cheeks with her hands. "I'm so sorry." In her limbo afterlife, Liza apparently hoped to maneuver her son to the answers. With Justine's intervention.

"I kept a lid on my temper, but the revelation blew it to the ceiling." He swiped a hand across his forehead. "This closure was supposed to allow me to move on. Now I have a new regret."

"Liza doesn't—wouldn't—want your regret." She bit her tongue at the telling verb tense. Though no way he'd guess why she said it. *Oh, your mom visits me regularly.* "I'm sure she just wants you to be happy."

"For years, I blamed her and convinced myself she married Roger and Terrence to secure money and social status. Now I accept how she sacrificed her own needs to try to give me stability." His tone remained bleak.

"Mothers will do that. At least the visit provided some answers and opened your mind to different interpretations of the past."

He pivoted to regard her. "Truthfully, I see him in a new light, too. But I blew up the opportunity to establish a relationship." His eyes focused back to the road. "While he finally acknowledged his paternity, I can't imagine he'd come clean to his daughters. I'd always be the dirty secret."

"That may be true. Now you'll never know." She pressed her lips together, unsure why she needled him.

Though Liza probably would've said the same.

He stared straight ahead and didn't answer. At least he didn't explode at her. She accepted the mute chastisement and turned her attention to the scenery. Dusk hovered, dulling the edges of the smatterings of houses and buildings along the interstate. Eventually the tendrils of light disappeared. Darkness surrounded the sleek car as they raced closer to LaPorte. Closer to— what? Would she see him again before he left for California? Her chest constricted. Darn it. Somehow, she'd let his prickly-engaging nature pry under her skin. Even if she got the new job, their brief interactions would stay with her. She'd compare other men to him. And other kisses.

Yet if this trip concluded their connection, she'd maintain her pride and walk away with her head held high.

****

They hadn't spoken for the past twenty minutes. As he pulled into town, Jackson wrestled between regret and relief. While he definitely appreciated having her along, the last comment prodded him toward a place he refused to go. He didn't give a damn whether Reynolds intended to reveal his existence to the family. The three women would be horrified, intent to protect their mother's memory and condemn his birth. Condemning him. He'd endured enough rejection for this lifetime.

In the same protective spirit, he'd say a final goodbye to Justine tonight. He stopped at a light and glanced at her. The woman wasn't his usual type, so why was he drawn to her? Besides being attractive, maybe the small-town values he scoffed at touched a chord. Reminded him of his grandmother's nurturing love.

Justine also came off as caring and kind, interested in the world around her. Interesting as a person.

But no way he'd let himself get caught up here. His life was in LA.

He pulled into her driveway and left the engine running. "Thanks again for coming with me today, and for all the help you've given with the clothing and the house. You've been a real sport to follow along on this crazy ride."

Her expression remained flat. "You saved me from Chicago traffic to get to the interview. I do appreciate that, and I'm glad you met with Mr. Reynolds." She focused on unclasping her seatbelt. "The past few weeks have been an adventure, for sure. I hope everything goes smoothly for you. And, well, have a good life."

"You, too." All right, she was going to make it easy for him. His reserve held until she looked up. He caught her soft eyes. That unexplainable intensity rolled between them again. A wave of desire followed, at the memory of their searing kisses. Compelling him to pull her toward him and kiss her breathless again.

Jackson fought the weakness, opened his door and jumped out into the cold. The door slammed behind him as he stomped across the short driveway to cool down, illuminated by a garage light.

She stepped out of the car, as well. On the opposite side of the hood, he returned to slam his palms down, hard enough that she recoiled. "You know damn well there can't be anything more between us," he ground out, frustration lacing the words. "My only goal at this point is to finish up here and get out of town as quickly as possible."

Her eyebrows arched. She mirrored his stance and

braced her gloved hands on the hood to glare at him. "Have I ever led you to believe I have any inclination to pine away for you?"

"No—"

"Then you have seriously overstepped. What a fricking ego." Pure disgust radiated from her thinned lips and narrowed eyes.

His own mock-anger wilted, along with the revved libido. He shoved his freezing hands under his arms and watched her dash away to fumble for the house key. His stomach roiled when she flounced into the house and issued her final retort. An impressive, echoing door slam.

Another sharp jab of pain twisted his chest. He'd been a major a-hole. Yet Jackson ignored the urge to run and bang on the door, to apologize. To probably make an even bigger mess of things. Instead, he pulled himself together enough to stomp back into the car and roar off into the night.

Chapter Forty-One

On Friday, Justine focused on projects in the museum's basement that would allow her to hide from everyone and everything. Since Carl was out at another county budget meeting, she feared if she stayed at her desk, July might roll in and comment on her bleary eyes. Sympathetic words would bring on the tears, and she'd indulged in too many the prior evening. Still feeling bewildered, and hurt, she leaned against the bar counter and rubbed her achy breastbone. Where in the heck did Jackson's tirade come from?

Did he regard her as some sort of lovesick fool? Well, screw him. She glared toward the Liza exhibit, semi-daring her to appear. Actually, she expected a ghostly visit the night before. Storming around the house must've scared her off.

Her head shot up at the sound of footsteps on the concrete. At least they were human. A middle-aged couple rounded the corner. "Good morning," she greeted. "I hope you're enjoying the museum. Let me know if you have any questions."

She gripped the dust cloth in her hand. When they exchanged polite comments and moved on, she skimmed it down the length of the bar. Cleaners came in regularly, but she liked to keep this surface shiny. "Darn you, Liza," she muttered, catching her downcast expression in the back mirror.

"What did I do?"

Irritation sizzled through her body. She tossed the cloth down and followed the voice to an alcove housing displays from Little Theatre and local service organizations. Liza perched on a mock throne from a past production of *Camelot.*

Justine stalked toward her, keeping her voice low. "You sired a presumptuous ass."

The apparition raised a dark brow. "Tell me how you really feel."

"If you're going to be sarcastic, we won't have this conversation. Between you and your son, I've had enough of being slammed around."

"Wait." Liza beckoned her forward with a wave, looking contrite. "I'm sorry. Obviously,

my own behavior isn't impeccable. I also must apologize for my boy. The scene outside your house was absolutely uncalled for." She rubbed her palms on her legs, clad in black fishnet stockings. "He has feelings for you, or he wouldn't have reacted so strongly."

Justine stayed outside the velvet rope separating the display from the public. "His feelings are very transparent. He can't wait to get the hell out of here, and he thinks I'm pathetic and desperate." She grimaced, stung by another surge of hurt and anger.

Liza rose and advanced—the first time she'd seen her up and moving. Which was way spooky but kind of cool. Justine fought the urge to reach out and test her substance. If her hand passed right through, she'd scream so loud July would call the cops.

The ghost halted an arms-length away. Her face remained solemn. "Please don't underestimate your connection with him."

Taking two steps back, Justine ensured the visiting couple had left the area. "No matter how much you might want your son to find happily ever after, he doesn't want that from me. I'll try to take my friends' advice to dwell on the upside of having met him. Once I get over being furious." She planted her hands on her hips, exhausted by the whole situation. "I don't know if this situation is keeping you from passing over, or whatever it is you should be doing, but you need to move on and let it go. Jackson found his father. They both donated wonderful items to the museum. We set up a lifetime commemoration to you. Soon he'll return to California, make a success of his new screenplay, and find the right woman."

"Neither of you will be happy." Liza's lips drooped. Her image began to fade. "I don't regret interfering."

"What do you mean? Can you see the future or something?" Justine reached out as the last trace of color poofed away.

"Hey, who are you talking to?"

She shrieked and whirled toward Carl's voice. His brow wrinkled as he stared into the alcove. "No. Were you talking to a ghost?"

"Maybe."

His eyes bulged behind his glasses. "Was he or she talking back?"

"Yes," she whispered, enjoying his obvious amazement.

"Come on. Follow me." He led to the nearby small conference room, ushered her inside, and shut the door. "Spill. You know I love to hear about the ghost sightings. I just wish I could witness them myself."

She sat across the round table, enjoying the moment

of drama. "Brace yourself for this one. I've been seeing Liza Maddox since I went to her house."

He clapped his hands rapidly. "This is better than I could have hoped for. Shame on you for holding out on us. Is she happy with the display?"

"I don't know. I guess so. She's more concerned about her son's wellbeing."

"That's sweet."

"Yeah. But I do not want to talk about him. In any way shape or form. I'd rather share about my interview yesterday." Justine took firm rein of the conversation. Otherwise, she might inadvertently over share about Jackson, and Lawrence Reynolds.

Carl's face fell. "Did they offer you the job?"

"No. Not yet anyway. The interview went well." She chewed on her lower lip. "I kind of expected to hear something by now."

He tapped his fingers on the table. "You know I want the best for you, Justine. Selfishly, I'd rather you stay here, but if they make the offer and you want to shake up your life, you should go for it."

Her shoulders relaxed at the confirmation of his support. "Thanks for being so understanding. I do need to challenge myself. What's happening with the county budget, by the way?"

He brightened. "At today's meeting, it appeared we'll suffer some cuts, but nothing drastic. Martin spoke up for us. The Liza event seemed to sway him into our corner."

She pushed out a relieved breath. "Thank goodness. If I do go, you should be able to hire a replacement."

"I don't want one." He flashed her a mischievous smile. "But if your mind's made up…"

"I think it is." Despite her pleasure at progressing through the interview process, she realized she hadn't really committed to the idea of changing jobs and moving. Till now.

Her cell rang an hour later after she settled at her desk to edit photos. The flashing number sent her pulse racing. The Drysdale Museum. Finally. She swept toward the conference room, gesturing to her phone when Carl looked up. She punched the button and answered the call as the door swung shut behind her.

"Hello, Justine. This is Samantha Chan. I'm pleased to tell you that the board has decided to offer you the position of curator. They were especially impressed by the success of your latest event." She halted, providing an opening for a response.

OMG. They wanted her. "That's wonderful news. Thank you so much. I'm excited for the opportunity." She bounced on her toes, indulging the euphoria of anticipation.

"Excellent. I'll email you a full compensation package. We can talk further after you've reviewed it." Samantha went on to state the pay offer, which left Justine's head spinning. Still, living in Chicago would cost much more money than LaPorte. She reiterated her grateful thanks and the anticipation of receiving the packet for review. After they clicked off, she trotted back to the office.

Her beaming face tipped Carl to the outcome. "I take it you're going big-time? Congrats." He stood to encompass her in a hug.

July swished into the office. "What's going on? Good news from the county?"

He shook his head. "The update's very positive from

them. But first, we have to celebrate. Our girl's leaving the nest."

****

That evening at home, Justine floated on a giddy cloud. The compensation package also included generous insurance coverage and vacation. Even Carl, who analyzed the offer, was impressed. She intended to pore over the pages again before accepting and signing off.

Soon after walking in her door, she called her parents and sister. They were shocked but happy at the announcement. Next, Marcy and Haley loaded their text exchange with gleeful emojis. When she finally settled down to eat dinner, anxiety mixed with the elation dimmed her appetite. She didn't have any friends in Chicago. Yet she did long to embrace a new adventure, as Liza had.

Her phone rang and she scrambled to reach it. Her nerves leaped with apprehension. "Oh, hi Harold."

"Time really flies around here, doesn't it?" He tried to sound jaunty. A hint of tiredness seeped through.

With so many consuming happenings in her life, she forgot all about him. "Sure does," she mocked an air of cheerfulness. "I imagine you're super-busy as I am." Too busy to get together, apparently. Which was fine. She already admitted the mismatch to her friends. Now to disengage from him, gently. But not this early in the conversation. That would be way rude.

He rolled into a few of his job-related demands. Half-listening, she tried to think of a way to deliver her big news. When he left her an opening, she blurted the decision. "Gee, I'm facing a huge change, myself. Today, I received a job offer from the Drysdale Museum in Chicago."

"Wow. Congratulations." Surprise colored the words.

"I didn't feel comfortable talking about the process until I had a clearer picture of the outcome. Truly, I didn't expect to be chosen." *Slow down, don't babble.* "Anyway, I'll have to start looking into apartments up there. I sure don't want to make the commute. Plus, a big city offers so much."

"The pace is hectic. Having moved from one, I can share that you'll be overwhelmed with choices. In a good way."

She tried to interpret the flat tone. Would she have to spell out her intention not to see him again? It wouldn't be fair to use him as a stopgap till she found true passion. Again. She rubbed her tightening chest. No, Jackson Maddox must be exorcised from her mind, along with his ghostly mother.

Caught up in those thoughts, she didn't respond to Harold's comment. He cleared his throat. "Am I off-base to assume you'd rather move without creating any stronger ties here?"

Relief flittered through her system. "We've had fun together, for sure. But yes, I think it would be easier. I really don't know how long I'll be here. I can't imagine making the commute for long."

"Don't worry. I understand. Our parents forced our hands in the first place."

"I didn't even know you were back." She stopped. He didn't seem to be too broken up or begging. No need to sugarcoat the situation. "They'll be disappointed, but they'll survive." Her mom had raised the question during their call and accepted her answer without much fuss.

"In the end, they just want to see us happy," he summed up.

Similar to the words she used with Jackson. *No, don't go there.* She again shook him out of her head. "My days will be crammed with wrapping details at the museum, and training, and settling in up there. You know though, if you're looking for someone to hang out with, I bet Haley would be happy for a break from tax season." She paused. "You two seemed to get along at the party."

"We're both number crunchers." He chuckled. "Seriously, I did like her. And I should probably say goodbye now, before the conversation gets awkward. Justine, best of luck. You'll love Chicago."

Chapter Forty-Two

While running errands after work on Saturday, Justine couldn't resist a quick detour down Michigan Avenue to drive past Liza's house. No one would notice her car slipping by on the dark street.

A "for sale" sign near the curb caused her to hit the brakes and pause for a stunned moment. The house was dark. He already flew the coop for California.

Tears pooled in her eyes. She dashed them away and drove, above the limit, down the quiet street. An unexpected wallop of regret twisted her into knots. Despite the flares of passion, they obviously weren't meant to be together. If only they parted on positive terms.

"Get ahold of yourself," she commanded aloud as she swung into her driveway. Jackson's parting shot was totally unreasonable and unfair. Before his final, slashing words could replay for the hundredth time, she garaged the car and jogged into the house. Despite the clock only nearing seven, she stomped up to the bedroom to put on her pajamas.

She hadn't eaten dinner. The quart of Coffee Fudge Sludge she dug into the night before beckoned. Celebration for landing the job. Spoon in hand, she returned downstairs to scoop the ice cream carton out of the freezer. The sugar overload calmed her as she settled onto the couch, curling her legs under a blanket knitted by July. Without interest, she surfed TV channels, searching for a comedy or a fakey reality show. Anything but a love story.

Two hours later, she'd started and paused four different shows. The sugar left her jumpy and unfocused. Maybe she should retreat to bed and read the historical drama downloaded on her new tablet. She stood, stretched her cramped limbs, and clicked off the living room light switch. What a waste of a Saturday night. In Chicago, she vowed to check out the nightlife.

Bam, bam, bam, bam, bam. Frantic pounding slammed against the door, driving her heart into her throat. Good Lord, did someone have the wrong address? Visions of a SWAT team routed to the wrong door swarmed her tingling senses. Should she answer it? Or pretend she wasn't—

"Justine, please open up. I saw you turn the light off."

Her hands fisted at her sides. Jackson Maddox pounded again. "I came to apologize. Please, hear me out."

Please. Not a word in his usual repertoire. She stormed up to the closed door but didn't open it. "Go away. I accept your lame apology."

A ripe expletive seared the air. There, that's the man she knew. Before he could disturb the neighbors, she cracked the door enough to hiss, "You don't need to pacify me."

His hand popped up to nudge the door in. She jumped back, anger sizzling at the invasion, as his face and body appeared in her foyer. "Did I invite you to come in? I don't think so!" The fool must be freezing without a coat.

"Just hear me out." He matched her forceful tone.

She sniffed and crossed her arms tight over her chest. "Really, there's nothing more—"

His tense expression adjusted to mirth. He dared to snicker. She followed his line of vision and squeezed her eyes shut. In the dim overhead light, he could see her fuzzy pajamas, decorated with shoes in every form and variation. Warm, but definitely not sexy. Her teeth clanged together. "Get out of my house." Now heated to a boiling point, she shoved on his chest to maneuver him toward the door.

He stood his ground and placed his hands on her forearms. "Not until you've listened to me." His hair was messy, as if he'd raked his hands through it, but she didn't smell liquor on his breath.

"Funny, there's nothing you can say that I want to hear." She stomped on his toes with her bare foot for emphasis.

He didn't flinch. "Then hear this." He hauled her up onto her tiptoes and meshed his seeking lips to hers. Heat sprang between them, immediate and undeniable, as he backed her against the wall. Without any underwear, her sensitive areas inflamed as they rubbed against his.

"Not fair," she whispered against his lips. He responded by sweeping his tongue into her mouth. "Mmmm." Crazy for more intimate contact, she slid her legs up around his waist. The hot, demanding kiss threatened to deprive her of oxygen. But what a way to expire.

A sliver of sanity intruded. Pulling away a fraction, she clung to his shoulders and gasped a breath. "Why are you here?"

His chest heaved to take in more air while he spoke

in short bursts. "I hurt you. I'm sorry. You didn't deserve what happened. I was scared, and an ass."

Justine's head and body reeled. She still exerted caution. Even pinned to the wall by a demanding, sexy, hard body. "So, what are you saying?"

"In the simplest of terms, I want to spend time with you. Be with you." Jackson cupped her face with gentle fingers. "If you'll give me a chance to prove I can be a decent guy."

She met his gorgeous blue eyes for several moments, trying to divine into his soul for the truth. The man wasn't prone to bull or empty praise. In her experience, he told the truth whether someone liked it or not. Satisfied with her gut reaction—and driven by her simmering body—she whispered, "I think I'd like that."

The corner of his mouth tugged up before fusing again with hers. She let down her guard to finally, fully, savor his taste. Her body softened against his hard angles while she skimmed one of her own hands through his mussed hair. When they eventually withdrew to grab a breath, she slid her legs back down his body to the floor. An enticing journey, reminding her of when he halted her fall in the closet.

His teeth now nipped past the collar of her robe. "I dig the flannel PJs, but in LA you don't have to wear anything to bed."

Her breath caught again as his smooth fingers slid the buttons of her top open, one by one. Anticipation gripped her, so strong that she trembled even before his hand caressed her breast. She moaned, low in her throat. "Bare naked is fine with me." Her eyes drifted closed as she arched her neck, encouraging the trail of kisses sweeping from her ear to her neck, to her sensitive collarbone. Suddenly, her legs were swept up in his arms. "Upstairs," she instructed, without caution or hesitation.

In the dark bedroom, her pajama top pooled on the carpet, followed by the pants. Her knees weakened when his hands and lips wove a trail of fire across her flesh. "Why are you still wearing clothes?" she asked, with a little pant.

"Because I want to make you crazy. Is it working?"

"Yes!" She grasped his shirt hem and tugged upward, tossing aside the garment to reveal tanned skin. Greedy for more, her hands slid down his stomach to stroke the bulge at his crotch. He groaned as her fingers worked the fly. The jeans tossed aside; his manhood sprang forward. *No underwear.* Her head spun at the thought—and at his impressive size. Craving immediate flesh to flesh, she melded her body to his. Their mouths met again, teasing, exploring. Muscles rippled under her hands.

In a smooth maneuver, he backed her down and onto the bed. In the light from the hallway, she saw his glasses arc across the room, enhancing the wicked glint in his eyes. His breath tickled her ear. "I want to make you scream."

Her hips rose off the bed at the flick of his tongue and lips at her center. Her legs fell open and she gasped out a wordless exclamation of pure pleasure.

She'd never been a screamer…till now…

Chapter Forty-Three

While Jackson showered the next morning, Justine hummed a tune and prepared to cook French toast. She rolled back the cuffs of the vintage dressing gown, enjoying the satin caress on her tender skin. After adding a dash of cinnamon to the egg and milk mixture, she pulled out four pieces of bread to await his arrival.

Unless the temptation of their freshly washed bodies sent them back to bed again. She shivered at the dart of heat to her center. Just in case, she didn't bother with undies. With a satisfied smile, she turned to get out the plates. Her hands flew up to cover her shriek. "You cannot be here this morning." Her eyes darted to the doorway. Good, she could still hear the shower running. Glaring at the interloper perched on the counter, she tightened the tie belt at her waist. Though the ghost likely already knew all her secrets. "Please tell me you didn't watch us last night."

Liza's face crinkled with apparent disgust. "Of course not. My circumstances may have forced me to become a voyeur, but I'm not kinky." A tiny smirk erupted. "Or at least where the two of you are concerned."

"Whoa. No details." Justine advanced to face her down. "You need to leave before your son comes in. If you're dying to talk to me, do it when he's gone."

"A poor choice of words, but I may not be able to

return. I sense the window of opportunity closing." Her features sagged. "To tell the truth, I'm a little scared to go, not knowing what I'll face. We've both heard which road is paved with good intentions."

Justine's annoyance fled. Empathy crept in. "You made mistakes but did what you thought was best. You've made a superhuman effort to come back and make things right."

Liza dropped off the countertop, though her heeled boots didn't make a sound. Today she wore a sassy red minidress. "My dear, you will be good for my son."

"There are no guarantees between him and me beyond this day," Justine countered—though she hoped she was wrong. "I'm moving to Chicago. He'll go back to LA."

"Jackson can write anywhere he chooses. Planes fly both ways." The apparition's chin quivered. "I do want to thank you for supporting him. For hopefully being open to loving him. I also have faith that someday he'll decide to try again with his father. You finally cracked his hard shell."

"Like an egg," Justine joked, before her heart stuttered. Liza began the familiar fade. "If I don't see you again, good luck." She clutched her hands under her chin as the last remnant of the red dress disappeared. Was the ghost gone for good? She might even miss her a little.

Her eyes widened in dismay. Jackson stood in the doorway with damp hair and raised brows. "Were you practicing your goodbye speech to me?"

Her eyes fluttered closed. Should she risk their newfound intimacy with such an earthshattering confession? The idea would blow his mind. Yet she had this talent, this gift, which appeared to be strengthening.

If they had any chance of being together, she couldn't hide this part of herself. "Sit down, please."

With a wary expression, he took the chair across from her.

She inhaled a deep breath. The kicky scent of peppermint body wash flooded her senses. No, she had to stay focused. "I wasn't practicing, and I wasn't talking to you. But I was talking to…someone."

"Bluetooth?" He glanced toward her ear.

"No."

"Skype?"

She shook her head. "When I told you some people have seen ghosts at the museum," she ventured, "that included me."

He halted. She could almost hear the wheels spinning. "Okay. I'll bite. Are you going to tell me a ghost story?" He winked and reached for her hand.

"Yeesss. But you probably won't like it." *All right, just say it.* "The main character is your mother." She winced, awaiting his reaction.

He yanked his hand back. "My mom? People have seen her at the museum? That's nuts."

So, no blurring of reality for him. Ironic, considering how screenwriters were paid to craft fantasies. "Not people, plural," she blurted. "Just me. And not just there. At her house." She waved her arm around the room. "Here, in my kitchen."

Now he shoved away from the table. "Ah crap. Are you telling me you were just talking to her when I walked in? Please don't do this, Justine. If you don't want to see me again, you don't have to run me off with wacko stories." The chair grated as he pushed farther back. "I'll grab my shoes and go."

Panic slithered through her chest. "No, please. Sit. I'm trying to lay myself bare here and share something scary, something I've only told Carl so far. Because the truth is too important to ignore."

His eyes darted to the doorway. He was going to leave. Suddenly a faint word sounded in her ear. *Paddington.* She flicked her gaze around the room. No Liza. But her voice whispered again in her head. *Paddington.*

"Paddington," she said aloud.

Jackson flipped toward her. "What did you say?"

"Paddington. I just heard the word. I assume you didn't?" Her hands clutched under the table, icy as the rest of her skin.

To her relief, he plopped into the chair. And buried his head in his hands. After several silent moments he looked up. "She bought me one of those bears when I was a toddler. I took the darn thing everywhere, till some of the fur rubbed off. Along with one eye. Some kids have a security blanket, I had Paddington. He stayed on my bed till I hit thirteen and thought I was too cool. I put him in the trash."

She didn't dare interrupt. Or move.

"When I first came in here after her...when I arrived, I found him on her bed. I took him up to mine." Tears glazed his eyes.

Her lips wobbled as her own vision blurred. "She rescued him."

"What did she want from you?"

The question caught her off guard. Had she fully changed his mind? At least the door cracked open. She weighed her words. "To watch over you while you were here. To support you if you decided to seek out your father. No, she didn't tell me his name either."

"Tell me more. If I'm going to be able to absorb and accept this, I need more details." He slumped in the chair. "I can't believe I'm saying these words. But unless you found the bear in the house—"

"I swear I didn't. You were with me the whole time, and I didn't creep in at night."

"I wouldn't have thrown you out." They shared a small smile. He rolled his eyes to the ceiling. "This goes against all my rational impulses, but if anyone had a strong enough personality to come back from the hereafter, it would be Liza. Without any definitive proof that ghosts don't exist, and loads of horror movies banking that they do, who am I to be a total cynic."

"Thank goodness," she whispered, hesitant to share more. The encounters could trickle out if they got to know and trust each other. Another wrenching thought compelled her as he resumed his seat, renewing a tremor of anxiety. "While I'm sharing stories, I also have to tell you that they offered me the Chicago job."

"Awesome." He pulled her up into an embrace, which, to her delight, slid into a sizzling kiss.

When they came up for air, winded and aroused, she reminded, "I'll be living in the Midwest and you're on the coast." She couldn't resist feathering her fingers over the stubble on his chin.

"I can write anywhere. Who knows, I might even change my mind about selling the house here." His hand teased inside the dressing gown, slipping it over her shoulder. "Why are we wasting time talking when we should be celebrating?"

Epilogue

March 2013

Justine swept an arm toward the hanging racks and shelves of labeled containers in the Drysdale Museum's climate-controlled basement. LED lighting tracks also illuminated additional furniture and treasures to interchange as displays adjusted.

"This area houses our vintage collection to outfit the mannequins. We gathered several new pieces since I started three years ago. Everything's been catalogued with the provenance. The file's in my computer." She straightened a couture 1940's gown on a padded hanger. "When you accept donations, you know to roll the fragile items in acid-free paper."

Her new assistant scribbled in her notebook. "You're the vintage expert, but I've studied and preserved all types of antiquities." She looked over her purple-framed lenses. "I can tell how much you enjoy the job. I bet you miss it when you travel to the coast with your gorgeous hubby." Victoria had exclaimed over the trio of framed photos on her desk upstairs, including one from their wedding.

"Jackson and I are done with long separations," Justine agreed. After five months, she still indulged a thrill at marrying the love of her life. Long-distance was bearable due to his job flexibility. They were both more than ready to live together permanently. "The Midwest will be our base and we'll trek out to California for extended trips as necessary. The success of his last two films leaves him in hot demand. Hollywood's fickle. When the bigshots beckon, you come."

"Are you keeping the Indiana house?" During the training period, they'd exchanged life stories.

"We are. You'd love the place. I'm so fortunate. Here, we're surrounded by antiques, tradition, and family. Jackson's California loft is sleek and minimalist, while the LA atmosphere is buzzing and trendy. After living in Chicago, I can deal with the craziness for a while."

Victoria smoothed a hand over her dark brown hair. "The board is great to allow you to telecommute during those periods."

"With our new grant that underwrites your hiring, I can leave knowing everything's in capable hands. I'm also excited to dive into my next new side adventure. In addition to historical consulting and freelance articles, I'm toying with writing stories or books. Starting with a little ghostly romance." She led the way out of the room to ascend the stairs. "He may be humoring me, but Jackson says he's impressed by what he's read so far." The grandfather clock in the upstairs hallway boomed the first of five gongs when they reached the landing. "This is a good time for us to break for the day. We're having dinner in the burbs with his family."

The woman closed her notebook as they walked along the broad wooden hallway. "I didn't know he had family locally."

"That's partly why we're keeping the LaPorte house." She didn't expound. While Jackson and

Lawrence had formed a tentative relationship a couple years prior, they kept the connection private. The gossip mill would grind with the news; they didn't owe anyone explanations. Except the Reynolds' daughters. After a handful of father-son discussions over six months, Lawrence introduced them to his family.

Justine termed their familial relationship as cordial, respectful, and growing in levels of warmth and trust. The women, of course, were stunned at learning about a half-brother. Deirdre, living closest to their father, came around first. The other two were more distant, both in their acceptance and in location. Hopefully, time would continue to heal.

The front doorbell of the museum tinkled. Her husband planned to pick her up before they locked the doors. "Have a good evening."

Victoria's face lit with interest. "Don't I get to meet him?"

"Sure. I don't mind showing him off." They rounded the corner to find him wiping his boots on the mat in the wood-paneled, two-story foyer. A chandelier rivaling the *Phantom of the Opera's* famed fixture glittered overhead. She adored the decadence of the mansion and counted her blessings at landing the job. Her co-workers were fun and helped carry the workload. Samantha was a fair and approachable boss. They weren't close friends, like she and Carl, but shared a vision for preservation efforts and public events.

Jackson stepped forward when they approached. Her heart gave a little leap when he placed his arm around her waist. She made the introductions, amused at how her replacement blushed and stumbled in her words. He sure hadn't had that effect on her when they met the first time. *Correction*, she also blushed and stumbled, but only because he came off so rude and snarky.

His hand tightened at her waist. "I'm glad you're here so Justine can relax at leaving her job for a while in capable hands."

"She's left big heels to step into. I know you two have plans, so again, nice to meet you. Have a wonderful night." The woman padded down the hall.

"She's a gem," Justine murmured. "Been working in museums since she graduated with her master's a decade ago. Let me grab my coat, and we'll head out."

He followed along the hallway to her office. They stepped onto the plush, burgundy and gold-patterned rug. Before she could move forward, he shoved the door closed and tugged her to his chest. "You're super sexy in that efficient, Miss Moneypenny work mode. I remember thinking the same thing out at the LaPorte Museum when I dropped off those photos three years ago."

"You remember that?" Pleased, she grasped the lapels of his overcoat. "I was pretty flustered at your appearance that day. I didn't believe I'd see you again after our snow-in."

In a sexy move, he twirled her around and backed her up against the door. His eyes were hooded as his finger traced her lips. "Did you really think you'd get rid of me so easily? Maddoxes are known for their stubborn, persistent nature."

"Both here and beyond." Their eyes held. The playful moment dimmed with her offhand comment. Yet she didn't regret introducing Liza into the conversation. After all, her intervention helped nudge along their romance and unfurled a path of new adventures. The spirit never appeared again after the final interlude in her kitchen, but no doubt tuned in with a loving, watchful eye.

Justine stood on her tiptoes to plant a kiss on Jackson's lips. She disengaged and swiped a smudge of lipstick off the corner of his mouth. "Come on. We don't want to be late for your family."

"Family." He didn't move and mulled the word. "Still kind of a strange concept for me. When we met, I didn't want to admit to being lost. Or maybe the right word is 'adrift.' Through you, I opened up to dig into and appreciate my history."

She warmed at the compliment and caressed his cheek again. "I'm proud of you for being willing to try to understand your parents' motivations. I hope you really do know that both of them loved you. They just couldn't figure out a way to be together."

"If they ditched everything and got married, it might not have lasted with all the drama."

"Sad, but possible." She regarded his matter-of-fact expression and squeezed his hand. "We should get moving. Rush hour traffic awaits." She spun away to grab her coat out of the office closet.

He helped her into it. "Deirdre's upbeat and fun. But part of me would rather have a quiet dinner together then make for an early night at home." He chuckled. "Who would've thought I'd ever refer to LaPorte as home or dig the slower pace? But sweetie, wherever you are, that's home for me."

"I couldn't agree more." She always melted when he revealed his soft side. Maybe they should drive straight home. Or just stay here for a few more minutes… No, important people were waiting to see them. Justine tucked her hand through his arm. Together they headed down the silent hallway.

A word about the author...

Sandra L. Young's passion for vintage fashion inspired her to write her debut "Divine Vintage" series, wrapping with The Ghostly Diva. She's gathered an impressive collection, wearing pieces onstage through years of performing in community theater. She also wears it out on the town for special occasions. Check out her garments featured at SandraYoungAuthor.com. And for all who have read and reviewed the Divine Vintage series, thank you so much. Lovely reviews fuel authors to keep diving into their imaginations for your reading pleasure!